CUPCAKE DIARIES

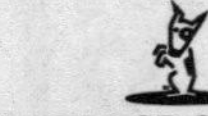

SIMON SPOTLIGHT
An imprint of Simon & Schuster Children's Publishing Division
1230 Avenue of the Americas, New York, New York 10020
This Simon Spotlight bind-up edition September 2016

For information about special discounts for bulk purchases, please contact
Simon & Schuster Special Sales at 1-866-506-1949 or
business@simonandschuster.com.
Text by Tracey West and Elizabeth Doyle Carey
Design by Laura Roode
Manufactured in the United States of America 0816 OFF
2 4 6 8 10 9 7 5 3 1
ISBN 978-1-4814-8437-4
ISBN 978-1-4424-2902-4 (*Alexis and the Perfect Recipe* eBook)
ISBN 978-1-4424-4612-0 (*Katie, Batter Up!* eBook)
ISBN 978-1-4424-4614-4 (*Mia's Baker's Dozen* eBook)
These titles were previously published individually by Simon Spotlight.

Alexis and the perfect recipe

Katie, batter up!

Mia's baker's dozen

by coco simon

Simon Spotlight
New York London Toronto Sydney New Delhi

Alexis and the perfect recipe

CHAPTER 1

My Sister Takes the Cake

My name is Alexis Becker, and I'm the business mind (ha-ha) of the Cupcake Club. The club is a for-profit group that my best friends—Mia, Katie, and Emma—and I started, and we make money baking delicious cupcakes!

I love figuring out how to run a business and putting together the different building blocks—math, organization, planning—that's why the girls can *count* on me for this kind of stuff. Plus, as you can tell, I love math-related puns! My friends are more creative with the cupcakes, so they come up with the designs and other artistic stuff. My one specialty, though, is fondant. I am very good at making little flowers and designs out of that firm frosting. Otherwise, I'm mostly crunching numbers and wondering how to make money. Mmm . . . money!

If the Cupcake Club was an equation, it would look like this:

(4 girls + supplies) x clients
= $$$$

Or really, more like this:

(Profit - supplies) / 4 = $

We actually have lots of fun doing it. Most of our clients are really nice people, which is much more than I can say for our latest client: my sister, Dylan. I can practically still hear her fuming.

"It is *my* party, *I* am the one turning sixteen, and I have budgeted *everything* down to the last party favor. I know *exactly* what I'm doing!" She was talking to our mom behind closed doors, but I heard every word since I was right outside her bedroom!

Dylan never gets out-of-control mad; she's always in total control. Except that ever since she'd started planning her sweet sixteen party (which was now four and a half weeks away), she'd been cranky *a lot*. But she never raises her voice when she gets mad. She lowers it to a whisper, and you can hear the chill in it as if actual icicles were hanging from the words. I had to put my ear to her bedroom door to hear everything that was being said. Knowledge is power; that's one of my mottoes, and I need all the information I can get. About everything.

My mother was sounding kind of amused by the fight, which was about two things: the guest list for the party and the cake. I had an interest in the outcome of both, since I wanted to be able to invite my best friends, and *we* wanted to bake the dessert for the party. (It wasn't about the money as we wouldn't charge a lot; it's just that it would be great exposure for our business!)

I could picture Mom trying not to smile and to take Dylan seriously. "Darling, I know how careful you are, and I am impressed, as always, by your work," she said. "I admire your attention to detail on these spreadsheets. However, not everything will be according to *your* plan, as your father and I also have a say in what works best for this family. Now let's take a look at this guest list again."

I grinned. Mom was on *my* side.

There were some muffled comments and I strained to hear them. Maybe I'd hear better if I put a glass against the wall like I'd seen people do on TV. Or maybe I should lie down and listen through the crack under the door. I pulled my hair into a ponytail, and then lay on the hall rug outside the door.

"The Taylors! *Mom!* The whole family? That wasn't in my head count!" The Ice Princess was losing her cool, but I didn't focus on that. All I could think of was that Emma's whole family might come. And *that* was very interesting.

Emma has three brothers. They've always all been in the background of things—rummaging around their mudroom looking for a lost cleat or watching TV in the living room. They're kind of like furniture. When we talk to them at all, it's just stuff like "Please pass the ketchup" or "Hey! We were watching that!"

Jake is much younger, so he's cute but not exactly a pal of mine, and Matt and Sam are older, so we don't really pay attention to them, and they don't pay much attention to us.

Until recently, that is.

What changed everything was that I had a little direct contact with Matt. He's eighteen months older, but only one school year ahead (he's in eighth grade at Park Street Middle School). Usually I am with Emma when her brothers are around, so I guess I see them from her point of view.

But this time I had to call Matt for help with something for Emma, and it wasn't until he said "Hello" on the phone that in one strange, sudden moment, *everything* changed.

So what happened? First off, I am very efficient. When something needs doing, I just do it. When someone needs calling, I just pick up the phone and dial. And that was what I had done, without even thinking about it.

But Matt's voice sounds much deeper on the phone than it does in person, and when I heard it, it threw me off and I panicked, like, *Who is this person I am talking to?* and *Why did I call him, exactly?* I kind of had an out-of-body experience. I suddenly realized I'd called a boy, and I almost dropped the phone!

But thanks to caller ID he already knew who was calling, so I couldn't exactly hang up. Then, just to confuse me further, in the course of our (very brief) conversation, Matt told me how worried he'd been about Emma, and that he felt bad for some things she was going through at the time.

I was shocked!

I didn't think boys *worried* about anyone! And feeling bad for someone? That is just unheard of! Suddenly Matt seemed like . . . a real *person*. With feelings! In the end, it was I who rushed us off the phone. I suddenly got really, really nervous and couldn't believe I'd had the guts to call Matt in the first place. You know in the old cartoons when the coyote runs off a cliff and his feet are still spinning, but he's in midair and he only falls when he realizes it? That's what happened to me.

And now, when I heard Dylan talking about the Taylors, all I could think of was Matt. And that gave me a funny feeling, like fish were swimming in my stomach.

I hope he comes to Dylan's party, I thought. *Or maybe I don't. Ugh! I don't know what I want!*

Suddenly the door flew open, and Dylan shrieked when she saw me lying on the floor. I blinked as the bright light from her room hit me.

"I hate this family!" Dylan wailed, stepping over me. She stomped down the hall to the bathroom and shut the door as hard as possible without actually slamming it.

"Alexis, honey, what are you doing there?" my mother asked in her "patient" voice.

I rolled up on one side and propped my head on

my fist. "Just interested in the outcome of everything," I replied.

My mother smiled at me and shook her head.

"What?" I said in my most innocent voice. "I just want to make sure that we get the job."

"You'll get the job, all right, but these better turn out to be the prettiest and tastiest cupcakes you've ever baked," Mom said. She's pretty tough. She's not a CPA and a CFO for nothing.

"Mom, please. We run a very professional outfit."

Dylan came stomping out of the bathroom and glared at my mother. "This is the person you'd like to entrust my dessert to? This . . . worm, lying on the floor like a two-year-old?"

"That's enough, Dylan. Don't speak like that about your sister," Mom warned. (She went to parent training when we were little, and she has all these certain voices and techniques she uses on us.)

"Yeah," I added. "I'm not two. Or a worm!"

Dylan drew back her leg like she was going to kick me, and I rolled away and sprang to my feet.

"Girls! Counting to three!" Mom yelled.

Dylan shook her head in disgust and stormed into her room, where she collapsed dramatically onto her bed. "The Cake Specialist said they'd even give me a discount," she muttered. "I would be the first discount they've ever given. They said I drive a hard bargain."

Mom patted Dylan. "I would expect nothing less, darling. But we need to support a business that is in our family. And I know the Cupcake Club will do a wonderful job for you."

"Wonderful!" I repeated, raising my arms in victory.

"Argh!" cried Dylan as she pulled a pillow over her head. "Just leave me alone!" After a moment she added, "And just make sure whatever you Cupcakers propose is in my party's color scheme of—"

My mother and I answered together, "We know, we know, black and gold!"

I put up my hand and my mother gave me a stiff-handed, silent high five. (She's not the high-fiving type).

"I saw that!" accused Dylan from under her pillow.

My mother and I exchanged a guilty smile.

"They'd better be the best black-and-gold cupcakes you've ever made!" said Dylan. "Or else!"

I rolled my eyes, and we left Dylan to her moping.

"Thanks, Mom," I whispered once we were out

in the hall with Dylan's door safely closed.

"You're welcome, dear," she whispered back. "But you owe me some pretty spectacular cupcakes!"

"Black-and-gold ones! Coming right up!" I said, and we laughed.

We started down the hall. I did a little cha-cha-cha step. I'm obsessed with all the TV dancing shows and like to practice dance moves whenever I can. Music and dance is kind of mathematical, which is why I love it. There's a logical and organized pattern to everything—the chords, notes, and dance steps.

"Is Dylan really mad, do you think?" I asked. All joking aside, I did not want Dylan as my enemy. She is my only sibling, and we are usually pretty good friends.

My mother thought for a moment. "She is getting everything she wants. The place, the music, the food, the date, the decor, the favors. Everything. Now, she is contributing quite a lot of her own money to it, so she does get her say. But I think she can accommodate me on a few extra faces and a special dessert."

"Sounds fair to me," I agreed, and I went to e-mail the Cupcakers with the good news. All we needed was a great idea, one that would keep Dylan from killing me. Oh yeah, and it had to be black and gold!

I just wished I could e-mail them about Matt Taylor being invited to the party. But what would I say?

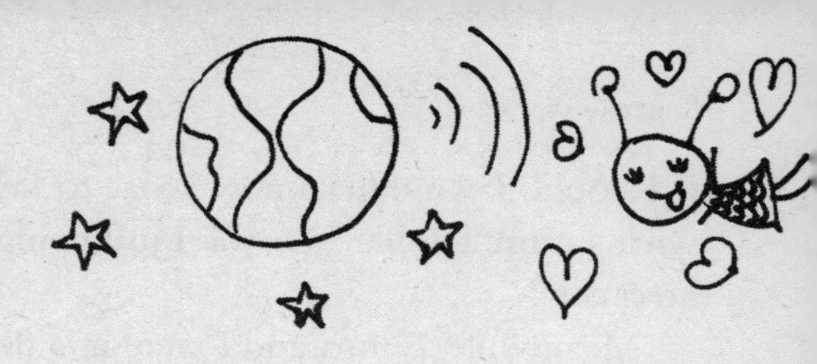

CHAPTER 2

Earth to Alexis

A couple days later we met at Emma's house. I have always liked baking there because her parents don't mind if things get messy. Mom kind of freaks out when we're baking in her sparkling clean kitchen. (Needless to say, I am not messy, but *some* people can be!) We were just brainstorming that day, but I was still glad to be at the Taylors'. I felt a buzz of nervous happiness and had taken a little extra time laying out my outfit the night before. I told myself it was just because it was a Monday and I wanted to start the week off looking good, but deep down inside I knew the real reason: I might see Matt! Was that weird or what?

Thinking about Matt in this new way was weird too. I wished I could tell someone, but even if I could, I wouldn't know what to say. Was this what a crush felt like? Or was I just being silly? I'm *never* silly!

Meanwhile, Emma and I were in a debate.

"*Please*, Alexis!" Emma was begging, and her big blue eyes widened as she looked at me.

"No," I said firmly, and drew myself up as tall as possible to look like I was in charge.

Mia and Katie were laughing at us as Emma and I argued about whether or not we could use real gold flakes in our proposed cupcake design for Dylan's party. It was true that they would look spectacular, but they were so expensive and, to be honest, I didn't want perfect Dylan to have *real* gold cupcakes! She was being such a brat about everything these days, it would feel like we were rewarding her for her bad behavior.

But of course Emma didn't see it that way as she huffed and crossed her arms. I could see the glimmer of a smile underneath, though, and I smiled at her, narrowed my eyes, and dared her to smile back. Finally she smiled back—victory!

Just then a voice asked, "Hey, what's the deal?"

Matt!

We hadn't heard him come in and now we all whipped around in surprise. My heart leaped as my stomach got all fluttery again. Matt has light, curly hair and blue eyes, and seemed to look especially cute today.

"Oh, Alexis is just being a tough CFO," said Mia.

"Well, someone has to be, or you'd all just be *giving* these cupcakes away," I said huffily. I wasn't really annoyed, but it made me feel less nervous to act like I was in front of Matt.

"You tell 'em, Alexis!" he said, smiling at me as he went into the kitchen. Was I imagining things or did his eyes twinkle? I was definitely feeling a little light-headed.

Emma grinned. "Huh! Look who's best friends now that you saved my life together," she said, reminding us about the time a few weeks ago when Matt and I worked together to help her out. "Usually he acts like he doesn't even know any of your names!"

Best friends! Hardly, but the idea of Matt and me linked in any way, shape, or form (plus, he'd smiled at me!) caused a warm feeling in my chest that quickly spread up into a blush.

Noticing how red I'd turned, Emma's grin quickly faded, and she gave me a strange look. Uh-oh. I ducked my head down and looked back at my leather-bound account ledger.

"Okay," I said, quickly trying to think of something else. "We have about twenty-five cents per cupcake to work with. Batter is ten cents per cupcake and frosting is five cents, so that leaves us with ten cents for any kind of decoration. By my calculations, the gold costs twenty cents per cupcake and that is just too much!"

"How does she figure this stuff out?" Katie asked the others.

"And why does she *want* to? That's the real question!" said Mia with a laugh.

"Ha-ha. Very funny. *Not*," I protested.

Even though I was talking to my friends, my mind was still on Matt. I heard his footsteps cross the floor above us, and I wondered what he had for homework and what subjects he liked. I also wondered what I would say to make conversation if he came back down. I chewed on my pen cap as I thought.

Suddenly I heard Katie saying, "Earth to Alexis!" and looked up to see everyone staring at me. Apparently Katie had been asking me a question.

I shook my head to clear my thoughts. "Oh, sorry. What?"

"Alexis, did you take your omega-threes today?"

Mia teased. "You seem really spacey!" She always makes fun of me and my vitamins, but I know they work. My whole family is about "optimizing our engines," so we eat superhealthy meals and exercise together, and we like to take supplements.

"Yes, I did," I replied, making a face at her. Usually I don't mind if my friends tease me, but I get annoyed when they make fun of me in front of other people—like Matt. I hoped he couldn't overhear any of this.

"Someone's a little testy!" said Katie as Emma frowned.

"What?" I asked, looking at Emma, and it came out a little harsher than I meant it to.

"Oh, nothing," Emma said, but I knew that wasn't true. Maybe she could tell that her brother was the cause of my freak-out.

Luckily Mia started talking about something else. "Hey, what are you going to wear to Dylan's party?" she asked. Mia is really into fashion, and her mom is a stylist, so clothes are always on her mind.

I was glad for the change of subject, even though it meant we hadn't yet figured out our budget. I told Mia that Dylan was going to set some things aside for me at Icon (Mia and Dylan's favorite store, but not mine), and I could bring the Cupcake Club with me this weekend to go try them on. As long as there wasn't anything too racy, that was good for me. Showing a lot of skin made me nervous. I wished I could get something at Big Blue, which was my favorite store since it was kind of preppy-casual, but they didn't have anything "special" enough for Dylan there. Or anything black and gold enough.

"So we'll go with you before we bake on Saturday, then," offered Katie. "Where are we baking again?"

It should really be my turn, but I didn't say anything for a minute, hoping Emma would offer. I looked down at the ledger.

Mia thought out loud. "Well, today is Emma's, tomorrow is my house, and Friday is Katie's, so . . ."

Everyone was looking at me, so I had to answer. "We could do my place, I guess. It's just that Emma is way closer to the mall . . . if we need to walk."

"Your dad would totally drive us! He's so nice about it!" Katie said. It was true. My dad was willing to drive us anywhere ever since he got his new car.

"I'd much rather be at your house," Emma added. "It's so peaceful and organized and clean! And there aren't any boys. . . ."

Yeah, that's not good news, I said to myself. Inside

I felt bummed that we weren't going to be at the Taylors', but I knew it wouldn't be fair not to offer, so I said, "Okay, my house it is."

Then we kept brainstorming and came up with three pretty good ideas for Dylan's party. Well, the other girls did most of the thinking. My mind was upstairs where Matt was the whole time. I kept wondering if and when he was going to appear again. And what I would say to him if he did.

If that afternoon was an equation, it would have looked like this:

(Friends + business) / cute boy = brain dead

Here's what we finally came up with:

Option A. Disco cupcakes: white cake with black vanilla frosting and Emma's coveted gold flakes strewn across the top.

Option B. S'mores cupcakes: angel food cake injected with liquid marshmallow and frosted with dark (black-looking) chocolate. They would have a sprinkling of graham crackers on top. They would probably be the best-tasting but not the coolest-looking.

Option C. Gift cupcakes: small yellow cupcakes peeled out of their wrappers and coated with raspberry jam, and then wrapped in a round sheet of black fondant tucked under at the bottom so they looked like a smooth hill. They would be individually wrapped like a gift with gold ribbon tied in a big bow on top. They would definitely be the prettiest ones.

It was a good day's work, though I hardly remember what was said after Matt showed up. Thank goodness I take good notes!

Unfortunately, Matt never came back down before we had to leave. I was tempted to call up the stairs to say bye to him, but that would have been truly weird. I did whisper it as I walked down their driveway, though. No one heard me, so why not?

CHAPTER 3

Project M. T.

My desk is my command center, and I take pride in keeping it superorganized. There are little drawers with all my supplies in tidy little boxes and packages. My pencil cup holds only Ticonderoga #2 pencils, all sharpened, points up, and my pen cup holds only blue erasable FriXion pens. I have a small container of white erasers (the best kind), and then there are my tools: very sharp Fiskars scissors for projects, a flat tin of rainbow-hued watercolor pencils (for graphs and pie charts), an electric pencil sharpener, a three-ring hole punch, a heavy Swingline stapler, and an old-fashioned Scotch tape dispenser.

My family shops the Staples sales religiously, and we are good with coupons and points and our club card. My parents figure that homework time spent looking for supplies is homework time wasted, so they like us to be well-stocked. When we run low on something, we just leave it on the kitchen island and our mom has her assistant reorder it immediately, putting it on her personal account. It's that easy, as they say on TV.

That night, though, despite my desk being fully stocked with supplies, my mind kept drifting away from my homework. It was really infuriating because I hate being unproductive. I had to admit that it was Matt who was distracting me. I was wondering if this was a crush. And if it was, what did I want to come of it?

Did I want him to be my *boyfriend*?

I wasn't sure, but I had to say *not really*. And to be absolutely honest, the idea of having a boyfriend kind of terrified me.

Well, then, did I want him just as a friend?

I was thinking definitely not just as a friend. Maybe something in between? It was hard to quantify it! My feelings about Matt would not organize themselves, and that was superfrustrating. I had no control whatsoever over anything—whether I'd see him, whether he'd speak to me if I saw him, and what we'd say. I played out all kinds of scenarios in my mind as I sat at my desk, watching my timer tick away the half hour I'd allotted to writing flash cards for my vocab test next Tuesday.

Now I was really frustrated. I sighed loudly, slapped the timer off, shuffled the flash cards into a neat stack, clipped them tightly together with a binder clip, and put them in my English bin on top of the desk. I was at a total loss. I grabbed a fresh sheet of white paper from the stack, and then reached for the calculator. Then I started fooling around with numbers, which *always* relaxes me.

I began scratching figures on the page as I thought. First, if I spend twenty minutes a day thinking about Matt, then that's one hundred and forty minutes a week, or two hours and twenty minutes. If I were working, say, at Big Blue for that long, I'd make twenty-five dollars, before taxes. If I were studying, I'd probably get an A on whatever it was. If I were exercising for those twenty minutes a day, and figured on a five minute warm-up and a five minute cool-down, then that was still ten minutes at my optimum heart rate, which was pretty good.

I rested my cheek on my hand and stared into space. Part of my brain was flashing a warning: "This is not scheduled into your planner for today! You are wasting time!" It was true, but I felt sluggish, like I had no control over myself. I certainly had no control over the object of my interest.

Or did I?

I sat up straight in my chair. That's it! What if I took a mathematical approach to my crush? What if I turned my mini obsession into a mathematically quantifiable experiment? I began brainstorming and scribbling onto my sheet in excitement.

My hypothesis was this: Could a crush be manipulated with results that can be replicated every time? Was there a predictable pattern of stimulus and response that I could plan and follow and chart, perhaps ending up with actual mathematical equations to predict Matt's behavior? In other words, could I come up with the perfect formula (or recipe, ha!) for getting Matt to fall for me?

This would be brilliant, I thought, as the neurons in my brain started firing up. It would also kind of justify any lazy daydreaming about Matt by turning those spacey moments into strategy sessions for my experiment. Let's see, what could I hypothesize and test?

What about wardrobe? I usually wear pants. It's kind of one of my trademarks. They are functional, comfortable, and easy to mix and match. But Dylan always wears skirts, and the boys flock to her. So, I wondered, what if I were to wear a skirt or a dress when I saw Matt? Would he react differently to me? Hmm. I wrote:

Project Matt Taylor

M.T., I thought. *More secretive.*

Then I scribbled:

Clothing experiment: Does he pay more attention to me if I am wearing pants or a skirt/dress?

I would need to conduct an experiment with each, where I timed the length of our interaction and compared the two figures. That would be easy. I could do it at school.

I chewed on my pen cap. What else could I test? Hair up or down? I almost always wore my hair in a ponytail or headband, but Sydney, the head of the Popular Girls Club in my class, always wore her hair down and boys paid lots of attention to her. Granted, her hair was long and blond and mine was long, frizzy, and red, but I could still do a hairstyle test. That sounded good, so I wrote it down.

Ooh! Another idea: comparing the frequency of who initiated our greeting, like in the hall at school. Sydney was giggly with boys, always starting conversations with them, while I only spoke to them if they spoke to me first. Maybe I could try to switch that up a little.

I decided to track my interactions with Matt (in the hall at school? At Emma's?) and collect the data and assess it. That was good.

This experiment called for a dedicated graph paper notebook, so I pulled one out of a cubbyhole in my desk and smoothed the cover with my hand. I could also write conversation starters in it (I had no idea what to say to him if I did see him), and maybe track things I could research that I know he's interested in, like sports and computer graphics. I was excited. At least now if nothing ever came of my interest in Matt, I wasn't *totally* wasting my time. I was practicing math skills!

Just then there was a knock on the door.

"Come in!" I trilled happily. I am always happiest when I am feeling busy and productive.

Dylan opened the door. "Dinner is in five minutes."

I looked at the clock, which read 6:55. We always eat exactly at seven. "Okay!" I said, still writing in my notebook.

My sister narrowed her eyes and folded her arms. "What are you working on?" she asked suspiciously. I guess it looked like too much fun to be homework. But I suddenly realized I did not want this notebook falling into the wrong hands, so I slammed it shut.

"Oh, just some cupcake ideas," I said casually.

"Stuff for my party?" Dylan asked.

"Not quite. Mostly budget stuff right now." *Please don't let her ask to see it.*

There was a pause before she asked, "When are we having the taste test?"

Okay, good, she didn't ask to see the notebook. "Oh, this Saturday. We're baking here, and then you can try all three of the options in the afternoon."

"But I have cheerleading practice on Saturday!" she said with a pout.

"Well, what time?" I asked patiently, ignoring her whiny voice. Sometimes I wondered who was the older sister!

"Four o'clock!"

"Oh, no prob," I assured her. "We'll be done making the samples by three for sure."

"Yeah, but I can't eat all that sugar and then go out and exercise. That will not work! I'm going to talk to Mom." Dylan immediately turned and walked away, not bothering to close the door. She was determined to make this hard for me.

"Whatever, Dyl pill," I said, annoyed.

"I heard that!" she called from the hallway.

"Good!" I whispered, and turned back to my desk, eager to get back to planning my experiment.

Tomorrow was the first day of Project M. T., and I decided that I would wear a skirt and see what happened. I was already dreading wearing the skirt—and what's more, I dreaded seeing Matt almost as much as I looked forward to it!

Who knew superorganized me could be *so* confused?

CHAPTER 4

Can He See Me Now?

Brrring!

The bell rang, and Eddie Rossi slammed his book shut and whipped it into his backpack. I thought this was pretty rude to Mr. Nichols, who was kind of old but not totally boring. *I mean, how badly do you want to get out of here, mister?* I thought.

I stared at Eddie with my most disapproving glare, but he didn't look around. Just sat with his backpack on his back, his hands gripping the edge of his desk, poised to launch out of his seat and out the door. I'm usually not that devious, but for some reason, his attitude really bugged me today. So I raised my hand.

"Yes, Alexis?" asked Mr. Nichols.

"Oh, you forgot to assign the homework," I said,

and it didn't take long for Eddie to react. His head snapped around and he glared at me. I gave him a closed-mouth smile and shrugged. *That's what you get, Mr. Rude,* I thought. *Teachers are people too!*

"Ah, thank you, Alexis," said Mr. Nichols distractedly. "I almost forgot . . ."

On autopilot, I copied down the homework and then packed up my bag. Eddie had already sprung out of the room and down the hall. From the back row I could hear Sydney Whitman and Callie Wilson restart their almost incessant chatter. The day was one long gossipfest for them, about movie stars, kids they went to camp with, kids from school, boys—anyone and anything. And it all sounded so utterly mindless and unproductive.

"Good catch on the homework, Alexis!" said Callie brightly. I looked up at her to see if she was making fun of me. She didn't seem to be.

"Yeah," sneered Sydney. "I'd hate to get out of here without something to keep our skills sharp at home."

Well, Sydney's response wasn't surprising. I ignored her and kept stuffing my books into my bag. My cheeks felt hot, but I willed myself not to blush.

Then she started laughing hysterically as she

sauntered out of the classroom with Callie. The next class shuffled in, and I was going to be late. I had no choice but to fall into step right behind Callie and Sydney. I had worn a skirt today as part of Project M. T., and its unfamiliar swish against my legs made me feel insecure. I had worn my hair up, as usual, as a control, so I could isolate the effect of the skirt.

I wondered if I'd even see Matt, after all this strategizing.

Just ahead of me Sydney said to Callie teasingly, "I wonder if we'll see Mr. Hottie today?"

"Oh, I almost hope not! I look terrible!" moaned Callie, who couldn't have looked more perfect.

"When was the last time you saw him?" asked Sydney.

Callie made a sad face. "Last week. And I used to see him every day at camp! It's so unfair!" she wailed.

"Well, maybe you need to get your hands on a copy of his schedule and just make sure you're putting yourself in the right place at the right time!" said Sydney. "I mean, what are we here for, right?"

Wow, scary! I thought. *Is that what we're here for? To get boys to notice us?* But then I realized Sydney had a point. And if so, maybe I should be listening to these two. They did certainly know how to attract boys' attention.

Suddenly Sydney squealed. "Oh my God! Two o'clock! Two o'clock!"

What? What was happening at two o'clock?

Callie flipped her hair and I could see her straighten her clothes. She grabbed Sydney's arm and linked her hand through it, squeezing tightly. I hate when girls walk together like that—it's so annoying! Anyway, I watched to see what was happening.

And just then, I spotted Matt! My stomach felt like it dropped to the floor, and I was hot and cold all over. I'm pretty sure I had an insta-blush. I looked down at the linoleum tiles, then at the lockers on either side of me, the ceiling, anywhere but toward Matt, who was ahead and to my right, walking with a friend toward me. Should I say hi? What was my plan? Suddenly I couldn't remember what I had planned to do! Why didn't I have my strategy book with me? I stared—past my skirt—at my toes.

"Hey, guys!" Sydney called in a loud, high-pitched voice that was sickeningly sweet in a very fake way.

I looked up to see who she was talking to, and it was Matt and his friend!

Callie was pink and she was grinning from ear to ear. What was going on? In confusion, I looked back and forth between the two pairs of friends.

Matt and his friend smiled at Callie and Sydney and nodded in greeting. Matt's friend said something quietly to Matt and Matt nodded again, laughing.

I opened my mouth to say hi to Matt, but thought better of it. I snapped it shut and put my head back down. I couldn't tell if he had seen me. I wondered if either of the boys was the one that Callie liked from camp, and crossed my fingers that it wasn't Matt. Talk about variables! I definitely didn't factor *that* into my experiment!

Okay, calm down, I told myself. *Deep breaths, Alexis.* This was excellent data to collect. I didn't say hi first and he didn't say hi either. But if I said hi first, he certainly would have said hi back. And, maybe next time, he would say hi first. I mean, maybe he didn't even see me, right? And if he didn't see me, how would he know I was wearing a skirt?

How utterly humiliating.

Later, at lunch, I tried to casually grill Emma for information on Matt. I wanted to see if I could piece together whether Callie liked him, or the friend he was with in the hall. But I had to do all this without making Emma suspicious—and that was not easy.

I peeled off the top of my yogurt container and as casually as I could, I asked, "What are you guys thinking of for next summer?"

Mia sighed. "I'd really like to do a fashion design camp in the city," she said. "It's almost like summer school. The only problem is that it's expensive and my mom's also not wild about me sitting indoors under fluorescent lights all summer. I think I have Eddie on my side though, so we'll see." Eddie is her stepfather, and he is awesome.

"I think I might go to the camp that my mom went to when she was a girl," Katie said. "You know, the one she went to with Callie's mom?"

Bingo! "Oh," I said. "Is that the camp where Callie went last summer?"

Katie nodded as she unwrapped her sandwich. "It's supposed to be really fun."

"Right, I was at the same camp," I reminded her. "It was fun. You got to try all different kinds of sports and activities."

Emma nodded, swallowing a gulp of chocolate milk. "Matt went last year too, and he loved it. He was a lifeguard so it was, like, half-price."

What? Matt was at the same camp as me last

summer? Why didn't I remember this? I sputtered and almost choked.

"Whoa! Hands up in the air!" said Mia, patting my back.

Mortified, I looked around the lunchroom to make sure no one else had seen me. I coughed and cleared my throat.

"That's cool," I said in a froggy voice. "Did he . . . *ahem!*" I cleared my throat again. "Did he go with friends?" I asked as innocently as possible.

Emma looked quizzically at me, then slowly said, "Why, yes. He went with Joe Fraser."

"Oh!" I nodded and quickly looked down, pretending to scrape the bottom of my yogurt cup. So there was hope! Maybe that guy today was Joe Fraser! "Anyway, maybe you'll be in my bunk," I suggested to Katie.

"That would be great!" said Katie enthusiastically.

Emma was still looking at me, so I shrugged and added, "Or maybe I'll go to math camp . . . or this cool business camp I read about."

Katie looked puzzled, but didn't say anything.

"Oh, Alexis!" said Mia playfully. "Leave it to you to find a business camp for kids!"

"Speaking of which, are we meeting today?"

Emma asked, finally turning her attention away from me. Whew! There would be no more fishing for information about Matt today. Emma was definitely suspicious, and I knew in my heart of hearts that it would not be a good thing for Emma to find out that I had—yes, I had to admit it to myself after today's noninteraction in the hall—a *major* crush on her brother.

"Oh! It's supposed to be at my house, but my mom asked if we could move it because she's having a dinner party tonight," said Mia. "She doesn't want the kitchen all messed up. I'm so sorry!"

Katie spoke up. "We can't do it at my house either because my grandma is visiting and she will, like, take over if we have it there. I love her, but it's just a little annoying."

Here was an opportunity! I had to think fast. "Oh, bummer! I think Dylan has her study group at our house on Tuesdays . . ." I started to say. Didn't she? Yikes. I'd better check or risk getting caught in a lie. We all looked hopefully at Emma.

Emma sighed. "Fine, we can do it at my house again," she said. "I just think it's so boring and gross. I'd so much rather be at someone else's house where it's quiet and clean and private! Anyway, Jake might be there."

Jake was Emma's little brother, and he could be a bit of a bother.

"Thanks, Emma!" I said. I think I sounded a little too gushing, because she gave me another funny look.

"Okay, *not* a big deal," she said.

"Right!" I agreed, trying to stop myself from smiling too broadly. Tonight I might have another Matt encounter.

And then my heart stopped as I spotted Matt walk into the cafeteria with a group of guys. I could feel my face growing warm, so I quickly looked down at my lunch tray, hoping no one noticed. There was no way he'd come over here, I told myself. But if he did . . .

I reached up and pulled the elastic band out of my hair, casually fluffing my hair and rolling the elastic band onto my wrist. If Matt stopped by, he wouldn't see the skirt, but the hair might be quantifiable.

I watched as he went through the line, and half listened to Emma's summer plans. Suddenly Matt gestured to his friends and began making a beeline toward our table! My mind said "Oh no!" and "Oh yes!" at the same time I quickly sat up and tucked a piece of hair behind my ear. My stomach started doing flip-flops—and then he was next to me!

"Hey, guys," he said.

"Hi," I squeaked. He looked down and smiled!

"Emma," he continued, "Mom asked me to watch Jake on Thursday night, but I just got assigned a group project due Friday. Any chance you can watch Jake and I'll owe you?"

Emma frowned. "I guess so. But it has to be a date of my choice!"

"Fine. Thanks!" he said, and ruffled her hair before taking off.

Emma rolled her eyes. "Brothers," she muttered.

I was thrilled! He had acknowledged me! He had said hi first (sort of!). I couldn't wait to get home and log all this info into my notebook: Score one for "hair down," and none for "skirts." (Whew!)

Now I just had to wait and see if Matt would be at home later today.

CHAPTER 5

Collecting Data

We all arrived at Emma's after school only to find that it was definitely not an option to hold a club meeting there. Emma's mom was having coffee with a friend, and Jake had three little friends over. They had turned the kitchen into a "goo factory," where they were experimenting with every kind of oobleck and gunk that could be created from basic household ingredients.

> 4 little boys + gooey gunk =
> total mess

What was amazing was that Emma's mom didn't seem bothered by the mess. My mother would have needed serious CPR if that was going on in her kitchen!

But Emma wasn't pleased.

After I said a quick hi to Emma's mom, I casually (as casually as I could) walked out to the TV room, but no one was there. I went back to the mudroom to Matt's locker (the Taylors all had lockers to hold their gear), and I saw that it was empty. I sighed heavily.

Emma narrowed her eyes at me when I returned. "Did you lose something?" she asked, almost in an accusing tone.

"What? Oh. No . . . no. What?" I stammered awkwardly. "Hey, uh, we can go to my house instead. It's okay," I offered.

Emma was still staring at me.

"I thought Dylan had her study group there?" asked Mia. Mia kind of worshipped Dylan so she filed away every tidbit I said about her.

I shrugged. "Well, maybe they can sit in the den," I said, then heard Emma mutter something under her breath.

"What?" I asked. "Is something the matter?"

Emma looked annoyed. "I don't know why we didn't just go there in the first place," she said.

Now I felt a little annoyed. "It's not exactly ideal

if Dylan's there," I countered. "You know how irritating it is when your siblings are around. It can be really distracting."

"My point exactly," said Emma, looking right at me.

Wait, did she know? But she couldn't. I hadn't done anything to give it away, had I? I shifted uncomfortably and said, "Let's go."

We trudged over to my house. And thankfully (for not making a liar of me) but annoyingly, Dylan was there with her two best friends, Meredith and Skylar.

"Hey, kids," Dylan called out, acting super-friendly for the sake of my friends, I supposed.

"Hi. Are you having your study group here?" I asked.

"Yes," she replied. "We're also working on some new cheer routines."

Have I mentioned that Dylan is maniacal about cheerleading? Maybe more manic about it than about anything else! When she decided she wanted to try out for cheerleading, she was still in eighth grade, but she went to all the practices over at the high school *a year in advance* and videoed them on her Flip. Then she uploaded the videos and studied the routines on her computer and learned them all.

She practiced and stretched and ran and did their whole warm-up routine. And when tryouts started freshman year, they signed her right on. It was like she'd already been doing it for a year anyway. Now she's assistant cheer captain and she's only in tenth grade! Talk about an overachiever. Rah-rah!

"Can we use the kitchen to bake?" I asked. "We have one more test recipe to run through for your party proposal." I knew that if I made it about her, I'd have a better chance at taking over the space.

"Yay! Do we get free samples?" squealed Meredith, who had a major sweet tooth.

I smiled and nodded. You had to love a fan.

Dylan looked at me. I hoped she wasn't going to get all power-trippy on me and say no just for the sake of saying no. Luckily, she simply said, "Just let us finish our drinks, and then we'll move." In our house we aren't allowed to have food or drinks anywhere but the kitchen.

I nodded. That was fair. Maybe the old Dylan was back. She turned back to her friends, and we began dumping our stuff on the couch near the back door.

My ears pricked up when I heard Dylan ask, "So what did he say next?" I glanced back at them. Were they talking about boys?

Meredith smiled shyly in response. "He said he'd like to see me again!"

It sounded like I might get useful info from listening in. Just as I was turning my head to hear their conversation better, Katie asked, "Want to go watch TV? Maybe I can find a *Dancing with the Stars* rerun."

Besides the fact that I live for TV dancing shows, I normally would have said yes just to get away from Dylan and her posse. But today I really wanted to hear what they were discussing.

"Um, you guys go ahead," I said. "I'll just get some stuff set up in here first so we're all ready to go when they're done." I was determined to get as much info as I could from these veterans of the romance trenches.

"Do you need help?" Mia asked sweetly. But that was the last thing I wanted right now! Even though it was Mia, I didn't want to have to make conversation and not be able to pay attention to what Dylan and her friends were saying.

"No," I said more forcefully than I meant to. "Thanks," I corrected myself. "I'm good."

I watched as Mia and the others exchanged looks, then shrugged their shoulders before heading to the den.

I turned back to hear what Dylan and her friends were discussing, only to hear Emma ask me, "Do you have a copy of *Jane Eyre* here? I'm supposed to read two chapters for homework, but I left my copy at home."

Sigh. I love my friends, but they were really bothersome right now! "Sure," I said without even looking at Emma. "Upstairs on my desk."

With my ears tuned to my sister and her friends, I quickly busied myself with measuring out ingredients. The Cupcake Club buys in bulk at a warehouse club and then we divvy up the supplies between our houses. My house, though, holds the bulk of the stuff since I'm in charge of purchasing. I also set out our supplies and preheated the oven.

Room-temperature
ingredients x 5 minutes
of mixing with paddle
attachment = light cupcakes

I made sure everything was neatly aligned on the counter: mixing bowls, measuring spoons and cups, rubber scraper, stand mixer, and timer. I adore the order and mathematics of baking: Add this amount of something plus this amount of something else, cook at this temperature, and you will get this—every time! Now if I could just get the right recipe for Matt + Alexis! I laughed at the thought.

As I took stuff out of the cupboards, I tried to figure out what Dylan and her friends were talking about. Apparently there was an upperclassman Meredith had met at the library where she worked after school, and things were "getting hot" between them. Usually I would have found this kind of talk really boring and a waste of time, but today I felt differently. It looked like I could get a lot of useful info from them.

I quietly moved closer to the table, trying not to miss a word.

"So I wore the sweater you suggested," Meredith told Skylar.

Skylar nodded. "Good," she said. "And?"

"Well, it looked good, and like you said, it's very . . . soft and fluffy, and it's a girlie color. I guess guys really do like that stuff because he did touch my arm when we were talking, like he wanted to feel the material."

"And the perfume?" asked Dylan.

"Yes," said Meredith. "I did just what you said. I wore that vanilla spice from Bath and Body Works. I felt like a doughnut! But I noticed him kind of sniffing the air—in a good way!—when I bent over to stack some books on the cart."

"Well, I told you about the study! Men love vanilla and pumpkin pie above all other scents! It has been tested!" Dylan said, laughing. I was surprised. Boys love Dylan, but I never thought it was something she put any thought or effort into!

"They're all just little boys at heart. They want baked goods and fuzzy things!" Dylan added. She sounded so mature saying that, like she had done it all. She did have a lot of boy friends, but Mom and Dad had just started letting her go out on dates this year. I knew Skylar had a boyfriend over the summer, but I didn't think he was still in the picture. I remembered hearing about some breakup story, but that was way before I was interested in that kind of thing. Like, more than a week ago.

Okay, I thought, the baked goods part sounded easy, especially for me: smelling like them, providing them, describing them in tantalizing detail. No problem! Next I mentally raked through my closet. I didn't really own anything that could be described as fuzzy. I definitely had to do something about that.

My data collecting was going so well that I grew a little bolder. I jumped up to sit on the kitchen island to make sure I didn't miss a word they were saying. I couldn't tell if they noticed me and were ignoring me, or noticed me and were kind of putting on a show for me, or if they just didn't notice me at all (most likely). I waited for Dylan to order me to leave while they finished their drinks. But she didn't.

"And how about your hair?" Skylar asked Meredith. "Was it 'touchable'?" She made quotation marks in the air with her fingers.

Meredith nodded. "I didn't blow it out that day. I set it in rollers, just like we discussed, so it was all springy and curly. He said that it looked different and he actually told me he liked it!" She blushed. "So getting up extra early was worth it!"

"Good." Dylan nodded. "The *Seventeen* survey said that men prefer wavy or loosely curly hair above all else." Boy, I had no idea my sister knew so much about this stuff!

I started thinking about curls. I have a little pack of rag curlers my grandma gave me one Christmas when I was in a *Little House on the Prairie* phase. I had wanted to create curls the way the Ingalls girls did. I could find those and see if they still worked!

I wished I had my notebook so I could write all this stuff down. I tried to visualize equations in my mind to help me remember what the older girls were saying:

Fuzzy texture + girlie color = boy touching your arm

Loopy curls - straight hair = compliment

Food scents / vanilla + pumpkin = boys sniffing

I was intrigued by the studies the girls were saying they had read about boys and what they liked. I had no idea that actual research dollars were being spent on this kind of thing! But now that I thought about it, it made sense. For instance, perfume companies spend a fortune developing perfumes that are supposed to make men fall all over the women who wear them (if you believe the ads). So why wouldn't they put lots of dollars into researching which smells men like best? And shampoo companies of course research what kind of hair men like best. Then they release that information right at the same time they're releasing the new products that make women's hair do just that! I liked figuring out businessy things like this. When things fit neatly into place, it makes me very, very happy. But I also liked the fact that people—scientists, even!—were spending valuable time and money on just the kinds of experiments I was conducting myself. It made what I was doing seem worthwhile.

But more important, I couldn't believe that I'd never paid any attention to the magazines and websites that Dylan and her friends liked to read. It was crazy to think that they were chock-full of all this scientific information about attracting boys, and I'd never known it! Well, I made a mental note to borrow some magazines from Dylan and go online as soon as I could.

Just then Emma came back into the kitchen holding my copy of *Jane Eyre*. She also had a funny look on her face. But I didn't want her interrupting my fascinating information session, so I kind of ignored her. But she just kept standing there, like she wanted to say something to me.

"What?" I finally whispered.

Emma looked at Dylan and her friends, then she shrugged and turned to go back to the TV room. *Whatever,* I thought, and sighed loudly.

Dylan turned to me. "Is that really a hint?" she snapped.

"What?" I was alarmed. I wasn't trying to get rid of them! "Oh, no, not at all!" I said quickly. "Take your time. I wasn't rushing you. . . ." My fear must've been obviously genuine, because Dylan's face softened.

"We're ready, actually," she said. "Come on, girls. Let's go outside for a few minutes to work on cheering before we start the chem review."

Meredith and Skylar gathered their mugs and things and, still chatting, went out to the yard. I wish I could have gone with them. I had really gotten some good intel, but it only left me hungry for more.

Then Emma and Katie wandered in. "Ready?" they asked.

"I guess," I said, then realized how I sounded. What was I thinking? We were here to work on our business! We were here to make money! Why was I moping about some boy and filling my head with silly tricks and tips? This was so not me at all! "I mean, yes, I'm ready!" I said brightly. "Let's make some money!"

"Well, all righty then!" said Katie. And we eagerly set to work.

It wasn't until I got upstairs after everyone left that I found my Project M. T. notebook on top of my desk. I had forgotten to put it away last night, not thinking anyone would see it. My heart raced as I thought about Emma. She must have seen it; that's why she gave me that look.

I flipped through it. Luckily, I never mentioned Matt's name. I only called him "The Crush." I actually shivered in relief, but that was a close call. And now I'd have some sort of explaining to do with Emma if it came up (I certainly wasn't going to bring it up myself). I picked up the notebook and looked around the room. Everything in my room was as neat as a pin. All except one place.

I lifted a key out of my desk drawer and used it to open the top drawer in my antique wood dresser. It is a wide and deep drawer, and inside is total chaos. It's the only place in my world that's not organized . . . well, until now with this Matt thing. My messy drawer is where I stash makeup, cheap trinkets, sunglasses, and old candy. I dropped the notebook in and shoved the drawer closed, then relocked it. I was probably too late, but better late than never (which is definitely *not* one of my mottoes).

CHAPTER 6

Mall Madness

The music they play at Icon is so, so loud, and the air freshener or incense or whatever they use to scent the store makes me gasp for clean air. Plus, it's dark. I mean almost pitch-dark. It is not a place I like to spend any time. But there I was on Saturday, with all the Cupcakers (including Emma, who was being a little weird), looking at the dresses that Dylan had placed on hold for me as "pre-approved" attire for her party.

I couldn't believe it. All three of the dresses she chose matched her party decor: black and gold. Was she trying to tell me that I was simply part of the decor? Whatever it was, I was annoyed. Black is really not my color. I don't think it makes me stand out, and I would like to stand out a little—especially if Matt might be there.

Most of all it just got on my nerves that Dylan felt she could pick what I wore. As if otherwise I would wear something that would embarrass her.

Katie scrunched into the corner of the dressing room. "Can you make some room, please?" she shouted over the music. I don't think Mia could hear her, even though she was wedged right up against her. The attendant had warned us we wouldn't all fit, but we had insisted. I didn't want to do this alone.

The room was so tight that Emma was basically sitting on Mia's lap. I was in a corner, trying to pull the first dress over my head.

"What do you think?" I asked after I finally—after struggling for five minutes—got the dress on.

"What?" shouted Mia.

I sighed. Talking was pointless. I jerked my thumb at the door and then went out into the communal viewing area, which was packed with other girls. We waited our turn in front of the only mirror. Finally we got a spot with a spotlight right above it. At least I could now see myself!

I tipped my head to the side and looked at the dress. It was horrible, all black and droopy. Not my style at all.

"It's fine," I said with a shrug, "if lumpy is the look I'm going for."

"What?" yelled Emma.

"Never mind!" I shouted, then looked at the price tag. "Really never mind!" I added, though no one could hear me.

Katie, Emma, and I went back into the dressing room, but Mia decided to wait outside for my "reveal." I looked at the other two dresses. One was short and flouncy. It had a black tulle skirt and a gold bodice. It was kind of prom dressish. The other one was strapless (nightmare!) and long, with a slit up one whole leg. I couldn't imagine my mother approving that one, but it was the kind of dress that a guy might like to see a girl in. Hmm. That would be my next choice. I grunted my way out of the first dress and slid the leg-slit dress over my head. It was no more than a thin piece of satin, with some gold details at the top in a kind of bandeau bathing suit style. Luckily, because it was so slinky, it slid down easily.

I went back out to look at the dress, then gasped when I saw myself in the mirror. Mia, Katie, and

Emma gasped too. I looked like I was twenty-five years old!

"Wow! You're a hottie!" yelled Katie.

"Yeah, you just need to take off the socks!" Emma said in my ear. I looked down. I had on fuzzy pink crew socks. That part did not look so good, but the rest of me screamed *Dancing with the Stars*!

Mia was nodding, but she had her head tipped to the side. "You look amazing, but you do not look like Alexis Becker." She reached over to a dress hanging on a hook. "Here, I grabbed this from a girl who was going to put it back. Try it."

I looked at the dress in her hand. It was not black. It was not gold. It was not too mature. It was a deep raspberry pink V-neck sweater dress—fuzzy and touchable!

"Look," said Mia. "It has slits up each side to make it dressier, and you'd wear it with pale or gold heels, a gold belt—maybe a chain, even—and a great-looking chunky necklace. Go on! Try it!"

I took the dress from her and went back in alone. Seconds later I was out again and staring in the mirror. The color looked amazing on me. The fabric felt amazing. I really, really loved it!

Suddenly someone tapped me on my shoulder.

I turned around and it was Meredith, with Skylar.

"Hi, Alexis!" they yelled, waving.

"You look awesome!" said Meredith.

Skylar nodded. "If you don't get that, I'd love to try it on!" she said in my ear.

I smiled. "Sorry, but I am getting it!" I replied. "Even though it's not black and gold!"

"I can't hear you!" Skylar shouted, giving me two thumbs-up. "But you look great!" she yelled.

I suddenly felt warm and happy, even though I was a little nervous about what Dylan would say. But I decided that she couldn't control everything!

On my way to pay with the money Mom had given me, I looked around—and spotted the only other nonblack clothing in the store. It was a really nice ice-blue long-sleeved V-neck shirt. And it was marked down from $40 to $19.99! I held the shirt up in front of me. It was my size. And I did have enough cupcake money saved up. I decided I couldn't pass up this great bargain, so I looped it over my arm and walked toward the long line at the cash registers.

"We'll wait for you outside!" called Katie.

I nodded and waved to her. As the line snaked around, I looked at what other people were buying. I couldn't believe how many people liked dressing all in black, and they weren't all Goth girls! Icon clearly knew what they were doing and how much people like buying cheap black clothes in a dark, loud, and stinky store.

I stood in line and found myself right behind Sydney and Callie. Before I could decide what to do, Callie said hi. She's kind of nice. I think if Sydney wasn't around to boss her, and Katie was okay with it, she might even be good in the Cupcake Club, but that just won't happen. I just hoped she liked Joe Fraser and not Matt Taylor. I didn't think I could compete with her.

I looked at Sydney, but she ignored me and talked away on her phone.

Callie pointed at my clothes and said, "Those look nice."

I wasn't sure if she was being serious or ragging on me, so I simply shrugged. But it seemed like she was really interested in talking to me, so I asked, "What are you getting?"

She held up a silky black dress with gold detailing—it was my *Dancing with the Stars* dress!

I smiled. "Wow! That is some dress!" *For a grown-up,* I wanted to add.

Callie giggled. "I don't even have anywhere to wear it, but the price is good and when I tried it on, it looked"—her voice dropped to a whisper—"amazing, if I do say so myself!"

"Yes, it would look great on you," I said, trying to be nice. *Just don't wear it in front of Matt Taylor,* I added silently.

Just then the line began to move, and Sydney hung up her phone.

"See you later!" said Callie.

I waved and turned away, then looked back to see Sydney grab Callie's elbow and whisper something in her ear. Callie looked at me guiltily and then at Sydney. She shrugged but her smile faded. Sydney probably yelled at her for talking to me. *Whatever,* I told myself. But I did feel bad for Callie.

After I paid I caught up with the others outside the store.

"Do we need to go meet your dad now or do we have time to go look at stuff at Claire's?" asked Mia. "They have some chunky necklaces that would look pretty with your dress. Then we still need to find a gold belt and some gold shoes." She thought for a moment, then added, "Kitten heels, I think."

"Let's go meet my dad," I replied. "I can't spend any more money! I'd rather be making money!"

"We know!" said Emma, and we all laughed.

I was just about to tell them about Sydney and Callie when who should come around the corner in front of us but Matt and his friend (was that Joe?)! I froze. How did I look? Was I wearing anything touchable? Pink? How was my hair? Did I smell good? What would I say?

"Hey," said Matt. "What's so funny?" (Ooh, score one for Matt saying hi first! Even though it was to all of us, it still counted! I would need to write that down in my notebook.)

"Hey," Emma replied. "Oh, we were just laughing about Alexis."

"Tsk, tsk, tsk, Alexis! Always making the crowd laugh," Matt said with a wink at me. I almost died! But I wished Emma hadn't said that they were laughing at me. What was I? Some kind of clown? Hmm. Okay, maybe it was all right if he thought I was funny. I mean, funny isn't bad, is it? Anyway, I was happy just to hear him say my name. I giggled and nervously looked around.

Then I caught Emma's eye. And I could tell that she knew. Cripes. What was I going to do now? I looked down at my shoes, which were my dorky-looking Merrells. I would absolutely have to ditch them forever when I got home. I looked up again and willed myself to say something, anything, when suddenly someone called out, "Hey, boys!"

Ugh! Sydney! She and Callie walked up to our group, but their eyes were only on the boys.

Matt turned around. "Oh, hey," he said very casually. I caught his friend looking over at Mia (what is that all about?) and then at Callie and Sydney. Ignoring the rest of us, Sydney linked her arm through Matt's and gave it a squeeze. I started to tense up.

"What are you boys up to?" Sydney asked in a very flirty way, flipping her hair from one side to the other. "Have you eaten lunch yet?"

"What? Oh." Matt looked unsure. "Not yet. Have you guys?" he asked us.

Opportunity knocking! I started to shake my head no, but Emma spoke up. "No. We were just leaving. See ya!"

And she started walking away! Mia and Katie followed her, but I was stuck in my spot. *Wait!* I wanted to yell. *Let's stay! Let's have lunch with them!* Joe seemed to feel the same way because he looked disappointed as Mia walked away.

Sydney was now sort of pushing Callie at Matt, and they were both looking embarrassed.

"Bye!" Matt called to us.

"Later," I said in as casual a tone as possible. I

turned to go with my friends, and I was trying my best to look like I didn't care at all that I just lost out on a chance to have lunch with Matt.

We rode the escalator down in silence to meet my dad in the parking area. I hated Sydney, but that was nothing new. I also kind of hated Matt now. And Emma. Why couldn't she have said, "Oh, sorry, Sydney Horrible Whitman, but we are all going back to my house with my cute brother and his cute friend and we are going to hang out all day and play Wii and you are so not invited." *Why couldn't she have done that?*

Outside my dad waved from his spot in the pickup area. He looked so happy to see us that I felt a tiny bit better.

What cheered me up more was when he said, "Want to go to Harrison's for lunch?"

Harrison's Roast Beef is my absolute favorite lunch place in the whole world. It would be hard to stay upset if I was going there. Plus, if we all went to lunch together, it meant Emma would not catch me alone and have a chance to grill me about what she found out today.

So I called back, "You betcha!" to my dad, and we all hurried to the car.

I'll have another chance to say hi to Matt again soon,

I told myself. *And maybe I'll be dressed better then, anyway,* I thought, looking at my boring outfit. Maybe it was a good thing this happened. This way I could keep up a mysterious air and let Matt think I'm really funny without me having to actually prove it. ("Better to remain silent and be thought a fool than to open your mouth and remove all doubt." That quote is one of my mottoes.)

CHAPTER 7

My Sister Really Takes the Cake!

During lunch at Harrison's my father and I told the Cupcakers about the dance we were planning for Dylan's party. We had been practicing most nights after I finished my homework.

"You have to see how graceful Alexis is!" my father bragged. "She can really cut a rug." He nodded proudly. Some people might say he is a total nerd, but I love him.

"Oh, *Dad*!" I said, like I was embarrassed, but I wasn't really. Our dance was the one thing that I was feeling really good about, as it took me away from all the crazy feelings that were going through my head: my dislike of Sydney, my crush on Matt, my frustration with Emma, the nervousness I was feeling about Dylan and the cupcakes we were about to present to her.

We had a great time at Harrison's. Dad kept us laughing with his corny jokes.

When we got home, Dylan and Mom were at the kitchen table, addressing the last of the party invitations on black envelopes with gold gel pens.

"Hello, Mom! Hello, Dylan!" I called as we walked in.

Dylan nodded at us without saying a word before going back to writing. The scent of the pens was so strong that I could feel it going to my head and making me a little light-headed. I was dying to see if Dylan had addressed the invitation for the Taylors yet; I wouldn't believe Matt was actually invited until I saw it in black and . . . gold. I craned my neck to see where she was on her list (created as an Excel spreadsheet on the computer, of course).

Dylan looked at me. "What?" she demanded.

"Oh, nothing!" I replied, waving my hand, and got ready to start baking.

"Just get going on the cupcakes, because I have to leave for practice at three thirty, and an athlete can't practice on a system filled with sugar."

"Ah, don't worry, we'll be done in plenty of time," I said, smiling at my friends.

Just then Mom asked, "So how did the dress turn out, Alexis?"

I could feel my face grow instantly hot. Should I make up a fib?

"Oh, you know . . ." I was stalling for time, but Katie cut in.

"Oh, Mrs. Becker, you have to see the dress that Alexis bought! It looks so beautiful on her!"

I glared at Katie and elbowed her. Poor Katie looked at me in pain and surprise. Luckily my mother was looking down, so she didn't see this exchange.

What? Katie mouthed at me. I shook my head vigorously, but they had already heard Katie.

"Are you going to show us the dress?" asked Dylan.

"Not right now," I said briskly. "Let's get the cupcake samples ready, and then I'll model it if you have time before practice." This made sense to Mom and Dylan, so they both nodded and went back to what they were doing. Now I could focus on the cupcakes! I would deal with what was sure to be a dress crisis later.

Without any more interruptions, my friends and I were able to work quickly to turn out samples for three different cupcakes: the disco, s'mores, and the gift one. Much as I hated to admit it, Emma had been right about the gold flakes. They looked magical and I knew Dylan would totally go for them. The s'mores were tasty but not elegant, just as we had suspected, and my little gift idea looked great, but not very appealing.

We stood holding our breath as Dylan and my parents inspected our treats.

"Oh, girls, these are lovely!" Mom said.

"I'll take them all," said Dad as he playfully lifted the platter, pretending that he was going to run off with it.

"Dad!" I called out just as Dylan took the plate away from him. Suddenly everyone was really quiet and serious as Dylan examined the cupcakes from all angles, tilting her head this way and that like a judge on a cooking show.

"Oh, Dylan, come on!" I said. My sister could be so exasperating!

But Mia grabbed my arm and whispered, "The customer is always right." Since that is one of my own mottoes, I didn't say anything else. I set my mouth in a firm line to keep it shut and crossed my arms in front of me.

Then Dylan leaned over the platter and smelled the cupcakes. I was about to have another outburst, but my mom shot me a look. What was wrong with Dylan? Why couldn't she say "Wow" or "Hmm . . . not what I want," like normal people would?

After what felt like several long minutes of sniffing, Dylan asked, "Do you have a knife?"

I groaned. I couldn't believe she asked for a knife! We were at home, and Dylan knew very well where the knives were. I was just about to say something when Mia replied cheerily, "Yes, we do!"

She picked one from the butcher block and handed it to Dylan with a flourish. Dylan cut each cupcake in half, and then in quarters. They looked really awful all splayed out like that.

"Dylan, honey, what are you doing?" Mom asked.

"I want to see what they look like inside," Dylan answered. "Then I'm going to taste them, but it's not like I'm going to eat an entire cupcake of each!"

"Well, I'd love to try one—a whole one," Dad said. "I've been waiting long enough. Do I have your permission, your highness?" He looked at me and the other Cupcakers and wiggled his eyebrows.

Dylan rolled her eyes. "Okay, let's sample."

My father took a s'mores cupcake, which he'd been eyeing the entire time, and took a huge bite.

"I'm not usually a fan of marshmallows, but this is dynamite!" he said. "I vote for this one."

My mother also picked the s'mores cupcake, and agreed with him. "Oh, the cake alone is so wonderful, but the marshmallows and the cracker crumbs make this absolutely delicious!"

I smiled. I knew those would be the tastiest.

Dylan took a bite of a sliver of the gold flake cake. She chewed it thoughtfully as we waited for her comment. When she put down the rest of her sliver, Emma asked anxiously, "Is it not good?"

"Oh, no, it's fine. I'm just not a big dessert person," said Dylan with a shrug. Argh! I wanted to scream. Poor Emma looked disappointed.

Next Dylan tried the gift cake. She pinched off a bit of the fondant and nibbled on it. Then she took a tiny bite. She bobbed her head from side to side as she chewed, as if she was weighing it against the previous cupcake. Finally she swallowed and turned toward the cabinet.

"Well?" I asked.

Without answering me, Dylan took her time getting a glass and filling it with water. Then she held one finger up while she drank and we all waited.

"Fine," she said finally.

"Fine?" I asked, annoyed. "What does 'fine' mean? Do you like it or not?"

"Dylan, try the s'mores one. You will love it," said my father.

"Okay, okay," she said, like she was doing us a huge favor. As with the other samples, Dylan took a small bite, and we all watched as she chewed. Now, I spend a lot of time around people eating cupcakes, and I know what I see. I could tell that Dylan *loved* that cupcake! Her features softened, her eyes lit up, and her mouth lingered over the bite before swallowing it. I'm sure I even saw a slight smile on her face when she was done.

"So?" My mom asked, as sure as we were that Dylan's choice would be the same as hers and Dad's.

Somehow the Dylan who enjoyed that very delicious s'mores cupcake two seconds ago was able shake her head and look sympathetic. "I am so sorry, kids, but none of these is right for my party," she said.

There was silence for a moment. We were all stunned, even my parents.

"Wh-wh-what?" I stammered. "What do you mean? You loved that last one! I saw it on your face!"

Dylan shook her head again with a look of

pity. "No, Alexis, the problem is that the tasty one is ugly and the pretty ones aren't very tasty." She shrugged. "Back to the drawing board?"

"Argh!" I screamed.

"Girls, girls, you all did a wonderful job. Dylan, how about a thank-you, first of all, to the Cupcake Club," instructed my mother. I could tell she was mad.

"Thank you," Dylan muttered without looking at us.

My friends were all standing there, not sure what to say. I was mortified. Who was this mean girl and what had she done with my sister, Dylan?

My mom took Dylan by the arm and led her out of the kitchen, which was a good thing, for Dylan's own safety.

"Well, I loved them!" Dad said enthusiastically. "How could anyone possibly choose? Now, let's see, if I was having a birthday . . ." He was clearly trying to make us feel better, but it was not helping.

"It's okay, Dad. We'll just clean up," I said, gently shooing him out.

Later, as I was washing off the frosting bowl, thinking about how mean and ungrateful Dylan was, my party dress popped back into my mind. *Ha!* I thought. *I'm glad I got a pink dress! Why should I have to go along with everything Dylan says and wants, any-way? I'm sick of having to do everything she says.* Now, instead of dreading what she would say about my dress, I couldn't wait to see her face when I put it on!

CHAPTER 8

Hello, New Me!

Right before Dylan left for cheerleading practice, she sent out an e-mail my mother made her write. It was to everyone in the Cupcake Club:

> Dear Cupcake Club,
> Thank u 4 the cupcakes u baked 4 me.
> I'm sorry if I was a difficult customer, LOL.
> I'm sure we will reach an agreement at some point.
> Dylan

It felt a little halfhearted, if you ask me. Note that she said "*if* I was a difficult customer" not "*that* I was a difficult customer." That is pure Dylan. Anyway, I figured that my parents are the real clients and

I knew we could find something that would work for everyone. I just felt bad about Emma and her gold flakes, not to mention embarrassed in front of my friends that I had such a jerky sister.

The others were nice about it, though, and in the end we were all laughing. Plus, they got me excited about my dress, and I actually tried it on and modeled it for my parents a few minutes after Dylan had left for practice. My parents loved it, and my mother said, "eh," when I told her that Dylan would probably be really mad. My father twirled me around, and we both decided it was perfect for our dance. I only hoped Matt would like it as much as everyone else did.

My father and I were still twirling, and my friends and mother were talking in the living room, when Dylan suddenly rushed in, breathless. I froze.

"Has anyone seen my other sneaker?" she cried in despair.

Then she saw me and narrowed her eyes. "*What* are you wearing?" she asked.

All the courage I felt before about standing up to her left me. "Um . . . ," I said.

"It's her dress for your party!" Mia sweetly answered.

"Yes, doesn't she look amazing?" Katie added.

Oh, great. I braced myself for a big speech from Dylan.

"What?" she shrieked before stamping her foot. "It's pink! This is not one of the dresses that I picked out! You know what the party colors are—"

Before Dylan could launch any more ugly words at me, Mom grabbed her and pulled her out of the room. Again! My friends and Dad and I were all speechless for a minute.

"Whoops," Emma finally said.

"I should not have said anything!" Mia said, looking really upset.

"Don't worry, girls," Dad said, "I apologize for Dylan's rude behavior . . . again. Don't ever turn sixteen!" He left the room to look for Mom and Dylan.

"Wow," I said. "Sorry about that. I guess I knew it would come, sooner or later."

No one knew what else to say, so we stood around awkwardly until Emma suggested that they leave. I hated for my friends to leave on such a sour note, but it was probably a good idea.

As the girls headed out the door, Emma turned to say, "Thank you for a lovely afternoon." And we all started laughing, hard.

"Oh! Don't forget these!" I said, handing each

of them their black-and-gold party invitations. "Dylan can't wait to see you all at her party next month! Just don't forget to wear pink!" This got us all howling again.

"What are we doing tomorrow?" asked Katie once she stopped giggling.

"Is Dylan free?" Mia asked with a straight face, and we all fell down laughing.

When we finally stopped laughing, my friends left, promising to talk again later. I cringed at the thought of them discussing Dylan. Ugh. Emma was lucky she had brothers.

Mean sister + friends
witnessing = total
embarrassment

As mad as I was about Dylan's behavior, I didn't feel like asking Mom what happened when she talked to Dylan. I needed a break from thinking about her. All I could think about was working on Project M. T. But first I had to throw my Merrells to the back of my closet. "Buh-bye," I whispered. "See you guys some time after never."

Then I opened my locked drawer and took out my notebook, grabbing some forbidden SweeTarts along with it. I sat at my desk and first logged in my most recent encounters with Matt, noting who said hi first and (possibly) why. Then I turned on my computer and googled some studies about how to attract boys.

I found out some crazy stuff! Like girls care more about boy's looks than boys care about girl's. And that boys like faces that are symmetrical. That is their main thing, not that they actually realize it. Just the researchers did.

Hmm. I wondered about my face. Do I have a symmetrical face? Doesn't everyone? I mean, I have two eyes, two eyebrows, two nostrils. I stood up and looked at myself in the mirror. I looked pretty symmetrical. But was I really?

I clicked on the lamp and propped my chin on my fists. I wanted to examine myself scientifically. Here's the data I collected: My left eye was a little bigger than my right eye if you looked really closely. Also, my left eyebrow kind of had a pointed arch while my right one was more of a smooth arch. Eek! Was that bad? My nose looked the same on both sides, and my cheeks, ears, whatever. I couldn't tell if one was off.

I went back to the computer. How symmetrical did you have to be? I googled again and learned that on a scale of one to ten, Angelina Jolie is only a 7.67 in symmetry. The researcher said she lost points because of those lips. Gosh. If Angelina wasn't a perfect ten, that was not good news for me. I am no Angelina Jolie, that's for sure.

I read on. Another article said boys liked makeup on girls, but only two kinds: foundation to even out skin tone, and eye makeup, to darken the eyes. My skin is pretty even, but eye makeup was something I could try.

I reached into my top drawer and took out an eye makeup kit that Mia had given me at a sleepover. It had dark shadow, light shadow, medium shadow, eyeliner, and mascara. I had no idea how to use any of them, but how hard could it be? If I needed help, there was a little map in the box that showed how to put it all on.

I suddenly decided I needed a total makeover.

Makeup + hairdo + new outfit = gorgeous and noticeable Alexis!

I grabbed the eye makeup kit, along with the curlers from my grandmother, the new ice-blue shirt, and purple beads I already had, and hustled down the hall into the bathroom. I ran a shower, shampooed my hair, and then, following the directions on the package, I rolled my hair up in the curlers and used a blow-dryer. Next, I put on the blue shirt and beads, and began applying the eye makeup.

I used eyeliner to draw a thick line along my upper and lower lashes, just as I'd seen my old babysitter do when I was younger. I stood back to look at what I'd done. Wow, I looked a lot older! Then I leaned back in and brushed light shadow just below my (asymmetrical) eyebrows and then, following the diagram in the kit, medium shadow in the creases of my eyes, and finally, the darkest shadow along the rim of my lid. Finally, I opened the mascara and brushed my eyelashes to a staggeringly long length.

I stood back again. OMG.

I either looked like a raccoon or a supermodel. I couldn't decide which. I turned my head all the way to the left and looked back at the right side of my face; then I looked back at my left side. I liked the left better. Next, I looked straight at the mirror and sucked in my cheeks, trying to look vampire-ish. Then I tucked my chin under and looked up through my eyelashes. That was the best look, I thought. The only thing ruining it was the curlers. I put my hand to my head and touched them. They were dry. Time for the big reveal!

I loosened the curlers without looking, then I flipped my head down and ruffled my hair with my hands, finally flipping my hair back as I stood up and looked in the mirror.

Uh, wow? I had a huge head full of curls—and it looked ridiculous! Or maybe it looked great? I didn't know! I knew I looked different, that was for sure.

Just then there was a knock at the door. "Alexis, dinner," Dylan called.

Yikes! I had been so busy making myself over that I forgot what time it was.

What do I do now? Wash it all off and pull my hair back into some kooky kind of ponytail? Or go down there as if nothing was different? I didn't want to spill anything on my new shirt, though.

"What's for dinner?" I called back.

"Grilled trout, broccoli rabe, and quinoa," replied Dylan.

It sounded pretty stain-free. And it was only my family. They've seen me at my worst.

So I smiled and winked at myself as I took one

last look in the mirror. Then I gave myself a big spritz of the cinnamon bun perfume that Dylan had on her side of the vanity. Yum! I smelled like . . . the food court at the mall. Oh well.

"Ta-da!" I cried as I flung open the door, but no one was there.

Just then the phone rang. I looked at the caller ID. It was Emma.

"Hey!" I called out, when I picked up the phone.

"Oh, hello, dear. Is that Alexis?"

It was Mrs. Taylor! "Oh, sorry, Mrs. Taylor. I thought you were Emma!" I said, laughing. "Are you calling for my mother?"

"Oh, no, don't bother her. I'm just calling to RSVP to the lovely invitation to Dylan's party! You were so kind to invite us all. We'd love to come."

"W-w-we?" I stammered.

"Yes, Mr. Taylor, Emma, and the boys and I. It sounds like great fun!"

I couldn't believe it! Matt was coming to Dylan's party! I had visions of seeing him at the party, of him seeing me in my new, fuzzy, touchable dress.

"Alexis . . . are you still there?" Mrs. Taylor asked. Oops!

"Oh, yes, I'm sorry," I said. "It's great that all of you can come!"

"Will you tell your mom for me, please?"

"Of course! She'll be so happy. Thank you! Thank you so much!" I gushed.

Mrs. Taylor laughed. "Actually, we thank you! We'll see you soon, dear."

I did a victory dance after we hung up, then ran down the stairs. "Mom!" I yelled. I couldn't wait to share the good news.

CHAPTER 9

The Beckers Try Harder

"Mom!" I skidded in my sock feet into the kitchen, breathless. "The Taylors can come! All of them!"

"Oh, that's wonderful, honey. Write it down in the RSVP notebook by the phone, then grab a plate," Mom said without looking at me. She seemed extra focused on tossing the salad. "We have a lot to discuss."

I frowned at what she'd said. Her tone told me someone was in trouble, and I knew it was not me.

But Dad did look up and did a double take when he saw the new me. "Whoa, tiger!" he said, laughing.

I wrote the first RSVP on the list and turned to face him. "Hello, Father," I said casually—just as

Dylan walked in and immediately screamed.

"Alexis! What on Earth did you do to yourself?"

At that, Mom finally looked up. "Oh, Alexis!" she exclaimed.

Suddenly I wasn't so sure about my new look. "What? Don't you like it?" I asked (fake) confidently.

Mom came over and lifted a curl. She let it go, and it sprang back against my head. "I love the curls!" she said. "I'm not wild about the makeup, though."

"I'm trying to play up my eyes," I said.

"Well, sister, they are played up, that's for sure," Dylan said with a snicker. Then she peered over my shoulder to look at the RSVP book. "Who called? The Taylors? Already? And they're *all* coming? Ugh! What's that smell? Are we having apple crisp for dessert?"

"It's my perfume," I said stiffly.

"All right, before any of this goes any further, I'd like you to get your food and sit down at the table. We are having a family meeting." My mother was using her firm voice (parenting class), sounding the way she does when I talk to her on the phone while she's at work.

Dylan huffed, but didn't say another word as she

sat down. I had to admit I was looking forward to seeing her in the hot seat.

"Girls," my mother began, "we are not acting as a fully functioning family unit. There is discord, agitation, unhappiness, malice, greed, envy, you name it." She looked at both of us until we returned her level gaze. As I was pretty guilt-free, I just sat there, but Dylan did squirm a little.

"Your father and I are disappointed in the turn things have taken. In our family, we do not condone speaking rudely to one another, nor treating one another dismissively or high-handedly, nor do we humiliate one another in public. The Beckers are loyal, supportive, and kind. The Beckers . . ."

"Try harder," I finished. It was our family tagline. Ever since my mom had read *The Seven Secrets of Successful Families*, we had to have a motto as well as other "guiding principles." Never mind that our tagline was the same tagline as some international car rental company.

"Exactly right," Dad said, nodding.

"And there hasn't been enough trying lately," Mom added, looking at me.

I was surprised. Why me? "I have been trying!" I protested. "I made the cupcakes, I went to that smelly clothing store—"

"Okay, Alexis. We know." My mother raised her hand. "Dylan—"

"Oh, it's always me!" Dylan cried. "Why is she never in trouble?"

"Because I'm perfect!" I gloated.

"That's enough, Alexis," Mom warned. "You need to be more gracious. We have seen to your wishes, inviting your friends to the party and hiring you to create the cupcakes—"

"Wait! That's not a done deal!" Dylan yelled.

"Yes, it is," said my father sternly. "And you don't have to yell."

"But they haven't even presented a good option yet—"

"I am sure that they will," Dad replied as Mom nodded in agreement. "The Cupcake Club will be providing the dessert."

Yay!

"That is so unfair!" Dylan said, leaning back and crossing her arms. "It's *my* birthday party! I should—"

"Dylan, listen to me," Dad said. "What is unfair is how you humiliated Alexis in front of her friends today. Twice. You put them through the wringer on timing and color scheme. Then you treated them like peons when you sampled their hard work. You acted like a spoiled brat and were totally ungrateful. These girls all look up to you, and any one of those wonderful cupcakes is worthy of your party. Then you were absolutely horrid about Alexis in her pretty dress. This party-planning has made you high-handed and inconsiderate. We understand that you want it to be a wonderful event, but nothing is perfect. You must understand that people will still like you even if your cupcakes don't look like they were made on TV and your sister doesn't match the color scheme!"

Dylan was looking down. It looked like Dad's words were sinking in.

"The most important thing in life is how we treat people," he continued. "And you have not been treating any of us nicely. So before things get any worse, your mother and I say stop! Stop it right now! And bring back the wonderful daughter we had before all of this started."

I looked sideways at Dylan, but couldn't tell what she was thinking.

A heavy silence hung over the table. Then finally, Dylan said, "I'm sorry," in a very quiet voice. "It's just . . . oh, never mind. I'm just sorry."

My mother came around the table to give her

a hug. She kissed her on the top of her head and said, "We love you, honey. The real Dylan. Not this party-planning nightmare person, do you understand?"

Dylan nodded, tears filling her eyes. My father reached over and took her hand. "We know you want this party to be special, and it will be," he said. "We will all work hard to make it so. You just need to do your part and be gracious. Take a deep breath and know that everything will be fine. Okay?"

Dylan nodded again, then picked up her fork. I think she finally realized how mean she'd been lately. My parents and I chatted about random stuff as we ate, but we all finished quickly. I went upstairs to shower again and get rid of the makeup. Then I changed into my pj's and went back to my room. When I got there, I found Dylan sitting at my desk! My Project M. T. notebook was on the table in front of her and she was staring at me.

"Oh my God," I said.

CHAPTER 10

Is She Really My Sister?

Dylan had the notebook in her hand and started walking around me. "What is this?" she asked in a teasing voice.

I thought I might throw up. I studied Dylan's face to see if I could tell which way this was going to go. Was she going to mock me? Pity me? Blackmail me?

"Um . . . ," I said, stalling for time.

"Are you . . . Do you like someone?" she asked.

I decided to take a breezy, confident tone. "Well, what if I do?" I asked.

"So what is all this . . . math and stuff in here?"

"Oh, just data!" I waved my hand dismissively. The less she thought I cared, the less she would press me. Probably.

"Who is it?" she asked.

I didn't know if the talk at dinner made her turn over a new leaf or if it made her resent me. I wasn't sure I should tell her. What if she ended up using it against me?

"Um . . ."

"You can tell me," she said encouragingly. "I won't say anything." Dylan even looked sincere, so I decided to tell her.

"Um . . . it's Matt." Maybe if I didn't say his last name . . .

"Matt Taylor?" she guessed immediately.

I looked down at my feet and nodded, feeling my cheeks suddenly getting hot.

"He's cute," she said, and for some strange reason I was happy that she "approved" of my choice. "Does he know you like him?" she asked, flipping through the pages.

"No!" I said quickly, horrified by the idea.

"Do you want him to know?"

"What? No way!" I'd rather die.

"So where are you going with all this?"

"I just . . . I just want him to notice me. And like me, I guess." There. I'd said it.

Dylan was quiet for a moment. Then she asked, "Do you want my help?"

I eyed her suspiciously. "What do you mean?" I could just picture her telling Matt flat out that I liked him, and that would be a disaster.

"I know what it's like to have a crush who hardly knows you exist, that's for sure!" Dylan said, laughing.

I paused. Was this a trick?

Dylan continued, "I also know some stuff about boys and what they like. And about how to present yourself." She looked at me critically. "And I do think you're ready for a more mature look. The makeover you did wasn't a bad idea. You just went too far, too fast."

I kept looking at her, not sure if I could really trust my own sister.

"Come on," she said in an encouraging tone. "I owe it to you. Let me try."

"Okay . . . ," I finally agreed. "But in the morning. I can't do it again tonight. I have too much other stuff to do."

"Fine. We'll get up early and do it, okay?"

I nodded, still waiting for this to turn into some sort of prank.

Dylan got up and headed for the door, then turned around. "And Alexis?"

"Yes?"

"I'm sorry."

Wow. An apology from Dylan, and I didn't even have to ask for it!

"For which part?" I asked.

"Everything." And she closed the door.

I sat down and sighed loudly, part of me wondering if I had just imagined the past five minutes. Dylan had really turned around! I started to finish entering the new data and notes on some new techniques, like hair-flipping, arm-grabbing, and lunch-inviting—not that any of them were my style.

I chewed on my pen cap as I asked myself the question Dylan had just asked. What did I want? What was my goal with Matt? Was it that I wanted him to just notice me? He already had. But wanting him to like me back seemed major, and maybe too big of a goal. Like more than I really wanted. I think.

My parents always tell us, when we have a big project due, to break it into smaller, more manageable chunks or goals. So if my big project is for Matt to fall madly in like with me, what would a smaller chunk be?

Chew, chew, chew. I looked at my pen cap. It was totally mangled. I twirled it around, and it looked like it was dancing. And then the answer came to me.

A dance. One wonderful, dreamy dance with Matt. Then he'd see how graceful and talented I was, and I'd have the chance to really charm him.

I smiled just picturing it, like a scene out of a Disney movie: *Cinderella*, *Beauty and the Beast*, *Enchanted*. One dance with the prince, and the rest is history. That was my goal.

Relieved to now have an actual goal, I put the notebook away, then did a huge e-blast to all of the Cupcake Club's previous clients, advertising our new flavors (s'mores being one of them), wrote out forty vocabulary flash cards, did a math crossword puzzle, reorganized my planner, and cleaned up my room.

Later that night, when I went to brush my teeth, I nearly tripped over a pile of teen magazines that Dylan had left outside my door. "Get Him to Notice YOU!," "7 Days to a Brand-New You!," "Flirty Tips & Tricks to Wow Him!" the headlines screamed. Well, I certainly had my work cut out for me.

The next morning Dylan gave me a crash course in flirtation and a real makeover. I think even my parents were happy that we were doing something together and not bickering. It was like when we were little and we used to play Barbie dolls together for hours. My Barbie would run the clothing store and Dylan's Barbie would come in to shop. My Barbie would bargain and haggle and put stuff on sale, and her Barbie would try everything on and leave it in a pile on the dressing room floor.

First Dylan and I looked through the magazines together to find a good new look for me. She talked about what I had heard her discussing with Meredith and Skylar, about pretty colors (no black, gray, or brown), touchable fabrics (fuzzy, floaty, silky, smooth), and patterns (floral is good; plaid, not so much). She went through my closet and also brought out some of her own(!) clothes to put together five new school outfits for me—complete with shoes and accessories!

I have to say, she was really getting into it, and she was being a big help. I think she liked that I was agreeing with everything she said.

Next Dylan made me shave my legs, which was gross and hard and took forever (I cut myself twice), but the result was pretty dramatic. She gave me a mud mask for my face and a quick manicure/pedicure (just clear nail polish because, she said knowledgably, boys don't like colored or fussy nails). Then she had me wash my hair and deep condition it, and she set it in hot rollers we borrowed from our mother. They were heavy and felt like they were pulling out my hair, but when she took them out, my hair fell in soft waves, like a Disney princess!

Finally she taught me how to put on makeup. "The point," explained Dylan, "is that no one should notice you are wearing makeup. You should look like yourself, only better."

Dylan gave me a tiny hint of pink blush to perk up my face and make me look healthy. (According to Dylan, boys respond to healthy looks. It has to do with the evolution of the species.) Then she gave me a cinnamon-and-ginger-laced pale pink lipstick with what she called "blue undertones" to make my lips plump up and my teeth look even whiter. Finally, she drew the faintest lines with brown eyeliner at only the outer corners of my eyes, and then she curled my eyelashes and lengthened them with a little brown mascara. When she turned me around to face the mirror . . . I loved what I saw! I looked great!

"Wow! Thanks!" I exclaimed. It was me, just a better-looking me!

Dylan smiled proudly at me, her handiwork.

"Now let's talk flirtation," she said. "There are two ways to get guys," she said, holding up two fingers. "You can be a normal girl or a supergirlie girl. The supergirlie girl technique tends to work well on younger guys and dumber guys; guys who don't really understand girls and are too shy to pursue them. The normal girl technique attracts the better guys, but it takes longer. Like sometimes years longer. Do you follow me?"

"Um . . ." I wasn't sure what she was talking about. "Do you mind if we go in my room, so I can write all this down in my notebook?"

Dylan laughed. "Fine, whatever," she said.

I made her wait outside while I took the book out of the drawer. "Okay!" I called, and she came in and continued her lecture. I scribbled madly, happy to have specific directions to follow.

From what Dylan was telling me, it seemed that Sydney and Callie go with the supergirlie girl technique, and I prefer the normal girl way.

The supergirlie girl approach meant you had to be aggressive, giggly, loud, super touchy-feely, overdressed, made-up, and perfumed, and you always traveled in pairs, never alone. Supergirlie girls often act grossed out or incompetent to try to get help from boys, and this would in turn make the boys feel good about themselves. However, the supergirlie girl way could backfire because it makes girls appear so different from boys, and some boys could get scared off. But it often worked because boys are so shy and clueless, especially when they're younger, that the girls just go after them and grab them, and the boys never see it coming. They think girls are supposed to be like that, and they're just happy to not have to do the work of asking girls out and stuff. The supergirlie girl approach was based on the idea that boys and girls are totally different and foreign creatures to each other, and girls had to do a lot of planning to get what they wanted.

Whew! I was so glad that Dylan explained all this to me. I never would have known. And I was beginning to think that there might be a perfect recipe for finding love after all.

The normal girl technique was more subtle. You dressed pretty but not overly fancy (you could still ride a bike or play catch in whatever you're wearing), and you might wear a little makeup, but never so the boys could notice it or, God forbid, see you putting it on. You are chatty and fun but not silly or giggly, and you are friendly but not aggressive. You don't travel in big packs and you try to be friends with a boy first. Some boys might be too clueless to realize when a normal girl likes them—that's the bad part—but in the long run, Dylan assured me, you attract better boys with this approach. Most important, the normal girl approach reminded you that boys are not that different from girls. They are people with feelings who are often shy and they just need to be treated with the same consideration you'd give a friend.

"I think I'd rather be a normal girl," I told Dylan.

"Good," Dylan said. "Slow and steady wins the race."

My hand ached after copying all of this down. I couldn't wait to put everything I learned into practice. I only wished I could discuss it all with my best friends.

"Thank you, Dylan," I said. "This is so helpful."

Dylan smiled, looking a little weary after sharing everything she knew.

Just then the phone rang. Would you believe it was Emma, inviting me over? I couldn't get the words out of my mouth fast enough. "Be right over!" I said, and hung up before I made the mistake of asking if Matt was going to be there. I was dying to, but slow and steady wins the race, I reminded myself. I might have to add that to my list of mottoes.

Dylan winked at me. "Go get him, tiger," she said.

"So, I'll let you know how it goes, in case he's there?"

"Who?" Dylan asked.

What? "Dylan!" I cried.

"Kidding!" she said with a laugh.

"Thanks again," I yelled as I ran down the stairs, hopped on my bike, and flew to the Taylors in record time.

CHAPTER 11

Slam Dunk!

"Hey," said Emma when I walked in. "You look nice." She circled me and took in my outfit and hair and everything.

My stomach was all butterflies, and I glanced uneasily around the kitchen. "What's up?" I asked. I wasn't going to tell her about the makeover. Not now, anyway.

And then Emma flatly said, "He's not here."

"Who?" I asked, a little taken aback.

Emma made a face. "Lover boy," she said, exasperated.

I blushed. "What?"

"I knew it!" shrieked Emma. "I was just testing you, but now I know for sure!"

"Know what?" I persisted.

Emma leaned in close. "I know you're in love with Matt," she whispered.

"Me? Matt? *What?*" I felt the heat rising in my cheeks.

Emma nodded, a look of satisfaction on her face. "I figured it out yesterday when we saw him at the mall. You got all blushy and nervous and then I saw that kooky notebook on your desk—"

"You did?" I interrupted.

"Ha!" said Emma. "So you are." It was a statement, not a question.

I sighed and looked down at my feet. "Yes. I'm sorry," I mumbled. It felt good to finally admit it, although it felt really weird. I looked at her. "I just can't help it!"

"It's a little awkward," she agreed. "And why Matt? I mean, Sam, maybe. He's cute and girls seem to really like him. But Matt? Smelly sock Matt? Computer geek Matt?"

"Cute, funny, nice Matt," I countered.

"Gross!" Emma exclaimed, playfully slapping me on the shoulder. After a moment she added, "Too bad Callie likes him too."

"Oh!" I said. "I wasn't sure if she liked him or Joe. I thought Sydney might like Matt."

"I can't believe you like my brother," Emma said as she shook her head.

"Well, it's not that surprising. I mean, you and I are good friends, and our moms are good friends. I guess the Taylors and the Beckers are just well-suited to each other!" Emma smiled. "I wonder if he likes you back?" Then she added in a mischievous tone, "Want me to find out?"

"No!" I screamed. "*Please* don't ask him, Emma." I was begging her, but part of me really did want to know.

"Well, at least he'll be at Dylan's party. Even if my mom has to drag him there," said Emma.

"You don't think he wants to go?" I asked, feeling a slight sting.

"No way! He and my mom had a big fight about it. Sam, of course, wants to go, because there'll be all those cute girls there. Jake will go anyplace where there's Mia or cupcakes, and both is even better. Matt is just . . . I don't know. I think he might be kind of shy about girls."

"Really?" I asked, surprised. From what I'd seen, he seemed pretty comfortable with the attention he got from girls. "He doesn't act that way."

Emma thought for a minute. "Hmm . . . I think what I mean is that I don't know if he's mature enough to like girls, you know. The thing he's really into is sports, especially basketball. So you could brush up on your dunking! That's something to put in your notebook."

The notebook! "Look, the notebook was just—"

"Pure Alexis," Emma said, laughing. "Always taking the business approach. Don't worry, I won't tell anyone about it. And I'm sorry for looking at it. I shouldn't have, but I thought it was a math notebook!"

"Yes, you shouldn't have," I replied. But I couldn't be mad at Emma. She was one of my best friends. Besides, I was happy we were talking about Matt!

"Let me see, what other 'data' can I give you?" Emma asked, looking upward and tapping her chin with one finger. "He loves cupcakes. And he's really into computer graphics. Maybe you could call him up and ask him to help on a project for the Cupcake Club? And then pay him in cupcakes?"

"Oooh! Good idea," I lied. As if I'd call him again.

Emma looked at me with a serious expression. "Can I ask you if you want him to be your boyfriend? I can't imagine Matt being anyone's boyfriend, but whatever."

I hesitated. Should I tell Emma my goal? She was my friend, but she was also Matt's sister. She looked at me expectantly. My goal was much easier to explain than any of my other feelings, so I took a deep breath and confessed, "I want to dance with him at Dylan's party."

Emma's eyes widened. "Wow. That's it? It seems like a small thing, but it actually may be impossible to accomplish. I don't think he dances."

I hadn't thought of that! "Well . . . ," I said, not knowing how to respond.

Suddenly the back door opened. "Hello!" hollered Matt.

"Eek!" I squealed. I was totally caught off guard, even though I had been hoping he would show up.

Matt was all sweaty from practice and had on a hideous pair of ripped sweatpants and a T-shirt. His hair was sticking up every which way. But he still looked gorgeous to me.

He seemed surprised to see me. "Oh, hey, Alexis," he said.

My heart leaped. He had said hi first! I couldn't wait to log *that* data in the notebook!

"Got any cupcakes?" he asked.

I laughed nervously. "No. Not yet." Should I ask him a question now? I didn't know what to do or say. Thinking of Sydney, I flipped my hair from one side to the other. "Huh," was all he said before heading for the fridge.

"Where's Mom?" he asked Emma.

"At Jake's practice," Emma replied, then she winked at me. "Hey, Alexis and I were just going out to shoot some hoops. Want to come give us some pointers?"

I stared at her. What was she doing? I couldn't believe what she had just suggested! I looked over at Matt, who was chugging a Gatorade. He turned and looked at us over the rim of the bottle. When he finished, he let out a really loud burp and grinned.

The burp was gross, and I wondered why he felt it was okay to do that in front of me. But then he said, "Sure," and shrugged, and the next thing I knew I was playing H-O-R-S-E in the driveway with Matt Taylor, man of my dreams! I silently forgave him for burping and quickly got caught up in the game.

I have to say that I am decent at basketball. Not sure why, but maybe because it's kind of like dancing to me. I don't know. Anyway, we were having a pretty good time. I think Matt was even impressed by my skills. This was definitely the normal girl approach, and it seemed to be working.

After about fifteen minutes, Joe Fraser showed up, and he joined the game too. I was so happy! Emma and I challenged the boys to a two-on-two, but they insisted we split the teams, so Matt and I played Joe and Emma. It was awesome. We were winning, 8 to 2, when suddenly somebody called out, "Yoo-hoo!"

Sydney and Callie!

Emma and I looked at each other and frowned. I couldn't tell if Matt and Joe were happy or annoyed. But the girls were definitely happy. They were super dressed up for a Sunday morning, in skin-tight jeans and tight sweaters with tiny down vests, and boots with high heels. Their hair was super-fluffy and they had on tons of makeup and perfume and dangly earrings. I wondered when Sydney had planned this little outing.

"Can we play?" asked Sydney in her high, flirty voice. Callie at least had the grace to look nervous.

Matt shrugged. "Okay." He didn't sound excited, but he didn't sound mad, either. I think he was just being polite. Emma, on the other hand, was really mad. Her face was set like stone.

"I think we need to play H-O-R-S-E again," said Matt.

"What's that?" Callie said, giggling.

Matt explained the game, and he went first, tossing the ball in high over his left shoulder, facing away from the basket. It was an impressive shot.

Sydney clapped and whistled, and Matt grinned. Why hadn't I thought to praise him like that? Then she stepped up to take the shot and threw it so badly that it just flew over her shoulder, landing nowhere near the basket.

"Whoops!" she said with a laugh, covering her mouth with a hand that showed off fresh scarlet nail polish. Sydney clearly didn't care that she had missed. In fact, she probably missed on purpose.

Callie took the ball. She bounced it once or twice, then flipped it over her shoulder, but her sweater was so tight it made her lose control as the ball left her hand; it fell weakly to the ground and rolled away. "Oh dear! I stink!" Callie said, but it was clear she didn't really care how badly she played either.

Now it was my turn. If ever I had wanted something in my life, this was it. I focused like a laser beam and took a deep breath, closing my eyes. Then I bent my knees like Matt had and lifted the ball in a gentle arc over my shoulder. *Slow and steady wins the race,* I told myself. I didn't dare to look, but when I heard the ball thump the backboard and

Matt yelling, my eyes flew open. Matt had both fists straight in the air. "Yes!" he cried. "You made it!" He stuck out his hand for a high five and I slapped it, laughing in giddy relief.

I stole a quick glance at Callie and Sydney and they were both standing there with their mouths open. Sydney started chewing on the end of a piece of her fluffy hair, probably wondering what she should do next. I had a new equation for my workbook:

Sports skills + comfortable clothes = boys impressed by YOU!

A few minutes later Mrs. Taylor pulled up to drop off Jake and pick up Matt and Joe to go to their friend's house for a school project. I didn't really get the chance to say good-bye to Matt, but it was all good. I was still on a high from my totally awesome shot.

"Let's hit it," Sydney said to Callie as soon as the boys left. Sydney didn't bother to say good-bye to Emma and me, but Callie turned to us with an awkward expression. "Well, thanks . . . ," she said.

"See ya," Emma muttered without bothering to look in their direction. We went inside, and Jake immediately went for the couch in the TV room. Emma started to make him a snack in the kitchen.

"Wow," I said.

"I can't believe you made that basket!" said Emma, laughing.

"Me neither!" I howled. "Talk about luck!"

"It was skill," said Emma. "And Matt was impressed."

"You think?" I asked, but I knew he was. My chest was bursting with pride and happiness.

As we headed to the TV room with drinks and Jake's snack, Emma said, "We still have to figure out Dylan's dessert. Let's get the others over here and bake."

"Yay! Cupcakes!" Jake yelled.

"Good idea," I agreed, thinking of the extra cupcakes we could leave behind for Matt!

CHAPTER 12

Confession

Of course, after that wonderful Sunday morning, I didn't see Matt for an entire week. I wore each of the outfits that Dylan had planned for me, and I took great care with my hair (down) and makeup, but no luck. My friends all noticed the change though, and Mia and Katie pestered me about my new look. I was happy that Emma did not let on about my crush, but it wasn't long before they figured it out.

It happened while we were sitting at lunch one day, when Sydney and Callie came over to our table.

"Hey, Emma," said Sydney. We all looked up in shock. Sydney usually just ignores us and rarely calls us by name.

"Oh, hey," Emma replied like she didn't care.

"We have a question. Someone said Matt is going to Dylan Becker's sweet sixteen on the twentieth. Is that true?" She was asking about my sister's party and she didn't even look at me! My blood began to boil.

Emma looked at me and raised her eyebrows. She turned to Sydney. "Yes. Our whole family is going."

"We're all going, actually," said Mia in a cold, snooty voice I'd never heard her use before.

I seemed to have lost my ability to speak.

Sydney and Callie exchanged a look. "Okay, thanks," said Sydney, before she and Callie walked away, their heads bent close as they whispered.

"What was that all about?" I burst out. "Wouldn't you think they would ask me? It's *my* sister they're talking about! And why do they want to know, anyway? It's not like they're invited!"

"They have some nerve," said Katie, shaking her head.

"I am so sick of those two. They just can't leave Matt alone. Someone keeps calling and hanging up, and I swear it's them!" Emma complained.

My stomach flip-flopped. They were calling Matt? That was pretty major!

"Has he actually *spoken* to them on the phone?" I asked, probably with a little too much feeling, because Mia and Katie turned to me with raised eyebrows.

Emma shrugged. "I'm not sure," she answered.

I could feel Mia still watching me. Then she asked with a shy smile, "Alexis, is there something you want to tell us?"

I was so bothered by Sydney that I simply admitted, "Yes, I have a crush on Matt." Then I added, "I'm sure you all already know."

"I didn't tell them!" Emma cried out defensively, even though I didn't look at her.

Katie immediately jumped on Emma. "Wait, you knew?" she asked.

Uh-oh. This had the makings of a cupcake war. I had to stop it before it went too far. "I'm sorry, guys," I told Katie and Mia. "I was going to tell you guys, but there just never seemed to be a right time."

"Well, there was clearly a right time to tell Emma, it seems!" Mia said, sounding a little offended, but I don't think she was actually mad.

"Oh, no, I guessed, actually," Emma said, "and made Alexis fess up. Then she swore me to secrecy. It is just too weird. I can't imagine anyone liking my brother, but now it seems he's getting all this attention from girls."

"Humph!" I said, and crossed my arms.

"So what are you doing about this crush?" Mia asked me.

"I've been doing some research," I said without thinking, and my friends all burst out laughing.

"Research!" Mia yelled. "Alexis, that is just so typical of you!"

"Wait, is that why you've had this sudden makeover and everything?" Katie asked.

I nodded shyly and muttered, "A lot of good it's doing. I've barely even seen him since."

"But it worked when you did see him!" said Emma.

"You think?" I asked, hoping that all my work wasn't going to waste.

Emma nodded. "Hello? He came out and played basketball with us!"

"You don't think he was just . . . bored or trying to be nice?" I pressed.

Emma shook her head. "Uh-uh. He would never be nice for no reason."

"Actually, I think he's really nice. Like when he helped you—"

"All right, all right! We know *you* think he's

nice," interrupted Emma. "I guess he is a little bit. I'm just not sure he's worth the time and effort, that's all."

"Yes, well, if he was a client, I think I would have stopped my aggressive marketing efforts by now," I said, and everyone laughed again.

"So when you say you have a crush on him, what does that mean?" asked Katie.

"Oh, I think he's cute. I want him to like me back. And . . ." I looked over at Emma, and she finished what I was too embarrassed to say.

"She wants to dance with him at Dylan's sweet sixteen."

I bit my lip nervously, unsure how my friends would react. But I didn't have to worry.

Mia clapped excitedly. "Ooh! Once he sees you dance he will fall head over heels in love with you!"

Katie grinned. "Are you going to ask *him*?"

"I haven't quite worked that part out yet," I admitted.

"Between the dancing and the cupcakes, I know he'll be wowed," said Katie loyally.

"Anything we can do to help?" asked Mia.

As much as I wanted to keep talking about Matt, I suddenly remembered there was something more important that we needed to do. "Yes! Let's figure out those cupcakes!" At least that was something that I could control. "Dylan has been on a rampage, so we need to sort it out before she goes nuts. The only thing is, she's also been really nice to me lately, with the makeover and stuff. I think she's just stressed. Let's give her the works!"

"The works?" Katie asked.

"I've been thinking," I said. "Let's forget about the budget for now. Instead, we should wrap up all of our great ideas into one slam dunk of a cupcake."

Emma smiled. "So what is it?"

"The s'mores disco gift cupcake. Chocolate cupcake filled with marshmallow, topped with chocolate frosting with graham cracker and gold flake crumble, and tied with a gold bow. She'll love it. And it will cheer her up."

The girls all agreed, so we made plans to start working on the cupcakes soon.

Dylan had, in fact, been even crankier than ever this week. As the RSVPs for her party rolled in, she became compulsive about checking voice mail and the list. I wondered if there was someone special she was waiting to hear from. Dylan is class president and assistant cheer captain, so I knew she wasn't exactly lacking for friends or popularity. But as I watched her flip through the RSVP notebook one afternoon, I kind of felt sorry for her.

"What's up?" I asked.

"Nothing," she replied. *Flip, flip, flip.*

I tried again. "Are you waiting to hear from someone?" I asked.

Dylan stopped flipping and sighed heavily. "*Don't* ever fall in love, Alexis."

"Too late, Dyl, I'm a goner," I said. "Who are you in love with?"

"Never mind," she said. "Nothing will come of it. He hasn't even RSVP'd."

"Sounds like a jerk," I said. The invitations had been out for days. Whoever she was talking about should have already received it.

But Dylan had bristled. "No, no, no, he's not a jerk," she replied defensively. "He's just very busy! I'm sure he'll . . . he'll let me know soon."

"Okay!" I said brightly, not wanting to upset her. But inside I thought, *Why do boys cause such heartache?*

That night, when my mother came in to say good night, I told her, "Mom, I think I know why Dylan's been such a jerk lately." I'd been puzzling over it all evening, and I was pretty sure I was right.

"Why? I'd love to know!"

"I think she's in love with someone and he might not love her back."

"Hmm . . . that *would* explain a lot."

"I think she wants everything to be perfect at the party so he'll fall in love with her."

"Oh! Is he coming?"

"Well, that's the other thing. He hasn't RSVP'd."

"Poor Dylly."

I nodded and sighed. At least the love of my life was coming. Granted his mother had RSVP'd for him, but it was a start!

"Well, I'll see if I can discuss it with her," Mom said before pulling the covers up tight under my chin. "I love you, sweetheart. Thanks for the tip."

"Of course, Mom. Love you, too."

CHAPTER 13

BF not F :(

The day of Dylan's party was gorgeous: The sky was blue, the sun was shining, and birds were literally singing in the trees. It promised to be a beautiful night. But first there was lots of baking to be done!

The Cupcake Club met at Mia's that morning, which was a good thing, even though I was bummed not to have a chance to see Matt. It was better, because I could focus on making our cupcakes.

We ended up going with my idea of combining all three original cupcake ideas. Dylan had surprised us when she said she "loved" this idea. But these were going to take a lot longer to decorate, so we had to be really organized.

We had an assembly line going once the cupcakes were baked and cooled. I lifted them off the cooling rack in their gold foil papers and filled them with liquid marshmallow using a baker's syringe. Then Katie would frost the cupcakes with dark chocolate frosting, and Emma would add the crumbled graham crackers and gold sprinkles. Finally Mia would tie the base of each one with a big gold ribbon, and set it back on the cooling racks to pack later.

Even though I wasn't anywhere near Matt, I was glad to have him on my mind as Katie and Mia kept asking me questions.

"What position does he play on the basketball team?" Mia asked.

"Oh, point guard, I think," I said.

"Center," corrected Emma.

"Right. I always get those mixed up."

"Have you been to any of his games yet?" asked Katie.

"No, but I think I'm going to go this week. Anyone want to go with me?"

"I always go," said Emma, "if I can. We have a rule in our family that if you can possibly make it to a sibling's game, you have to go, to show support."

"Let me know if he ever needs any extra support!" I said, laughing. "I can always sub for you if you can't make it!"

Emma's response was to playfully stick her tongue out at me. I stuck mine right back at her.

"So what are his favorite cupcakes we've made so far?" Mia asked.

I didn't know the answers to any of their questions, but I wanted them to think I knew something about Matt.

"Oh, I think the . . ." I looked around.

"Bacon," said Emma. "He liked the caramel cupcakes with the bacon caramel frosting. He had me make them for his team dinner."

"Runs in the family!" Mia laughed. The recipe had been Emma's idea.

"He also liked the mini vanillas we made for Mona," I added.

Emma shook her head. "That boy would eat anything if you frosted it."

The vanilla minis were *my* recipe! "Well, he certainly wolfed them down," I retorted.

"Alexis, you don't live with him like I do," Emma insisted. "He even eats burnt cupcakes, as long as they're loaded with frosting."

"Wait a second," I protested, suddenly getting

mad. "Are you comparing my vanilla minis to burnt cupcakes?" I couldn't believe Emma was so rude! She was supposed to be on *my* side.

"Okay, you two," Katie said as she exchanged a look with Mia.

"I just don't know who made you the Matt expert all of a sudden," said Emma. "You barely know him!"

"That's not true!" I said. But it kind of was.

"The only times you ever interact with him, I'm there! So how could you suddenly have this great romance blooming?"

Now I was really mad. "There's no 'great romance blooming,' Emma. I just think he's really cute. And the time when I decided I liked him, you *weren't* there!"

"Well, it's annoying! I'm sick of hearing you talk about him like you own him! You're no better than Sydney Whitman!"

"It's Callie who likes him." I spat the words out furiously.

"Well, it's Sydney who's doing all the work!" said Emma. "Just like me for you!"

"What?"

"Stop, you guys!" cried Katie. "Come on!"

Emma and I glared at each other.

"Speaking of work, we have a whole lot of cupcakes to bake," said Mia, sounding like a parent. "And we need to get them all done today. Business first, Alexis. That's your motto."

"So let's just focus on what we need to do, okay?" Katie added.

I nodded without looking at Emma. I decided I would not speak to her. In fact, I would not speak at all.

Emma muttered something, but I didn't care to ask what she said. I was all business now. For the next few hours, I worked quickly to fill two hundred cupcakes, and by noon we were done. I only talked when Mia and Katie spoke to me. No one was happy that things were tense, but it wasn't *my* fault!

Mom came to pick up the cupcakes and take them to the restaurant. Mia, Katie, and Emma had plans to dress together for the party, and I wasn't happy about that. I didn't want them to all be having fun without me (or worse, talking about me), but I couldn't ditch my family, and it would just be too hectic to have my friends get ready at my house, what with Dylan's chaos going on.

Dylan's crush still had not RSVP'd, which made him uncrushworthy in my book. But I think she was still hoping. Every time the phone rang that afternoon, she dashed to check the caller ID (not that she'd answer the phone, because that would seem desperate).

Meredith and Skylar came over to get ready with Dylan, almost like bridesmaids before a wedding. They were all in black and gold, of course, and when they were ready, they offered to help me with my hair and makeup. Of course I said yes!

Meredith was working on my hair with rollers. "Is there anyone special coming tonight that you're looking forward to seeing?" she asked.

I narrowed my eyes at Dylan. "Did you tell her?" I snapped.

"No, Alexis," Dylan calmly replied. "I didn't say anything to anyone."

"Chill, Alexis, she didn't," Meredith said, a little taken aback. "I was just asking to make conversation, like they do at the hairdresser."

I felt bad. "Oh, sorry. Actually, there is one guy I like. He's . . . he's my friend's older brother. But she's mad at me right now for liking him."

"That's ridiculous! She doesn't own him!" said Meredith.

"I know!" I felt myself getting riled up all over again.

"And it's not like she could marry him, anyway!" she added, laughing.

"You're so right!"

"That happened with me at day camp one summer," Skylar joined in. "I lost a friend that way. I totally regret it."

"What do you mean?" I asked.

"Well, I was about your age, and there was this really cute junior counselor named Tom. And his sister Madison was my best friend at camp. But I became so obsessed with Tom that every time I called Madison, every time I went to their house, it was like it was really to catch a glimpse of Tom. Madison ended up feeling like I was using her just to get to Tom."

"Were you?"

"No! I really liked Madison! It was just inconvenient that the guy I liked happened to be her brother!"

"Well, it was also probably convenient, too," I said knowingly.

Skylar nodded. "Sure, because I got the insider's perspective, and I got to see him casually, without having to go on a date or anything. I could see him in his normal environment."

"But you lost a friend," said Meredith.

"Yes, a good friend," Skylar replied. "And I was so over him by the end of the summer."

"How did you get over him?" I asked.

"We finally went on a date, and I realized we had nothing to talk about when Madison wasn't there."

Just then the phone rang. I was holding the cordless in my lap, and I flipped it over to see what the caller ID said.

"Hanson?" I said aloud.

Dylan screamed, "It's him! Get it! No wait, don't!" But it was too late.

"Hello?" I said.

A deep voice kind of stammered, "Uh . . . hi . . . is Dylan there, please?"

I looked at Dylan and she was shaking her head no.

"Um, no, I'm sorry, she's out right now," I lied. "May I take a message?"

"Yes. This is Noah Hanson. I'm so embarrassed. Dylan invited me to her party, and the invitation got mixed up with my mother's bills, and I only just opened it. I know it's too late to say yes, so I was just calling to apologize. Will you tell her, please?"

I froze for a second.

"Hello?" he said again.

"No! Come! It's not too late! It's . . . a buffet. One more person won't make a difference. Don't worry. Just come! I'm sure she'd be happy to see you." I said, crossing my fingers. *Please say yes, please say yes.* I hoped for Dylan's sake.

He paused. "Well, if you think it's okay . . . Um, who is this?"

"I'm Alexis, her sister, and my mom is here, and she's nodding, so it's totally fine for you to come," I lied again, holding my crossed fingers up in the air. I looked over at Dylan. Her face was hidden in her hands as she waited for the final verdict.

"Oh, okay, that's really nice," Noah said, sounding very relieved. "Thanks! So, I'll be there at seven, right?"

"Yup, seven it is. See you there!" I sang out and uncrossed my fingers to switch to a thumbs-up sign before hanging up.

"Yessss!" Dylan screamed as soon as I put the phone back on its base. "Oh, Alexis, you are the best! Thank you, thank you so much!" She jumped up and grabbed me in a big hug.

She and Meredith and Skylar started yelling and dancing around together in a circle. "Yay! Noah's coming!"

At that moment Mom poked her head in to see what the noise was all about. "He's coming," I whispered. She didn't need to ask who.

"Phew," she said, and with a wink, she closed the door.

This was going to be a great night.

CHAPTER 14

Nothing > Friends!

Girls, you look spectacular!" my father said proudly as he wrapped his arms around Dylan and me for the photographer.

"Gorgeous," my mother agreed.

"You two look pretty great, yourselves," I said. And they did.

We had arrived early, along with Meredith and Skylar, to make sure everything was set up just right. I checked the cupcakes first, of course, but the restaurant had arranged them beautifully on three tiers of a gold cake stand. They looked really pretty and I knew they'd taste even better!

Dylan looked really happy about the cupcakes and gave me a hug as we stood in front of the display. "Thank you," she whispered. She looked really beautiful in her gown, and I even started to tear up a little. I think I was just relieved that we were done with all those weeks of arguing, the cupcakes were done, and this day was finally here!

I watched as Dylan glanced nervously at the front doors. I knew how she felt. I kept waiting to see handsome Matt walk through the door myself (never mind that he'd be with Emma!) and had gone to the ladies' room twice to check my appearance in the mirror.

I had worn my hair down and in loopy curls (thanks to Meredith). I had on a little bit of Mom-approved makeup and a tiny bit of vanilla spice perfume (thanks to Dylan). I was wearing the fuzzy pink dress (thanks to Mia) with a gold chain belt of my mother's and some gold sandals of Dylan's. I had a chunky ice-cube necklace from Mia, and it looked fantastic. I had to admit, I was looking pretty good.

The band was warming up, and my father asked them to play a little bit of "The Way You Look Tonight," so we could practice our dance. They played the whole thing and when we finished our dance, the whole band applauded!

Just before seven, people started to arrive. That's when I got really, really nervous. Luckily,

Mia and Katie arrived together right at the start. Emma had gone home after getting ready, so she could come with her family. I wasn't sure what I would say to her when she came. Still, I watched the door eagerly for the arrival of the Taylors—and for Noah!

Mia and Katie were getting a soda by the bar and I was saying hi to Dylan's godmother when Sydney and Callie walked in! And would you believe Callie was wearing that black *Dancing with the Stars*-type dress from Icon!

I rushed over to Dylan. "Look who's here!" I said angrily, grabbing her arm.

She looked at the door, just as a gorgeous, tall, blond guy walked in.

"Noah!" she screamed.

"Noah? No, no, not him!" I said. "He's cute though! No, Sydney and Callie are here! There they are!" I pointed across the room to where they were standing.

"Did you invite them?" Dylan asked as she hurried to the door to meet Noah. She didn't seem concerned at all that the devilish duo had crashed her party!

"Of course not!" I said, trying to keep up with her.

"Callie is Jenna Wilson's little sister, right? Jenna's here," said Dylan. Of course! Callie's older sister was on cheerleading with Dylan. So of course she'd be invited, but that didn't explain Callie and Sydney.

"Why don't you go find out why they're here?" Dylan said just as we got to the door. "I'm going to say hi to Noah."

I watched as Noah kissed Dylan on the cheek, and then Dylan took his hand, guiding him toward the drinks. I was happy for Dylan that Noah showed up, but superannoyed that she wasn't mad that Sydney and Callie had shown up at her party uninvited! (And after the hard time she'd given me about inviting my friends!)

I stared at Sydney and Callie for a minute, trying to figure out what I wanted to do. Just then Callie pulled Sydney with her across the room, toward an older girl who I now recognized as Callie's sister. Jenna had been talking with her friends, and turned around when Callie tapped her on the shoulder. Jenna seemed genuinely shocked to see Callie and Sydney and looked really annoyed.

Mia and Katie came over. "Did you invite them?" Mia asked, nodding her head toward Sydney and Callie.

"As if!" I said.

"Then why are they here?" Katie asked.

"I . . . ," I started to say, but then something—or rather, some*one*—caught my eye. It was Emma, with the rest of the Taylors. I wanted to run across the room to greet them, but then I remembered my fight with Emma, and I held back.

I checked my dress and my hair, patting everything nervously as the Taylors walked toward me. Jake looked really cute in a little jacket and tie, and Matt and even Sam looked, frankly, gorgeous in their suits.

"Hi, Alexis, darling! Don't you look beautiful!" Mrs. Taylor said, greeting me with a kiss. Mr. Taylor did the same as Mrs. Taylor looked around the room. "Now, where's your mom? Wow, it looks wonderful in here! What a lot of planning you've all done! Oh, there she is. I'll go say hello. Come on, sweetie." And Emma's parents took off, leaving their kids standing with me.

Jake went up to Mia and tugged on her dress to say hi, and they and Katie began chatting about law enforcement, Jake's favorite subject.

Sam said, "Great party. Oh, wow, there's Dylan!" and he walked over to her.

Then it was just me, Matt, and Emma. It felt

really awkward. I hadn't made eye contact with Emma yet.

"Hey, would you guys like a soda?" I finally said, looking somewhere between the two of them.

"Sure," Matt answered. "Why don't I get something for you two?"

Emma and I looked at each other, and suddenly we both burst out laughing. Hard! We couldn't stay mad at each other, especially not on such a big night.

Emma put her arm through mine. "Sure," she told Matt. "I'll have a Sprite."

"Me too, thanks," I said, giving him my best smile.

Matt grinned, and as he walked away I pretended to swoon. "He is too cute!" I whispered. "Sorry!"

"It's okay," said Emma. "I'm sorry I was so mean earlier. I guess it was just a little hard to take."

"I know I've been kind of annoying about it," I said, thinking about the story Skylar told earlier. "Anyway, I would never sacrifice our friendship for love. If it came down to Matt being my boyfriend or you being my friend, I'd pick you. I swear."

Emma looked like she didn't believe me, but she hugged me and said, "Thanks, but I don't think you need to make a choice. I love my brother too, you know." She swatted my arm playfully, then gasped.

I looked over to see what she was looking at and rolled my eyes. I had, for five minutes, forgotten about Sydney and Callie, but there they were, still standing around. "Yeah, can you believe they had the nerve to show up?"

"Unbelievable!" Emma said in a disgusted tone. When Katie and Mia came back (without Jake, who was now with his mother), we started trying to figure out what we should do. We decided that Emma would say something to Sydney, since Sydney had approached her about the party in the first place. I wondered if we should kick them out, but Mia thought that wouldn't be very ladylike and suggested we tell the manager that there were crashers.

Emma took a deep breath before crossing the dance floor toward Sydney and Callie, who had just spotted Matt. I watched in horror as they surrounded him, and Sydney snaked her arm through his. It made me wonder about Emma's comment about Sydney doing all the work for Callie. Maybe Sydney secretly liked Matt herself.

When Emma joined them, she began talking, and they were all listening to what she was saying. Then Sydney began gesturing and telling some sort of story. Matt watched the whole thing in silence, I was glad to see, and when the bartender handed him the sodas, he took them in his hands and took a few steps away from the group.

Emma must have made Sydney and Callie feel bad enough to leave, because Callie suddenly grabbed Sydney's arm and was pulling her toward the door. I hoped they would leave!

When Emma and Matt came back with the drinks, Emma looked really mad, but Matt was laughing.

"I hate those two. They are so evil!" Emma exclaimed. "They said Callie's sister, Jenna, had 'lost' her precious cell phone, so they had to deliver it to her. They didn't want to look out of place, so they dressed up."

I looked at Sydney and Callie, slowly making their way to the door. "I wonder how it got 'lost' in the first place if it was so precious?"

"Exactly! So I told them to go," said Emma.

Matt was still laughing. "The drama with all you girls!" he said. "I can't believe it. It's so dumb!"

"Believe it, mister," said Emma as she took our drinks from him.

"Thank you," I said to Matt. But as I took a sip, I saw my mother talking to Sydney and Callie at the door. She seemed to be guiding them toward the refreshments instead of the door! What was she doing?

Now Sydney and Callie headed toward us. That made me madder than ever, and when I am mad, I think the adrenaline makes me do things I would normally be too afraid to do! I looked over at Matt, and he was looking at them, then at Emma, then at me. And right then he and I both said at the same time, "Wanna dance?"

I couldn't believe it! I know where my courage came from (the adrenaline from being mad!), but I will never know what made Matt ask me to dance. I don't know if Emma said something to him before the party, or his mom, or if he decided it himself, but whatever it was, the timing was great.

Matt and I laughed and hit the dance floor just as Sydney and Callie arrived where we'd been standing. Emma winked at me and went off with Mia and Katie to get some hors d'oeuvres.

The truth is, Matt and I didn't have anything to say to each other. We smiled a lot, and since I am a good dancer, I think I impressed him. He is an okay dancer, but for someone so athletic, he's not that great. I don't want to say I fell a little out of love with him right then, but between Emma's and my friendship being on the line, us having nothing to say to each other, and him being only a so-so dancer, my crush kind of lost a little fizzle that night. And I was okay with that. I was proud to have set a goal, and to have reached it!

As Matt and I danced, I thought about all of my equations and my research. Oh, I was superhappy the whole time I was with Matt, but I decided that when it comes to love, there is no perfect recipe. There are so many ingredients, and things just have to happen naturally. If you need to force them or manipulate them, then they just aren't meant to be.

There was a lot of crushing going on that night at Dylan's party: I liked Matt, Callie liked Matt, maybe even Sydney liked Matt, Dylan liked Noah, Sam liked Dylan . . . and I'm sure there were a lot more equations that may not have a solution. All I know is this:

Nothing > friends

I repeat: Nothing is greater than friends!

CHAPTER 15

Later that Night . . .

Dylan's friends freaked out over the cupcakes. People came up to her all night to rave about them, and in the end, Dylan declared that the s'mores disco gift cupcakes made the party. That and Noah coming. They had a plan to go to the movies the very next night, which just goes to show you that if something is meant to happen, it just does.

For me, what made the party were the dance with Matt, the look on Callie's and Sydney's faces when he and I danced, making up with Emma, Dylan loving the cupcakes, and my big moment on the dance floor with Dad. Everyone gathered around and cheered. We were so good! We would have won if it was a contest! At the end he gave me a big hug and said, "Alexis, you are wonderful.

Just the way you are!" I looked over and saw Matt smiling at us, and I smiled back.

When we got home that night (along with Meredith and Skylar, who were sleeping over), I opened my locked drawer and took out the Matt notebook. It had been fun doing the research online and reading all the studies and their results, but it had been hard to quantify the results in a real-life setting. I needed data that was more concrete. And real feedback. Like tonight. I had reached my goal, and I could cross it off in my planner. Matt and I had danced together.

I read a quote somewhere that said, "The essence of mathematics is not to make simple things complicated, but to make complicated things simple." Someone named Gudder said it. I think he or she was right. The whole math thing complicated a simple crush. But on the bright side, I got a great makeover, some good love advice, and a dance with a cute boy. It was all good.

I wasn't sure what would happen next with Matt, if anything, or if I even wanted anything to. I needed a new goal, whether it was love-related or not, because when it comes down to it, I am all about setting and reaching my goals. Failing to plan is planning to fail. That's one of my mottoes.

So maybe it was time to focus on business again, instead of love. One thing is for sure: If I'd spent as much time on the Cupcake Club this month as I did on Matt, my friends and I would all be a lot richer!

I ripped the pages out of the Matt notebook. Then I dumped them into the shredder under my desk. It was time for a new goal. I picked up my planner again and on a new goal page I wrote:

SELL MORE CUPCAKES!

I sent an e-mail to the Cupcake Club:

> Great work! Thanks for putting up with Dylan. And me. Now on to the next assignment!
>
> xoxo,
>
> Alexis

Then I grabbed some SweeTarts and went to see if anyone wanted to watch *Dancing with the Stars* with me.

Katie, batter up!

CHAPTER 1

My Cupcake Obsession

My name is Katie Brown, and I am crazy about cupcakes. I'm not kidding. I think about cupcakes every day. I even dream about them when I sleep. The other night I was dreaming that I was eating a giant cupcake, and when I woke up I was chewing on my pillow!

Okay, now I *am* kidding. But I do dream about cupcakes, I swear. There must be a name for this condition. Cupcake-itis? That's got to be it. I am stricken with cupcake-itis, and there isn't any cure.

My three best friends and I formed the Cupcake Club, and we bake cupcakes for parties and events and things, and sell them. We're all different in our own way. Mia has long black hair and loves fashion. Emma has blond hair and blue eyes and lots of brothers. Alexis has wavy red hair and loves math.

I have light brown hair, and I mostly wear jeans and T-shirts. I'm an only child. And I hate math. But I have one big thing in common with all my friends: We love cupcakes.

That's why we were in my kitchen on a Tuesday afternoon, baking cupcakes on a beautiful spring day. We were having an official meeting to discuss our next big job: baking a cupcake cake for my grandma Carole's seventy-fifth birthday bash. But while we were thinking about that, we were also trying to perfect a new chocolate-coconut-almond cupcake, specially created for my friend Mia's stepdad and based on his favorite candy bar.

We had tried two different combinations already: a chocolate cupcake with coconut frosting and almonds on top and then a coconut cupcake with chocolate-almond frosting, but none of them matched the taste of the candy bar enough. Now we were working on a third batch: a chocolate-almond cupcake with coconut frosting and lots of shredded coconut on top.

I carefully poured a teaspoon of almond extract into the batter. "Mmm, smells almondy," I said.

"I hope this batch is the one," said Mia. "Eddie finally started taking down that gross flowery wallpaper in my bedroom, and I have to find some way to thank him. I would have paid someone a million dollars to do that!"

"You realize you could buy a whole new house for a million dollars, right?" Alexis asked. "Probably two or three."

"You know what I mean," Mia replied. "Besides, you know how ugly that wallpaper is. It looks like something you'd find in an old lady's room."

"Hey, my grandma Carole's an old lady, and she doesn't have ugly wallpaper in *her* house," I protested.

Emma picked up the ice-cream scoop and started scooping up the batter and putting it into the cupcake pans.

"We need to find out more about your grandma," Emma said. "That way we can figure out what kind of cupcake cake to make for the party."

"Right!" Alexis agreed. She flipped open her notebook and took out the pen that was tucked behind her ear. Sometimes I think Alexis must have a secret stash of notebooks in her house somewhere. I've never seen her without one.

"First things first," Alexis said. "How many people are coming to the party?"

I wrinkled my nose, thinking. "Not sure," I said.

Then I yelled as loud as I could. "Mom! How many people are coming to Grandma Carole's party?"

My mom appeared in the kitchen doorway. "Katie, you know how I feel about yelling," she said.

"Sorry, Mom," I said in my best apology voice.

"The answer is about thirty people," Mom said. "So I think if the cupcake cake has three dozen cupcakes, that would be fine."

"What exactly is a cupcake cake, anyway?" Mia asked. "Do you mean like one of those giant cupcakes that you bake with a special pan?"

"I was thinking more like a bunch of cupcakes arranged in tiers to look like a cake," Mom replied.

Mia nodded to Alexis's pen and notebook. "Can I?"

"Sure," Alexis replied, handing them to her. Mia began to sketch. She's a great artist and wants to be a fashion designer someday.

"Like this?" Mia asked, showing Mom the drawing. I looked over Mia's shoulder and saw the plan: three round tiers, one on top of the other, with cupcakes on each.

"Exactly!" Mom said, smiling and showing off a mouth full of perfect white teeth. (She *is* a dentist, after all.)

Alexis took back her notebook. "Excellent," she said, jotting something down. "Now we just need to decide what flavor to make and how to decorate it."

"What do you think, Mom?" I asked.

"Oh, I'm staying out of this. This is your project," Mom replied. "I think I'll let you girls come up with something. You always come up with such wonderful ideas, and I know Grandma Carole will love whatever you do."

"All done!" Emma announced, putting down the ice-cream scoop.

"Mom, oven, please?" I asked.

"Sure thing," Mom said, slipping on an oven mitt. She put the chocolate-almond cupcakes into the preheated oven, and I set the cupcake-shaped timer on the counter for twenty minutes.

Mom left the kitchen, and the four of us sat down at the kitchen table to work out the details.

"So what kind of flavors does your grandmother like?" Alexis asked.

I shrugged. "I don't know. She likes all kinds of things. Blueberry pie in the summer, and chocolate cake, and maple-walnut ice cream . . ."

"So we can make blueberry-chocolate-maple cupcakes with walnuts on top!" Mia joked.

"Hey, we thought bacon flavor was weird and that worked out well!" said Emma. It was true. Bacon flavor was a really big seller for us.

"You know, we don't know anything about your grandma," Emma said. "Maybe if you tell us something about her, we can get some ideas."

"Sure," I said. "Hold on a minute."

I went into the den where Mom and I keep all our books and picked up a photo album. We have lots of them, and there were pictures of Grandma Carole in almost all of them. I turned to a photo of me and my mom with Grandma Carole and Grandpa Chuck at Christmas. Grandma Carole looked nice in a red sweater and the beaded necklace I made her as a present at camp. Her hair used to be brown like mine, but now it's white.

"That's her," I said. "And that's my grandpa Chuck. They got married, like, forever ago, and they have three kids: my mom and my uncle Mike and my uncle Jimmy. She used to be a librarian."

"Just like my mom!" Emma said, smiling.

I flipped the pages in the photo album and found a picture of Grandma Carole in her white tennis outfit, holding her racquet.

"Mostly she loves sports and stuff," I said. "She runs, like, every day, and she won track medals in high school. She goes swimming and plays tennis, and skis in the winter, and she likes golf even though she says there's not enough running."

"Do sports have a flavor?" Mia mused.

"Um, sports-drink-flavored cupcakes?" Alexis offered.

"Or sweat-flavored cupcakes," I said, then burst out giggling.

"Or smelly sneaker-flavored cupcakes," Mia said, laughing.

"Ew, sweat and sneakers . . . those are so gross!" Emma squealed.

"But I guess she does like sports most of all," I said. "She's always trying to get me to do stuff with her. Because I am *soooo* good at sports." I said that really sarcastically, because the exact opposite is true. Now it was Emma's turn to giggle.

"Yeah, I've seen you in gym," she said.

"It's even worse than you know," I confessed. "When she tried to teach me to ski, I wiped out on the bunny hill—you know, the one for little kids? I even sprained my ankle."

"Oh, that's terrible!" Emma cried.

"And when I played tennis on a team with

Grandpa, I accidentally whacked him in the head with my racquet."

Mia put a hand to her mouth to try to stop from laughing. "Oh, Katie, that would be funny if it weren't so terrible!" she said.

I nodded. "He needed four stitches."

"So I guess you don't take after your grandmother," Alexis said.

"Well, not the sports thing," I admitted. "But everyone says I look exactly like she did when she was younger. And she's a good baker, too. She used to own her own cake baking business."

Alexis stood up. "You're kidding! Why didn't you tell us?"

"I just did," I said.

"But she's a *professional*," Alexis said. "It's not going to be easy to impress her."

"Yes, the pressure is on," Mia agreed.

I hadn't thought of that before. "Well, we'll just have to make a superawesome cupcake cake, then."

Alexis sat back down. "Okay, people, let's start jotting down some ideas."

We tried for the next few minutes, but nobody could think of anything. Then Emma looked at her watch.

"You know, I need to get home," she said. "It's my turn to make dinner tonight."

"We need some more time to come up with ideas, anyway," Alexis said. "Let's schedule another meeting."

"Let's do it tomorrow," I suggested. But Alexis and Mia had whipped out their smartphones, and Emma took out a little notebook with flowers on it—and they were all frowning.

"Alexis and I have soccer practice tomorrow and Thursday, and a game on Friday," Mia reported.

"And I have concert band practice on Wednesdays and Fridays," Emma said. Emma plays the flute, and she's really good at that.

"Sorry, Katie. You know spring is a busy time of year," Alexis said.

"Yeah, sure," I said, but really, I didn't. I don't really do anything besides the Cupcake Club, and it's not just because I have cupcake-itis. I'm no good at sports, and I'm not so great at music, either. When we learned how to play the recorder in fourth grade, I ended up making a sound like a beached whale. My teacher made me practice after school, after everyone went home.

Just then the cake timer rang. I put on a mitt and opened the oven door. All the cupcakes in the pan were flat. They should have gotten nice and puffy as they cooked.

"Mom!" I yelled.

Mom rushed in a few seconds later. "Katie, what did I tell you about—Oh," she said, looking at the deflated cupcakes.

"What happened?" I asked.

"This looks like a baking powder issue to me," she said. She put the pan of flat cupcakes on the counter and picked up the little can of baking powder. "Just as I thought. It's past its expiration date. You need fresh baking powder for your cupcakes to rise."

I felt terrible. "Sorry, guys."

"It's not your fault," Emma said.

"Yeah, and anyway, Eddie's not finished taking down that wallpaper yet," Mia said. "We can try again next time."

"Whenever that is," I mumbled.

Emma, Alexis, and Mia started picking up their things.

"We can talk about your grandma's cupcakes at lunch on Friday," Alexis said. "Everybody come with some ideas, okay?"

Emma saluted. "Yes, General Alexis!" she teased.

"Ooh, if Alexis is the general, can I be the cupcake captain?" I asked, and everyone laughed.

When my friends left, the kitchen was pretty quiet. Mom went into the den to do some paperwork, and all that was left was me and a pan of flat cupcakes.

As I cleaned up the mess, I thought of Alexis and Mia and Emma all going off and doing stuff—stuff that I couldn't do. They were all multitalented, and the only thing I was good at was making cupcakes. It made me feel a little bit lonely and a little bit like a loser.

In fact, it made me feel as flat as those cupcakes.

CHAPTER 2

Do I Really Look Like a Deer?

After I cleaned up I did my math homework while Mom made dinner, but that did not exactly improve my mood. In fact, when I sat down to eat I was feeling flatter than ever, even though Mom made tofu and broccoli in sesame sauce, which is superdelicious. (And please don't go hating on tofu. It's got a bad rap, but that stuff is pretty tasty. You should try it sometime.)

But that night even the deliciousness of tofu couldn't get me out of my mood. Mom noticed right away. She always does. I think it's because it's just the two of us in the house most of the time. Dad left when I was little, and I don't have any brothers or sisters, like I said before. If I had a big family, like Emma's, I could probably sulk through dinner without being spotted. But Mom started with the questions right away.

"What's wrong, Katie? Did you get enough sleep last night? You weren't up reading under the covers again, were you?"

"No, Mom, I'm not sleepy," I said.

"Are you feeling sick? Does your throat hurt?"

"No," I said, picking at some tofu with my fork. I didn't look up from the plate.

Then Mom changed her tone. Her voice got softer. "Okay, honey. If there's something you want to talk about, I'm here."

That understanding mom voice always gets me, even when I don't feel like talking. I put down my fork.

"It's kind of hard to explain," I said. "It's just . . . Mia and Alexis and Emma all do other stuff besides the Cupcake Club. Like play soccer and flute, and Emma walks dogs . . . and I don't do anything. Besides the Cupcake Club, I mean."

Mom didn't say anything right away. Then she said, "Well, you do well in school, and the Cupcake Club takes up a lot of your time. But maybe doing a different kind of activity isn't a bad idea. Is there something you're interested in?"

"That's the problem," I said. "I'm not good at

sports. I'm just not. I'm the worst in my whole gym class. And I could never play an instrument like Emma. Remember what happened when I learned the recorder?"

Mom cringed. "Oh dear. I see what you mean," she said. "But sports and music aren't the only things the school offers. I'll tell you what. After dinner let's get on the computer and look at the school website. Okay?"

"Okay," I agreed. It actually sounded like a good idea. Why hadn't I thought of that before? There had to be something that I would like.

So after we ate (I ate every single piece of tofu on my plate) and cleaned up the dishes, Mom set up her laptop in the kitchen. I'm not sure why, but we seem to do everything in the kitchen. It's like if the house had a heart, it would be the kitchen, you know? (Okay, I know that sounds a little weird. Maybe I'm eating too much tofu.)

Anyway, we went on the Park Street Middle School website and clicked on "Activities and Clubs." There was lots of stuff to choose from. We went down the list alphabetically.

"How about the chess club?" Mom asked.

"Boring," I said.

"The drama club?" Mom suggested. "You're

very funny, Katie. You're always entertaining your friends."

That was a pretty nice compliment, I thought. But I had one objection. "I can be funny in front of my friends. But on a stage? No way. I would totally freak out."

"Are you sure?" Mom asked. "You don't know until you try."

I tried picturing myself in front of an auditorium full of people, and I got sweaty just thinking about it. "Nope."

"All right," Mom said. "How about the debate team?"

I shook my head. "If I don't want to be funny in front of people, I certainly don't want to debate in front of them. Plus, I'd have to research topics and gather information. You need to put a lot of work into getting your point across."

"Well you certainly did a good job getting your point across that you don't want to debate," Mom said with a smile. "How about the math club?"

"That would be 'no' with a capital *N*," I said.

Mom sighed. "Well, there must be *something* here you'd like to do," she said. "Why don't you take a look?"

As she turned the laptop to face me, the phone

rang. Mom got up from the table and picked up the phone on the wall.

"Hi, Mom," she said, and I knew she was talking to Grandma Carole. "Yes, the girls met today, but we're going to keep your special dessert a secret. No, I won't give you any hints!"

Then Mom took the phone into the living room, and I knew she was trying to talk to Grandma without me hearing. I strained to listen, but Mom was talking in her low phone voice.

Then she came back in the kitchen. "Katie, Grandma wants to talk to you."

I took the phone. "Hi, Grandma."

"Hello, Katie-kins!" Grandma Carole said. She has called me Katie-kins since I can remember, and she is the *only* one who calls me that—so don't get any ideas. "So, your mom tells me you're trying to find an after-school activity you can try."

"Yeah," I said. "But I'm having a hard time."

"What about sports?" Grandma asked.

"Well, I'm not exactly great at sports," I said. "Remember Grandpa's stitches?"

"Accidents happen," Grandma said. "And you're young—like a baby deer finding her legs."

A baby deer? I thought. This conversation was getting a little weird.

"Haven't you ever seen a baby deer on one of those animal shows on TV? At first when they try to walk they are really wobbly. But after just a little while, once they gain confidence, they are frolicking in the woods with all the other deer. You just need practice—and confidence. Maybe you'd feel more comfortable joining a team with your friends. Do your friends play any sports?"

"Mia and Alexis play soccer," I replied. "But I stink at soccer."

"Nonsense!" Grandma Carole said. "Have you ever played before?"

"Well, a couple of times in gym, and—"

"That's all? That's not a true test," she interrupted. "Soccer is a wonderful game. Doesn't it look like fun when you see your friends play?"

"It kind of does," I admitted.

"Life is not worth living if you're always sitting in the stands, Katie," Grandma said. "Go out there and try out for the soccer team. I bet you will surprise yourself."

"Maybe I will," I told her. Grandma Carole was so convincing, I was starting to feel like I could kick a goal from all the way across the field.

"I love you, Katie-kins. Now will you give me a hint about my birthday dessert?"

I laughed. "Nice try, Grandma! Not a chance. It's a surprise."

Grandma chuckled. "Okay then. It was worth a shot. Please give me back to your mom."

"Bye, Grandma. Love you, too," I said and then handed the phone to Mom. She was smiling.

I was smiling too. I didn't feel flat anymore. I had a plan. Tomorrow at lunch, I would talk to Mia and Alexis about soccer.

CHAPTER 3

I've Got a Plan

The cafeteria at Park Street Middle School is pretty much like any other cafeteria. Lunch ladies serve food from behind steamy serving tables. It's superloud, and at some point spitballs will be thrown (usually by Eddie Rossi and his friends). And even though the seats aren't marked, everyone sits in the same place every day.

Take the Popular Girls Club (PGC), for example. They have the best table in the cafeteria, the one closest to the lunch line, where you can see everybody who goes by. Sydney Whitman, their blond-haired, blue-eyed leader, always sits in the right corner seat. Her friend Maggie sits next to her, and Bella sits across from Maggie. Callie, my former best friend, sits across from Sydney. The rest of the seats are empty—unless Queen Sydney gives her royal permission for someone to sit there.

Even though Callie's not my best friend anymore, she's still kind of my friend, so I always say hi to her on the way to my table. Callie always says hi back, but Sydney usually rolls her eyes or else she whispers something to Maggie and they laugh. I just ignore them. It makes life easier that way.

Anyway, I think the Cupcake Club table is the best one in the cafeteria even though it's kind of way in the back. But it's a little bit quieter back there, so Mia, Alexis, Emma, and I can talk cupcake business without anybody bothering us. (Well, most of the time. There was that one day when Eddie shot a spitball at us from ten tables away. Gross, but impressive.)

This Wednesday I found Mia at the table. She usually gets there first. Alexis and Emma were in the hot-lunch line, like they always are.

"Hey," I said to Mia, who was opening the lid of her plastic lunch container. I noticed what looked like little pies inside. "Pie for lunch?" I asked.

"They're empanadas," Mia explained. "They're kind of like pies, but they don't have to be sweet. These are chicken and cheese. My dad and I visited my *abuela* last weekend, and she sent me home with a bunch."

Now, I only started taking Spanish this year, but I hang around with Mia enough to know that "*abuela*" means "grandmother."

"Cool. Your grandma bakes too," I said.

"Want a bite?" Mia asked, holding out one of the empanadas.

"Sure," I said. I opened my lunch bag and took out some carrots and some homemade oatmeal cookies. "Only if we can trade."

"Deal," Mia said with a grin.

Alexis and Emma walked up carrying trays of spaghetti and salad.

"I love spaghetti day," Alexis said, sliding into her seat. "It actually tastes like food."

"If the other stuff doesn't taste like food, then what does it taste like?" I asked.

"I'm not sure," Alexis replied. "Alien brains, maybe?"

Emma giggled. "It's not that bad."

Alexis and Emma started to eat their spaghetti. I decided to come right out with my idea. It was all I could think about all morning.

"So, I was talking to my grandma last night," I said.

"About cupcakes?" Alexis asked.

"Not exactly," I answered. "We were talking about why I don't participate in activities, like sports. I know I'm terrible at them, but grandma thought maybe it's because I haven't played a lot. You know, just to have fun."

Emma nodded. "That could be it. I've been playing basketball and Wiffle ball with my mom and dad and my brothers since I was little. Maybe that's why I don't stink at it."

"And in Manhattan, I joined my neighborhood soccer league when I was five," Mia added.

"Yeah, so, I was thinking maybe I could try soccer," I said a little shyly. "I mean, I know I'm no good or anything but—"

"Katie, that would be so cool!" Mia said, her dark eyes shining with excitement. "I would love it if you played with us!"

"Definitely," Alexis agreed. "That would be so much fun if you were on the team!"

"And don't worry about not being good," Mia said quickly. "Alexis and I can help you. Right, Alexis?"

"Of course," Alexis said. "We have a game on Saturday, so maybe that afternoon we could practice with you."

"Perfect!" I said happily.

It made me feel good to see Mia and Alexis so excited about me being on the team. And with their help, maybe I could be a halfway decent player. I actually felt a little bit excited about trying out. Maybe this wouldn't be so bad after all.

"You know, you should come to my house tomorrow after school," Emma said. "You could play some basketball with me and my brothers. Just for fun, like you said. Who knows? If you're good, you could try out for the team next winter."

The idea of playing basketball with anybody—especially teenage boys—would normally make me very nervous. But for some reason I felt like I could actually do it. Maybe my friends' enthusiasm was rubbing off on me.

"Okay," I said.

The little voice inside me was saying, *Basketball? Are you crazy? You couldn't make a basket if you climbed on a ladder!*

It's just for fun, I told the little voice. *I've got to try, just like Grandma said.*

CHAPTER 4

It's Supposed to Be *Touch* Football

There was one thing that Grandma Carole hadn't psyched me up for: gym class. There are lots of reasons why I hate gym class more than any other class, even math:

1. I stink at all sports. (Yes, I'm trying new ones. But right now I stink at most of them.)

2. The teacher, Ms. Chen, has no heart. She's not mean, exactly, but when you mess up, she doesn't say, "Oh, don't worry about it, honey," like my mom would. Instead she says, "Look sharp, Katie!" or "Get it together, Katie!" If Ms. Chen wasn't a gym teacher, I think she would be an ice princess living

in an ice castle, with her glossy black hair pulled back and a white sparkly dress, and everything she touched would turn to ice.

3. Both Sydney *and* Maggie of the Popular Girls Club are in that class, and I only have one friend in gym with me: Emma.

4. Back in September my friend George Martinez started teasing me by calling me "Silly Arms," after that sprinkler thing with the arms that wiggle all over the place, squirting out water. I guess that's what I look like when I play volleyball. Anyway, I didn't mind when George said it, but now other kids call me that too.

So two periods after lunch I was in the gym, wearing my blue shorts and my blue T-shirt that says PARK STREET MIDDLE SCHOOL in yellow writing on the front. Emma and I were sitting on the bleachers, waiting for class to start.

Sydney and Maggie were the last ones out of the locker room. Maggie has frizzy brown hair that's always in her face, but Sydney always manages to look perfect, even in a gym uniform. Her straight, shiny hair is never out of place. I'm not sure how she does it. I think she must have been born that way. I can just picture Sydney as a little baby in the hospital. All the other babies would be screaming and crying, and little Sydney would be quietly smoothing her perfect hair.

Ms. Chen marched out of the gym teacher's office carrying her clipboard, and Sydney walked up to her with a big smile on her face.

"Ms. Chen, what are we doing today?" she asked.

"Flag football," Ms. Chen replied. She nodded over at George Martinez and Ken Watanabe. "George, Ken, get the flags from the supply closet."

"Flag football! Awesome!" Ken shouted. He and George high-fived as they raced to the supply closet.

I groaned as the boys ran off.

"It won't be so bad," Emma said, but she didn't sound convinced.

"Honestly, I will never figure out how to play that stupid game," I said. "Are you supposed to run around and grab other people's flags? Then why is there a ball involved?"

"It's like football, but instead of tackling the player with the ball, you grab their flag," Emma explained.

I shook my head. "You might as well be telling me how to build a rocket right now," I said. "I do not get it. It's too confusing."

"Then just run around and stay away from the ball," Emma suggested.

"Now *that* sounds like a plan," I agreed.

Ms. Chen blew her whistle, and we both jumped up and ran to line up on the black line that goes all around the edges of the gym. Ms. Chen took attendance and then made us warm up with jumping jacks, push-ups, and sit-ups.

I'm pretty good at jumping jacks and sit-ups, but that whole push-up deal is not so easy; maybe because my arms are so skinny. I am usually on my third one while the class is finishing up number ten.

"Look alive there, Katie!" Ms. Chen called out.

Or I will turn you into ice, I thought. *Actually, that wouldn't be so bad. Then I wouldn't have to play flag football.*

Then it was time to choose teams. She made George and Ken captains. George picked me to be on his team, which was nice because he didn't even pick me last. But then he picked Sydney and Maggie, and Ken picked Emma.

"Oh this is great. We're on a team with Katie,"

Sydney said loudly, in a supersarcastic voice.

I looked at Emma across the room.

Help me! I mouthed and then frowned, but all Emma could do was make a sad face back.

We were the red team, so we each had to strap this red belt thing around our waists and then stick a red scarf thing, the flag, in it.

Just stay away from the ball, I kept telling myself. *Everything's going to be all right.*

Boy, was I wrong.

It didn't start out too bad. Our team had the ball first, and George threw it to Wes Kinney, and he ran toward the other team, and Ken chased him and pulled his flag. I didn't have to do anything.

Then the other team had the ball, and Ken threw it to Aziz Aboud, and then Aziz threw it back to Ken, and then Wes grabbed Ken's flag and yelled out, "Revenge!"

Then it was our team's turn again, and before Ms. Chen blew the whistle I saw Sydney whispering to George. Then the play started, and George pretended like he was going to throw the ball to Wes again, only he handed it to Sydney.

I was kind of running around in a circle, minding my own business, when I heard Sydney yell, "Katie! Catch!"

The next thing I knew, I saw a football flying toward my head.

"Ow!" I cried as the ball smacked me on top of the head.

Sydney giggled. "Oops! Sorry, Katie. I guess my aim is off today."

Yeah, right, I thought as I rubbed my sore head.

"Shake it off, Katie!" Ms. Chen yelled.

See what I mean? No sympathy.

Ms. Chen blew her whistle again, and I resumed my plan of running around aimlessly.

Emma ran up to me. "Sydney *so* did that on purpose!" she whispered.

"I know!" I hissed back. "And she doesn't even get in trouble!"

For the next few plays I was Sydney's target. She kept getting the ball, and every time she got it she threw it to me no matter where I was.

"Come on, Silly Arms. Try to catch it!" George called out.

"Yeah, Silly Arms!" Sydney repeated, and she and Maggie burst into giggles.

Wes rolled his eyes. "You guys are so dumb," he said, and I thought he was actually standing up for me. But then he said, "Why would you even throw it to Katie? She can't catch anything. She couldn't catch on fire if she wanted to."

I could feel my cheeks getting red. This game was turning into my worst nightmare. When did it suddenly become "Let's Pick on Katie Day"?

Luckily, the next time Sydney had the ball, Eddie ran up to her and grabbed her flag. Eddie is kind of a jerk, but he's the tallest boy in middle school, and I guess he's pretty handsome. He even grew a mustache last summer, but his mom finally made him shave it off.

Anyway, Sydney got all giggly and pushed into Eddie after he got the flag. The next time Eddie had the ball, Sydney and Maggie chased after him, and then instead of grabbing his flag, they kind of fell into him, and all three of them fell onto the floor.

Ms. Chen blew her whistle. "Break it up, people!"

From then on all Sydney and Maggie wanted was to get the boys' attention, which was fine with me. The next time Sydney got the ball she ran right *at* Eddie and Aziz instead of trying to avoid them. The boys started tackling her, and Sydney started shrieking.

"My hair! You're messing up my hair!"

Ms. Chen blew her whistle. "Eddie! Aziz! On the bench!" she yelled.

Grumbling, the two boys walked to the bleachers. I couldn't believe it. Sydney was the one who started everything, and once again, she didn't get in trouble at all! I know Mom says I shouldn't say "hate" about anyone, but I really do hate Sydney Whitman.

The rest of the game was a mess. Even though the blue team had lost Eddie and Aziz, our team couldn't score because Sydney and Maggie kept bumping into George and Wes and the other boys and giggling.

Finally the game ended.

"Blue team wins by two points!" Ms. Chen announced, and the blue team cheered.

Wes punched me in the arm. "Thanks a lot, Skinny Arms," he said in a mean voice.

"Yeah, thanks for making us lose, Skinny Arms," Maggie added, and everybody on the red team laughed.

Well, everybody but George. "Hey, she's Silly Arms, not Skinny Arms!" he yelled. I gave him a look. Then he came up to me and said, "It wasn't your fault, Katie." But I didn't say anything to him. Everybody else thought I made the team lose, and that was so unfair. It was Sydney's fault! But if I said anything, Sydney's crew would back her up and I'd just end up looking like a sore loser.

I felt like crying, but I didn't because I knew that would only make things worse. So I ran into the locker room without looking back.

I was going to have to get good at sports soon or the rest of my life was going to be miserable.

CHAPTER 5

Outshined by a Kindergarten Kid

The next day after school I walked home with Emma. She seemed really excited. As for me, I wasn't as confident as I had been the other day at lunch. My stomach had been in nervous knots all day. Me, play basketball? What was I thinking?

"This is going to be fun, Katie, I promise," Emma said. "Nothing like gym class."

I wanted to believe her, and I knew that Emma's brothers were basically nice. Jake was in kindergarten, and he's really cute and sweet. Her oldest brother, Sam, is in high school, and he plays sports and works at the movie theater, and he's smart and nice, too.

Then there's Matt, who's one grade above us in

middle school. Alexis had a crush on him a few months ago, and I'm not sure why. I guess he's cute, but he's definitely not as handsome as Sam. And he's a total slob. And sometimes he says mean things to Emma. But most of the time he's pretty nice.

"Okay," I said, taking a deep breath. "Just for fun. I can do that. At least Ms. Chen won't be there telling me to look sharp."

"And Sydney won't be there either," Emma promised. Then she started talking in a silly high voice. "Oh, help! Help! My hair!"

I laughed. Emma is one of those people who never says anything bad about anybody, but Sydney was being so ridiculous lately that even Emma couldn't help it.

"Well, I don't care if my hair gets messed up," I said honestly. "I'd just like to make at least one basket for a change."

"I'm sure you'll do great," Emma said confidently.

When we got to Emma's house, her three brothers were already playing in the driveway. Matt was dribbling a basketball between his legs, and Sam was holding up Jake, so he could make a dunk shot. Jake dropped the ball through the hoop and then clapped his hands.

"I did it!" he cheered.

Sam swung Jake around and put him on the ground. Then he saw me and smiled. "Hey, Katie."

"Hey," I said back, and my heart was beating really fast, and my palms started to get sweaty. I didn't mention this before, because it's kind of embarrassing, but I guess I have kind of a crush on Sam. Mia does too. He's got blond hair, like all of the Taylors, and he always smells nice; not sweaty like Matt. And, I know, he's in high school and I'm in middle school, so I couldn't date him or anything. (Actually, the whole idea of dating kind of terrifies me, anyway.) But still, I can't help how I feel when I'm around him sometimes.

Then Matt ran up to the basket and did one of those shots where you jump up and sink the ball from the side. He was showing off, I think.

"So let's get this game started," he said. "Boys against girls, right?"

"Seriously?" I asked, and I suddenly felt cold and clammy. How were Emma and I supposed to play against two older boys who were practically professionals?

"Don't worry, you can have Jake," Matt said with a grin. He tossed the ball to Emma. "Girls first."

Emma took the ball to a chalk line drawn across the driveway.

"This is the foul line," she explained. "Every time we start, we start from here."

"Got it," I said.

"I've got Katie!" Matt called out, and he ran and stood next to me.

Sam stood facing Emma, blocking her. Jake was running around yelling, "Throw it to me! Throw it to me!"

Sam was a lot bigger than Emma, but Emma was fast. She ducked to the left, and before I knew what was happening, she threw the ball to me!

To my surprise, I caught it. And then . . . I stood there.

"Go to the basket, Katie!" Emma called out.

I turned around and started to dribble the ball. One . . . two . . . and then Matt slapped the ball away from me.

"Oh yeah!" he cried, dribbling up to the basket. Then he sank a shot cleanly through the net.

"Two points!" he cheered, and he and Sam high-fived each other. Then Matt took the ball to the foul line.

"Block him, Katie," Emma instructed me. "Don't let him get past you."

I stood in front of Matt, like I had seen Sam stand before, and kind of spread my arms wide and bent my knees.

"Katie, you look like a gorilla!" Matt teased. "Come on, try and get the banana."

He held up the ball, like he was going to throw it, and I jumped up to block it. Then he darted to the left and bounced the ball toward the basket, sinking another shot.

"And he scores again!" Matt congratulated himself.

"Dude, you're hogging the ball," Sam complained.

"I can't help it if I'm awesome," Matt replied, and Sam punched him playfully in the arm.

Then it was my turn to take the ball to the foul line. Matt was guarding me, and I was really stressed out. Sam was so tall that I couldn't even see Emma, and Jake was running in circles again, yelling, "Me! Me!"

I just stood there, trying to decide what to do. Matt started tapping his foot impatiently.

"Sometime this century, please," he said.

I had no choice. I bounced the ball to Jake, and he caught it! Then he ran up to the basket and chucked the ball underhand with all his might.

The ball rolled around and around on the rim—and then it went in!

"Yay, Jake!" Emma cheered.

Jake ran up and high-fived her. "I'm awesome too!" he bragged.

I was happy for Jake, but even more embarrassed than ever—a kindergarten kid was better than me!

Still, it was kind of fun, even though I was terrible at it. The next time our team got the ball, Emma threw it to me, and Matt accidentally knocked into me while he tried to block me.

"Foul!" Sam yelled. "Katie, you get a free shot from the foul line."

Matt tossed the ball to me, and I stood on the chalk line, facing the basket. Everyone was staring at me, and I could feel my palms getting sweaty again. I wasn't sure if I was holding the ball right or how to shoot. I swung the ball underhand and then let go. The ball soared through the air and . . . crashed into the garbage cans on the other side of the driveway.

"Wrong basket, Katie!" Matt teased, and my face went red.

Sam ran and got the ball. "She gets a do over," he said.

"No fair!" Matt cried. "Why?"

"Because I said so," Sam told him. (Didn't I tell you he was nice?)

Sam stood behind me and reached over my head and put the ball in my hands. I could feel my heart getting all fluttery again. He placed my hands on the right spots on the ball and then he grabbed my arms.

"Pull back, then push up," he said, moving my arms the right way as he talked. "Let go when you're at the top. Don't aim for the basket, aim for the spot on the backboard just above the basket."

What I heard was "Blah, blah, blah, blah, blah" because I couldn't concentrate with Sam so close to me. Then he stepped back.

"Okay, give it a try, Katie," he said. "You can do it!"

I took a deep breath and tried to throw the ball the way Sam showed me. The ball soared through the air . . . and dropped down at least three feet below the basket.

"Painful!" Matt called out. "Better luck next time, Katie."

Sam tried to cheer me up. "Don't worry about it, Katie," he said. "Anybody who can make cupcakes like you can shouldn't worry about whether they can make a basket or not."

"Thanks," I said, but it didn't make me feel much better.

Making cupcakes was not going to help me solve my problem!

CHAPTER 6

What's the Point?

Even though I was terrible at basketball, I didn't give up. I didn't make any baskets at all during the game, but Emma and Jake made some. In the end Sam and Matt beat us by six points.

"Good game, Katie," Matt said, giving me a fist bump. "You looked better the more we played." That's when I figured that his teasing was part of the game, like what my friend George does. He didn't give me a hard time about losing or playing badly, and I was grateful for that.

Then Sam had to leave for work, and Matt had to go to a practice, so Emma and I did our homework in her kitchen while Jake colored next to us.

"So, what did you think?" Emma asked.

"Well, it was kind of fun," I admitted. "But I definitely stink at basketball. There's no way I can try out for the basketball team."

"Oh, you weren't so bad, Katie," Emma said kindly.

I shook my head. "Emma, I tried to make a basket in your garbage cans," I said, laughing. "I'm bad."

Emma started to smile. "Well, maybe you wouldn't be a good fit for the basketball team," she said. "But I hope you'll play with us again sometime."

I thought about Jake being so cute when he made a basket, and Matt goofing around, and Sam showing me how to shoot the ball. . . .

"Sure," I said. "That would be fun."

Then my cell phone rang, and it was my mom calling to tell me she had pulled up outside. I packed up my books in my backpack and said good-bye to Emma and Jake.

I climbed into the car with Mom. Even though she wasn't wearing her dentist jacket, she still smelled a little bit like a dentist's office—a mix of mint and . . . teeth. "Did you have fun?" she asked.

"Yes," I said. "But I stink at basketball. Everything

is still the same. I have no other talent, and I will always be a loser in gym. I don't even know why I'm trying. What's the point?"

"Well, sometimes the point is just to have fun," Mom said. "And I wouldn't give up yet. There are still lots of other things you can try."

"I guess," I said, and I sank down into my seat.

When we got home I helped Mom make dinner—a big salad with chicken and avocadoes and tomatoes and lots of other good stuff in it. Before we sat down to eat, I saw that I had a text from Grandma Carole on my phone.

How is your sports quest going?

I quickly wrote her back.

Terrible. Played basketball today. Couldn't make a basket.

Then I got another text from her.

Keep trying! I am sure you will find your talent.

Maybe. I just hoped I'd find one soon.

Tx Grandma. ♥ you.

She texted me back.

♥ you too Katie-kins!

But even Grandma's texts didn't make me feel better. During dinner I didn't feel like talking much, and so most of the time all you could hear was me and Mom crunching on lettuce. But then Mom had an idea.

"I was thinking of going for a run after dinner," she said. "Do you want to join me?"

I didn't. I was still bruised and sweaty from playing basketball, and besides that I was cranky.

"I just don't get the idea of running," I said. "You run and run and then you end up in the same place where you started. What's the point?"

"The point is that running is really good for your cardiovascular system," Mom said in her I'm-going-to-teach-you-something voice and then she proceeded to tell me how great running is for your health and stuff. It still didn't make me feel like running. "Plus, you just feel great after."

"Not now," I said. "Maybe some other time, okay?"

"Okay," Mom said, and her voice changed. I could tell she knew something was bothering me. "How about when I get back we make some cupcakes? I've got this green-tea recipe I want to try. And if you say 'What's the point?' I'll probably scream."

I had to smile. "There is always a point to making cupcakes," I said, and I realized I meant it. Even if baking cupcakes didn't help me be good at sports, at least it was something I was good at. And that was something to be proud of, right?

Even Sam thought so.

CHAPTER 7

I Hate to Admit It, but Sydney Is Right

Mom and I made a batch of green-tea cupcakes with cinnamon and other stuff in the icing. The green tea tasted weird and good at the same time, and the sweet cinnamon icing tasted really good with it. I brought four cupcakes into school the next day—Cupcake Friday.

I decided to have some fun with the cupcakes. When we were done eating lunch, I handed one to each of my friends.

"Okay, welcome to everyone's favorite game show, *Guess That Cupcake!*" I said, using the banana from my lunch as a microphone. "Take a bite and see if you can guess what flavor it is!"

Alexis answered first. "No idea, but it's green, so . . . cucumber?"

I shook my head. "Nope! Emma?"

"Um, maple?" Emma answered.

"Not maple," I told her. I turned to Mia. She was taking a second bite, and she had a thoughtful look on her face.

"Hmm," she said, thinking out loud. "I think this is . . . green tea."

"You are correct!" I cried. "How did you know?"

"My dad and I get green tea when we go out for sushi," Mia replied. "So what do I win?"

Whoops! I hadn't thought of that. I handed her the banana. "You win this delicious banana!"

"A banana? I've always dreamed of owning a banana," Mia joked, and I laughed with her.

"So is this a flavor your grandma likes?" Alexis asked, opening her notebook.

"No, that's just something my mom wanted to try," I replied. I reached into my lunch bag and pulled out a piece of paper. "I made a list of Grandma Carole's favorite flavors last night."

Alexis took the list from me. She looked impressed. "Thanks."

"Maybe Alexis is rubbing off on you," Emma suggested.

Alexis turned over the list. "Katie, this is written

on the back of your math quiz," she said.

I shrugged. "I'm recycling. Anyway, check it out. There're some good flavors in there."

"Blueberry, chocolate, raspberry, lime, and . . . chubby?" Alexis asked.

"That's *cherry*," I said. "Although chubby cupcakes would be awfully cute, wouldn't they?"

Alexis sighed. "I think there are some good flavor combinations here," she said. "We need a baking session. How about Sunday?"

"That's perfect," Mia said. "Because tomorrow we'll be teaching Katie how to play soccer before our game."

I had almost forgotten about that. "Oh yeah, sure."

Then I heard a loud voice behind me.

"Watch out for Silly Arms, Mia." It was Sydney, of course. "She'll spill her lunch all over that designer sweater you're wearing."

I turned and saw that Sydney was standing with the whole PGC—Maggie and Bella, who were giggling, and Callie, who looked like she wanted to sink into the floor.

"I'm not worried, Sydney," Mia said. She's one of the only girls in school who can stand up to Sydney. They were kind of friends, once, but I don't think that worked out too well.

Sydney rolled her eyes. "Have you seen this girl in gym? Loser! She's a safety hazard. The school should make her wear a helmet just to walk down the hall."

"There are no losers at this table," Mia said, and she looked angry. "I think you need to apologize to my friend."

Mia is so brave! I love her so much. I wanted to hug her. Then Callie spoke up, and I thought she was going to defend me too. After all, we were best friends for, like, twelve years. But instead she just tried to distract Sydney.

"Hey, Syd, Eddie Rossi told me he wanted to talk to you before," she said.

Sydney took the bait. "Really?"

"Yeah, I think we should go see him now," Callie told her.

"Bye, Mia," Sydney said, as if she had just been talking about tuna fish instead of insulting me.

Sydney marched off across the lunchroom and Callie and the rest of the PGC followed her. Callie kind of glanced over her shoulder at me with a worried look, but I just turned away. I guess by distracting Sydney she was trying to help me out, but frankly it just didn't seem like enough.

"Oh, Katie, Sydney is just awful!" Emma cried.

"Don't worry," Alexis said. "One day, when we're all cupcake millionaires, we'll buy a big billboard that says 'Sydney Is a Loser.'"

I turned to Mia. "You are awesome for standing up for me. Thanks."

"It's okay, Katie," Mia said. "You're the one who's awesome. Don't listen to her. She doesn't know what she's talking about."

"Actually, she does," I pointed out. "She's right. I'm a total spaz. I probably should wear a helmet."

"You're letting her psych you out," Mia said. "You'll see. Tomorrow, when we play soccer, you'll see you're not a spaz."

"I really hope so," I said. "You know, I started out just wanting to be good at something besides cupcakes. But now I feel like I've got something to prove. I'll never get through middle school and high school if I can't get through gym. I'm tired of being teased, you know?"

My friends nodded sympathetically. Alexis was punching in numbers on a calculator with a serious expression on her face. Then she looked up and smiled.

"The way I see it, there's about an eighty percent

chance that you'll be good in at least one sport," she said. "Maybe it will be soccer. I haven't worked out the numbers for that yet."

"Those odds sound pretty good to me," I said. "Just keep your fingers crossed. Or else the next six years of my life will be totally miserable!"

CHAPTER 8

I Discover My Secret Skill

You can do it, Katie-kins!

I tried to imagine Grandma Carole's voice cheering me on as Mom drove me to Mia's house for my soccer lesson.

"I'll pick you up at four, okay?" Mom asked as we pulled up in front of the big white house.

"Okay," I replied. "Hopefully I won't have some freak soccer ball accident and end up in the hospital or anything."

"Don't worry. I'm sure you'll do fine," Mom said. "Just remember to have fun! And don't forget to wear your mouth guard!" With a mom as a dentist, I practically have to wear a mouth guard to walk down the hall.

Remember to have fun. Who says that? Moms,

that's who. Why on Earth would someone have to remind you to have fun? Shouldn't fun just . . . happen?

I heard noises coming from Mia's backyard, and when I walked back there, I saw Mia and Alexis. Alexis was setting up orange cones all over the biggest part of the yard. In the side yard next to the garage, Mia's stepbrother, Dan, and some other guy were playing catch with a softball.

Alexis marched up to me. Like Mia, she was wearing her red soccer shorts and her practice T-shirt. But Alexis had a whistle around her neck and a clipboard in her hand.

"Okay, so we're going to start with some drills," she said crisply.

I had to laugh. Alexis sure loves being in charge—no matter what is going on.

"Um, hi, Alexis, nice to see you, too," I said.

She gave a slightly embarrassed smile. "Sorry, Katie, don't mean to get carried away. It's just kind of fun getting to be a coach instead of listening to a coach, you know?"

"Anyway, drills are a good idea," Mia chimed in. "That's how we start all our practices."

I looked at the cones, which were arranged in a kind of zigzag pattern all the way across the lawn. "So what do I have to do exactly?"

"You just kick the ball around the cones," Mia said. "Like this."

She started dribbling the ball, kicking it a short way and then running after it and kicking it some more. She wove around all of the cones perfectly. The way she did it, it looked kind of easy.

"Okay," I said. "I'll try it."

Mia kicked the ball to me, and I gave it a kick. It went skidding across the grass, nowhere near the cones.

"Just small kicks," Alexis said. "And kick with the inside of your foot, not the toe."

She ran after the ball and dribbled it back. I saw what she was talking about.

"Cool," I said. "Here we go."

I kicked the ball like Alexis had shown me, and it didn't go sailing away this time. I kicked it toward the first cone—and knocked the cone right over.

"That's okay, Katie!" Mia called out. "Keep going."

I made my way to the second cone, but this time I tripped when I was trying to kick the ball. I stumbled into the cone and knocked that one down too.

I was starting to get discouraged, but I could hear Grandma Carole inside my head.

Keep trying!

So I gave it my best. I promise you. But I barely made it through the course. By the time I got to the last cone, I had knocked over almost every one.

"If this was a game where you got points for knocking down cones, I'd be an all-star," I joked.

"Don't worry, Katie," Mia said, trying to keep me from being too discouraged. "Nobody gets it the very first time they try."

"It just takes practice," Alexis said. "I would recommend going through the course four or five more times."

Mia must have seen the look of horror on my face. "Or how about a kicking lesson?" she said. "We can practice passing. We'll kick the ball back and forth to each other as we make our way down the field."

"Okay," I said. "As long as there are no cones involved, I should be fine."

Once again Mia and Alexis demonstrated for me. They each got on opposite sides of the yard, and Mia kicked the ball hard. It skidded across the grass in an almost perfect straight line to Alexis.

"Okay, now I'll kick it to you, Katie," Alexis said. "And you can kick it to Mia."

"I'm ready!" I called out, trying to sound confident.

Alexis kicked the ball, and I ran to meet it. Then I kicked it as hard as I could in Mia's direction.

Only the ball did not go in Mia's direction. Instead it sailed backward, over my head, and bounced into the side yard where Dan and his friend were playing catch. Dan's friend ran to get the ball.

"Sorry!" I called out.

"Hey!" Dan called out in a teasing voice. "Now we're going to throw our ball at you!"

He lobbed the softball right at me, and I reached up and something amazing happened: I caught it!

Then something even more amazing happened. Without even thinking I threw the ball back to Dan. The ball did not fly backward over my head. It did not knock over any cones or garbage cans. Instead the ball soared in a beautiful arc and landed right in Dan's glove!

"Hey, you've got a pretty good arm," Dan said, and he sounded impressed. "Are you on the softball team?"

"Um, no," I answered shyly. "I've actually never played softball before."

"Really?" Mia asked, running up next to me.

I thought about it. "Well, sometimes we play Wiffle ball in gym. But I always stand way, way back in the outfield. And usually the guys think I can't catch the ball, so if it comes to me, they jump in front of me and catch it."

Alexis looked confused. "I don't get it, Katie. You can't catch or throw a football like that. So why did you catch that softball?"

I shrugged. "I don't know. Footballs are kind of . . . wobbly," I guessed. "They confuse me."

"Maybe it's because a softball is more cupcake-size," Mia teased. "It's got to be cupcake related somehow."

"It doesn't really matter *why* you can do it," Alexis said, and she sounded excited. "You *can* do it! And it's spring, which means that softball tryouts start soon. Katie, I think you've found your talent."

It seemed too good to be true that I could actually be good at a sport. Maybe my catching and throwing the ball perfectly was a fluke, a one-time thing.

"Let's make sure," I said. I called out to the guys. "Dan! Over here!"

Dan threw the ball to me again, and once again, I caught it. I grinned.

I had finally found my secret skill.

CHAPTER 9

So Running Isn't So Bad After All

The first thing I did when I got home was call Grandma Carole.

"Hi, Grandma. It's me, Katie," I said.

"Katie-kins! What a nice surprise. Is everything all right?" Grandma asked.

"More than all right, Grandma," I said. "I found a sport I'm actually good at! I'm going to try out for the softball team!"

"Good for you, Katie-kins! I love softball. I bet you'll be hitting home runs out of the park in no time!" Grandma said. I could hear the excitement in her voice.

"Oh . . . ," I said.

"What's the matter?" Grandma asked.

"Well, you just reminded me of something.

I might be good at catching and throwing the ball, but I didn't really think about the hitting part."

"You'll be fine," Grandma said. "You just need a little practice, that's all."

"You sound so sure," I said.

"That's because I *am* sure. I can't wait to see you and hear all about it in person."

"Thanks, Grandma!" I said. "I can't wait to see you too! Love you!"

"Love you, too," Grandma said. "See you soon. Bye!"

I hung up the phone and tried to think positive, the way Grandma always did. But what I was actually thinking about was whiffle ball. Whenever we played whiffle ball at school, I always struck out. I started to feel nervous, but I knew I couldn't back out now.

"I'm very excited for you, Katie," Mom said as we ate our usual Saturday night pizza with mushrooms-and-sausage topping.

"But what if I don't make the team?" I worried. "Everyone's expecting me to become this great softball player. You should have seen the way everybody reacted when I caught and threw the ball."

"I don't think that's the case," Mom said. "Everyone's happy that you found something you're good at and that you like to do. If you don't make the team, at least you know you did your best."

I know Mom was trying to make me feel better, but a slow feeling of panic kept creeping up on me. "I need to start training, like, now," I said. "Can we play catch after dinner?"

"We could, but we don't have any balls or mitts," Mom pointed out. "I'm sure your friends will help you out. In the meantime why don't you go on a run with me tomorrow morning? That will definitely help you get in shape for the tryout."

Just the idea of running seemed superboring, but I knew Mom was right. And I was anxious to start doing something to help me train.

"All right," I said. "But maybe just a few blocks, okay?"

Mom smiled. "We'll see."

The next morning I was sound asleep when Mom came into my room and pulled open the curtains. The bright spring sunshine hit my face, and I groaned and rolled over.

"Rise and shine, Katie!" Mom sang. "It's time for our run!"

"Seriously?" I asked. "The birds aren't even awake yet."

"This is the best time for a run, trust me," Mom said. "Put on some shorts and your good sneakers, and I'll meet you in the kitchen."

I was still pretty sleepy when Mom and I left the house. Mom started jogging, not too fast, and I could keep up with her easily.

I'm not usually an early riser, but I must say it was nice to be up when most of the neighborhood was still asleep. And the air smelled so nice and clean! The sun had just come up, and everyone's lawn was sparkling with morning dew.

I was wrong about the birds. They were all awake, and I had to admit that all the singing and chirping they were doing was kind of pretty. Otherwise, the streets were pretty quiet, because most people were still sleeping.

We jogged down our street and then made a right and headed for the town park. I used to go on the swings and slide there when I was little, but I never noticed the path that went all around the park, weaving around the trees. I saw two squirrels chasing each other around a tree, and a big yellow butterfly, and then there was this bubbling creek we ran past that I didn't even know was in the park.

When we left the park I was sweating a lot and panting a little.

"Wanna go back?" Mom asked me.

To my surprise I didn't. I was actually liking this.

"No," I said. "Let's keep going."

In the end I had to walk the last few blocks home, but Mom said that was good, because we needed to cool down, anyway. My leg muscles hurt, but at the same time I felt good, like I was ready for anything.

"Thanks for coming out with me," Mom said. "Maybe we can do this again sometime."

"Definitely," I agreed.

Then I took a shower, which felt awesome, and then Mom and I went to Sally's Pancake House where I got a short stack of chocolate-chip pancakes, which tasted superdelicious. In the afternoon Mom drove me to Emma's for our cupcake baking session.

Before we make a cupcake for a client, we always test out the recipe first. We use the money from our profits to buy supplies and stuff, and whatever's left over we split among the four of us. We also take turns doing the baking at one another's houses.

At the end of our Friday meeting we had

decided to test a blueberry cupcake and a chocolate raspberry cupcake. When I entered Emma's kitchen, Alexis was already there, setting out the bowls and measuring spoons on Emma's big kitchen table. Emma was taking ingredients out of the blue plastic tub that we use to store our basic stuff.

I didn't see Sam anywhere, but I figured he was working. (And I would never ask where he was—that would just be too embarrassing.) I did see Jake. He was up on a chair, leaning over the table, so he could grab blueberries from the bowl.

Emma shook her head at him. "No, Jake! Those are for the cupcakes."

"There's plenty here for one batch," I said. I took a few blueberries from the bowl and gave them to Jake. "You can have these, and then you can have a cupcake when they're done."

"Thanks!" Jake said happily, and then he left the kitchen as Mia came in.

"My stepdad got all the really ugly wallpaper off of the walls!" she announced happily. "Now I just have to decide what color to paint my room."

"How about rainbow?" I suggested. "With stripes all across the wall."

"Or pink," Emma said. That's Emma's favorite color.

"I like white or cream walls," Alexis said. "It looks neat, and you can always decorate with posters or pictures."

Mia sat down on one of the stools around the counter. "It's just so hard to decide. I'm thinking maybe pale pink with an accent wall, or some kind of purple." Then she noticed all the cupcake supplies on the counter. "But enough about my room. We have cupcakes to design, right?"

"Right," Alexis agreed, getting down to business. "We're going to do some vanilla cupcakes with blueberry jam centers and vanilla frosting with fresh blueberries on top. Then there's a chocolate raspberry cupcake with chocolate frosting and fresh raspberries."

"They both sound *sooo* good," Mia said. "You know, I've been so busy worrying about my room that I forgot to come up with decorating ideas."

"I had one," Alexis said. "Since Katie's grandma likes sports so much, we could do the blueberry cupcakes, but instead of putting blueberries on top, we could decorate them to look like different kinds of balls. Like a soccer ball cupcake and a baseball cupcake, and we could dye the icing green to make a tennis ball cupcake too."

"That's pretty cool," Emma said.

"Definitely," I agreed. "I'm just wondering if it feels adult enough. Soccer-ball cupcakes and baseball cupcakes sound like something Jake would like, you know?"

"I see what you mean," Mia chimed in. "It's great for a kid's party, but maybe not a seventy-fifth birthday celebration."

Alexis nodded. "Yeah, that makes sense," she said. "But I will definitely put this idea in my kids' party file."

"I thought of something," said Emma shyly. "Your grandma was born right at the start of spring, so maybe we can do a spring theme. We could put birds and flowers on the cupcakes."

"That would be so pretty!" Mia said. "I can just picture it!"

"That does sound really nice," I agreed. "And I think that would go nicely with the blueberry cupcakes."

"And maybe the icing could be blue, like a robin's egg," Emma added.

"That is so perfect because Grandma Carole

always looks for the first robin of spring," I said. "She says it's good luck."

"I like it," Alexis said. "Okay, so let's scrap the chocolate raspberry for now. Mia, do you think you can come up with a flowers and birds design?"

"Sure," Mia said, nodding her head. "Maybe I can play with the icing today. We have blue food coloring, right?"

Alexis grabbed the bottle from the table. "Check," she said, holding it up. "Okay, so we have a plan."

For the next couple of hours we worked on our sample cupcakes. We made some basic vanilla batter, and when the cupcakes cooled, I got to use one of my favorite cupcake tools. It's a special tip you can put on the end of a pastry bag. You fill the bag with jam and then stick the tip into the cupcake. One squeeze, and your cupcake has a delicious jam-filled center.

We tested the cupcakes without frosting first.

"Yummy," Alexis said. "But tell me again why we're not using real blueberries in the batter?"

"We could, but it's tricky," I told her. "Since the blueberries are heavier than the batter, usually they fall to the bottom. You can coat them in flour first, but that doesn't always work."

"The blueberry jam is delicious," Mia remarked. "These kind of remind me of that peanut-butter-and-jelly cupcake your mom made for you on the first day of school."

Emma smiled. "Yeah, that cupcake sort of started everything, didn't it?"

"I guess it did," I said. I looked down at Jake, who had blue jam all over his face. "What do you think, Jake?"

"Awesome!" Jake replied.

"Okay, I've got two icings going," Mia said. "One is vanilla with mashed-up blueberries mixed in. The other just has blue food coloring."

The food coloring one looked pretty, just like a robin's egg. The blueberry one looked a little weird. It was more purple than blue, and there were some big blueberry chunks in it. But it tasted really, really good.

"I can't decide," I said. "One is the perfect color, but the other one tastes superamazing."

"I can't decide either," Emma agreed.

"There must be a way to combine them," Alexis suggested. "Katie, maybe your mom can help us. She is, like, the queen of cupcakes."

"And I am the cupcake captain, don't forget," I joked. "But, yeah, I'll definitely ask her."

Then I remembered something. "I need a favor from you guys," I said. "After we clean up."

"What is it?" Emma asked.

I grinned. "Wanna play catch?"

CHAPTER 10

Callie's Mad at *Me*? Seriously?

"Wow, it's true, Katie," Mia said as I tossed a softball to her from across Emma's backyard. "You really can play softball."

"Don't sound so surprised," I joked.

"You know what I mean," Mia shot back.

"I know," I said. "But it's not such a big deal. I can throw and catch. I'm not so sure if I can hit the ball."

"I'm sure Matt will help you with that," Emma said. "As long as you bribe him with cupcakes."

I was secretly hoping she would suggest Sam as a softball coach, but Matt would have to do.

"Sure," I said. "We can give him some blueberry cupcakes from today as a down payment."

Alexis looked at her watch. "Hey, I've got to get

home. We're having dinner early, and I want to get a good night's sleep tonight. We have a big game tomorrow."

"Where is it?" I asked. "Maybe I'll come."

Because I'm not good at sports, I have never much liked watching games on TV or in person. But my friends had been helping me so much, I felt like I had to support them.

"Cool!" Mia said. "It's at the middle-school field at six."

Mom said I could go to the game as long as I finished my homework. On Monday my mom had Joanne, who works with her at her office, pick me up after school. Joanne does that a lot because Mom still doesn't like me being home alone all that much. She took me to Mom's office, and I did my homework with the sound of dentists' drills in the background. I shuddered. Honestly I hate going to the dentist even though the dentist is my mom. But nobody was screaming or crying or anything, so I guess Mom was doing a good job. When Mom finished with her patients she dropped me off at the field.

It's a little weird going to a soccer game when you're not playing, because almost everyone watching is a parent or else a little kid who's been dragged to the game. In the stands I saw Mia's stepdad, Eddie, sitting with Alexis's mom, and I waved hi.

Then I heard a voice calling to me.

"Katie! Over here!"

It was Callie's mom. Mrs. Wilson and my mom have been friends since before Callie and I were born. She's almost like a second mom to me, which is why it's extra weird that Callie and I aren't best friends anymore. I kind of miss seeing her all the time.

So I walked over. "Hi, Mrs. Wilson," I said.

"Hi, Katie." She gave me a hug. "Are you here to see Callie play?"

Uh-oh. Tough question. "Well, sure, and I have two other friends on the team too," I said, only lying just a little bit. "Mia and Alexis."

"Oh yes, they're good players," Mrs. Wilson said. "Come here, have a seat. I haven't seen you in so long."

So I ended up sitting next to Mrs. Wilson for the whole game. That was good, I guess, because she explained a lot of the soccer stuff to me. Like how in the spring league the girls played other teams from Maple Grove. And how many points you got for scoring a goal and who could be on what side of the field when and stuff like that. It all sounded pretty complicated. Maybe it was a good thing I wasn't good at soccer!

Still, the game was pretty exciting. The ball kept going up and down the field. I noticed that Alexis was a really good kicker. She could kick the ball really far and fast. And I cheered when Mia made a goal.

I was kind of surprised to realize that Callie was the star of the team. She was superfast, and whenever someone passed her the ball, she was right on it. And she scored four goals! It was amazing. I cheered for her, too, and I think she heard me because she looked up. But mostly she concentrated on the game.

Even though the Rockets rocked, the other team, the Comets, beat them 8–7. At the end of the game the two teams lined up and then slapped hands as they walked past one another. I thought the Rockets would look sad, but when I ran up to Mia and Alexis after the game they looked pretty psyched.

"Alexis, that pass you made was amazing," Mia was saying.

"Thanks!" Alexis said, high-fiving her. "I think

this was our best passing game ever."

"You did great, guys," I told them. "Soccer looks pretty fun."

"It is," Mia said. "I'm glad you came."

Then Callie walked over, and she looked kind of mad. At first I thought it was because of losing the game. But it turned out she was mad at *me*.

"Katie, what are you doing here?" Callie asked. "You hate sports."

"Maybe I used to," I said, getting defensive. "But not now."

Callie shook her head. "I used to ask you to come to my games all the time. . . ." She looked at Mia and Alexis.

I couldn't believe what she was saying. *Yeah, and I was your best friend until you sold me out to be part of the Popular Girls Club,* I wanted to scream. Not to mention how just the other day she stood by while Sydney made fun of me, and she didn't say a thing! She had no right to be mad at me for this, not even a little.

"We all cheer for one another," Mia said, and she smiled at me. "And it's true, she's really good at softball."

"Yeah, she's even trying out for the team," Alexis said proudly.

Callie looked surprised and then she didn't look so mad anymore.

"Really? Wow, that's pretty cool, Katie," she said. "Good luck."

"Thanks," I said. "And good game. I can't believe how many goals you made."

Callie actually smiled. "Thanks," she said. She looked around, and I wondered if she was looking for her new friends, but there were just a lot of parents waiting around. "See you!" She waved, and then she ran off to see her mom.

"That is one complicated situation," Mia said, looking after Callie.

I shrugged. "I guess," I said. "But right now I'm a lot more worried about that softball tryout!"

Especially now that Callie knows I'm trying out, I thought. *If I don't make the team, I am going to look like a loser!*

CHAPTER 11

I'm Keeping My Eye on the Ball, I Swear!

"All right, Katie," Matt said. "Like I showed you. Bend your knees and hold the bat just below your shoulders."

"She's holding it too high!" Alexis said directly behind me.

It was Friday afternoon, the day before tryouts, and Emma had finally arranged to have Matt give me a batting lesson. During the week I ran with Mom a few times after work, and Mom got us a ball and gloves so we could practice catching. But so far, no batting.

And in case you're wondering what Alexis was doing there, she offered to come along and help.

"You can't have batting practice without a

catcher," she said, and I know she's right. But sometimes I wonder if she's really over her crush on Matt.

To be fair, though, Alexis seemed a lot more interested in telling me how to bat than she did in flirting with Matt.

"I am *not* holding it too high," I protested.

"She's good," Matt called back. "Okay, Katie, now keep your eye on the ball!"

"Sure," I said, but actually, I have a problem with that advice. Because when the ball comes at me, it's spinning really fast and it's all blurry and it just makes me nervous.

Then Matt pitched the ball to me underhand, like they do in softball, and I kept my eye on it, I swear—both eyes, even. And when it got close to me I freaked out a little and swung the bat way too soon.

Whump! I heard the ball land in Alexis's catcher's mitt.

"Steeeeee-rike!" Alexis cried, like some professional umpire.

"Too soon, Katie!" Matt called out.

"Yeah, too soon, Katie!" Alexis repeated.

"I know!" I said, a little frustrated. "It's hard to know when to swing."

Matt walked up to me and Alexis. "Okay, how about this?" he asked. "When you think you want to swing, don't. Count to two and then swing, okay?"

"Okay," I said, nodding. Then I got back into batting stance.

"Oh, you are holding it a little too high," Matt said. "Here, move your elbows, like this."

Matt got behind me and positioned my arms—sort of like when Sam was showing me how to shoot a basket. But I didn't have any heart palpitations or sweaty palms this time.

Is that all it means to have a crush on someone? I wondered. *Sweaty palms? Would Alexis get sweaty palms if she were standing here now?*

"Earth to Katie," Matt said. "Are you listening?"

"Oh, sure," I said. I placed my arms in the right position. "Like this, right?"

"Okay, let's give it another try," Matt said. "This time, count to two before you swing."

"Got it," I said.

Matt pitched the ball to me again. I kept my eye on the ball, and when it got close, I freaked out again.

"Strike!" Alexis cried.

"Why is it that it's good to get a strike in bowling

but bad to get one in baseball?" I wondered out loud, trying to distract Alexis and Matt from the fact that I was terrible.

"Well, this isn't bowling," Alexis said. "I know you can do this. Just keep your eye on the ball."

"I am. I swear," I protested. "That's not the problem."

"What happened to counting to two?" Matt called out.

"I get too nervous," I answered. "When the ball starts to get close, I feel like it's going to hit me in the face or something. So I swing."

"I am not going to throw the ball at your face. I promise," Matt said, rolling his eyes. "Geez!" Then he muttered "Girls!" in an exasperated voice.

"Hey, I heard that!" Alexis called out. "Katie's just nervous, that's all. This has nothing to do with her being a girl."

"That's right!" I agreed. Now I had something to prove. "Let's do this."

Matt pitched. I kept my eye on the ball. When the ball got close, I started counting.

One Mississippi, two Mississippi . . .

Thump! The ball landed in Alexis's glove before I could even swing.

"Ball one!" Alexis yelled.

"What does that even mean?" I said.

Matt shook his head. "Katie, I said count to two, not count to two million."

"I *did* count to two," I told him. "I counted by Mississippis."

"Well, no wonder," Alexis said. "That's way too long, Katie."

Matt gave an exasperated sigh. "Forget about counting. Just hit the ball when it gets close to the bat, okay?"

"Got it," I said. I got back into batting stance, more determined than ever.

Do not freak out. Do not freak out, I told myself. *Matt will not hit you in the face.*

Matt pitched. The ball soared through the air. I swung.

Crack! I hit the ball! It went careening to the left, and Alexis ran after it.

I started jumping up and down. "I hit it! I hit it! I hit it!"

"That was a foul ball," Alexis said, running back to me.

"Good job, Katie!" Matt said, and I felt like I was going to burst with pride. "Now next time straighten it out, okay?"

"Okay," I said, even though I had no idea what that meant.

So Matt pitched the ball a bunch more times. And after a while, I sort of got used to the ball coming straight at me. I lost my fear and just concentrated on trying to follow it with my eyes and hit it when it got close. I struck out a few times, and I had a lot more foul balls. But I "straightened out" after Matt showed me how, so I also hit a few good balls. One of them popped up in the air, and Matt caught it. But another one rolled on the grass, and Matt had to chase after it.

Finally Matt called it quits. "You're doing good, Katie. You'll be fine at the tryouts, I think," he said. "Just keep throwing and catching like you do."

"Thanks," I said.

He held out his hand. "And now I believe there was a payment involved?"

I walked over to the Taylors' deck and picked up the box I had brought with me.

"One dozen chocolate peanut-butter cupcakes," I said.

Matt smiled and took the box. "You are the best, Katie."

"Thanks," I said. "You are, too. And so is Alexis. She's a great catcher."

(Did you see what I was doing there? Just trying to help out a friend—just in case Alexis was still getting sweaty palms.)

"Yeah, thanks," Matt said. He turned and smiled at Alexis. "You can play on my team anytime."

Alexis blushed, and I felt like I had done a good deed.

In fact, I was feeling pretty good when Mom took me home. And Mom had a weird smile on her face, like she was keeping a secret.

"A package came for you today," she said as she unlocked the door.

"Really?" I asked. "What is it?"

"I'll let you open it yourself," Mom said, and she handed me a box that looked like a shoebox. I looked at the name on the return address: Carole Hamilton.

"It's from Grandma Carole," I said. Then I ran to the kitchen to get scissors, so I could cut through the tape.

The box was filled with crumpled-up newspaper. I felt around and pulled out a softball. There was a note on a small piece of blue paper.

Dear Katie-kins,

I am so excited that you are going to be on the softball team! I know you're going to do great.

This is a softball I saved from my high school championship team. It's very special to me, and I know it will bring you luck.

Love,

Grandma Carole

"Wow," was all I could say.

Mom read the note over my shoulder. "That's very special," she said.

I tossed the softball from hand to hand, thinking. Grandma Carole was counting on me to get on the team. I didn't want to disappoint her—or Mom or the Cupcake Club or Callie or even Matt.

I *had* to get on that team. Failure was not an option. But first I had to get rid of this nervous energy.

"Hey, Mom," I said. "Want to go for a run?"

CHAPTER 12

I Don't Totally Stink

Tryouts were Saturday morning at ten at the middle-school field. I was so nervous that I woke up at five a.m. Mom was still asleep, so I went down to the living room and stared at the ceiling until she woke up.

"Katie, you're up early," she said, yawning. "I'm going to make some coffee. What would you like for breakfast?"

My stomach felt like it was tied in a knot. "I don't think I can eat," I replied.

"You have to eat something," Mom said. "You need energy for your tryouts."

I groaned. I know she was right. "Then I guess, cereal, please."

I munched on a bowl of Grainy Flakes and

changed into shorts and a T-shirt for the tryouts. When we got to the field, there were a lot of girls and parents there. Most of them were lined up in front of a folding table set up over by the stands with a sign that read PARK STREET SOFTBALL TRYOUTS.

"I guess we should get in line," Mom said, so we did.

When we got to the front of the line, we saw a woman about Mom's age wearing a white polo shirt with a whistle around her neck. She had blond hair pulled back in a ponytail.

"Hi, I'm Coach Kendall," she said. Then she nodded to a young guy with brown hair bringing some equipment out of the locker room. "That's Coach Adani. We'll be running the tryouts today. I just need your name, age, and grade on the form, okay?"

I nodded, too nervous to say anything, and filled out the form. I forgot that anyone at Park Street could try out. There would be girls older than me too. Ones that had been playing longer. I gulped.

"I'll head for the stands," Mom said. "Good luck, Katie."

I'm sure she wanted to give me a hug, but

thank goodness she just waved and started walking away.

I headed for the baseball diamond on the field, where most of the girls seemed to be going. I recognized a few girls from my grade. There were Sophie and Lucy, who are nice but they're best, best friends and pretty much only hang out with each other. I saw Beth Suzuki, a girl from my Spanish class who trades notes with me sometimes. And then I saw Maggie Rodriguez from the Popular Girls Club.

I groaned. Just like gym class! She was going to give me a hard time, I just knew it.

But so far, Maggie didn't seem to notice me. In fact, I thought she looked as nervous as I did. She was kind of hanging off to the side and not talking to anybody, which was fine by me.

Before I could think too much about it, Coach Kendall and Coach Adani walked onto the diamond, and Coach Kendall blew her whistle.

"All right girls, line up!" she called, and we quickly got into a line.

"Coach Adani and I are going to put you through some drills today to see what you can do," she said. "First up, I want to see you run around those bases. Don't stop until I tell you. Let's go!"

I relaxed a little bit. Running—I could do that. Sophie was at the head of the line, and she started leading us around the diamond. For a while we all stayed in line. But then it was obvious that some of us were faster and some of us were slower. Without even realizing it, I was at the front of the line, right next to Beth.

We must have gone around about four times when Coach Kendall finally blew the whistle for us to stop. I stepped on home plate, and my heart was pounding. The run had me feeling good, and it also felt good to know that I was one of the fastest on the team. I couldn't help noticing that Maggie was the last one to finish, and she looked really winded.

"All right," Coach Kendall said. "Now we're going to try some fielding." She pointed to me, Beth, and another girl who I didn't know. "I want you to each take a base."

I started to feel nervous all over again. Beth ran to first base, so I took second, and the other girl took third. Coach Adani stood at home plate, and Coach Kendall stood behind him with a catcher's mitt.

"Here's how it's going to work," he said. "I'm going to hit out a ball. If it comes to you, catch it and throw it home."

This is it, I thought. *This is where I prove myself. Can I do it?*

Then I heard cheers from the stands.

"Go, Katie!"

I looked up and saw Alexis and Emma. I knew Mia was at her dad's in Manhattan or else she would be there too. I had my very own cheering section, and I couldn't let them down.

I put my hands on my knees and focused on Coach Adani. He hit a ground ball to Beth. She scooped it up and threw it back to Coach Kendall. The throw was a little wide, and Coach had to chase after it.

Then Coach Adani hit a pop-up to second base. Easy. I caught it and threw it to Coach Kendall—and it landed right in her glove.

I had aced it! I didn't feel so nervous after that. Coach Adani hit two more balls to each of us, and I caught each one that went to me. Then we left the field and the other girls got a turn.

I sat on the grass and watched the competition. Some of the girls, like Lucy, were really good. But a few girls couldn't catch very well. And Maggie . . .

well, Maggie was pretty terrible. But you could see that she was trying really hard.

Maggie missed the first two balls, and when she threw them back, they didn't go anywhere near home plate. And then when Coach Adani hit the third ball to Maggie, it went way to the left. Maggie actually jumped and then dove to catch it! It was pretty cool, and everybody cheered even though the ball ended up bouncing out of her mitt.

As I watched the rest of the fielding tryouts, I felt more and more nervous each minute. I knew what had to be next: batting.

And that's exactly what happened next. Coach Kendall put me and two other girls on the bases while the first group of girls came up to bat. Lucy went first, and she hit her first pitch way, way out into the outfield, which was awesome—but it only made me more nervous.

All I could think about was when my turn would be next. I was so distracted that I missed an easy pop-up that one girl hit right to me.

And then, before I knew it, I was standing at home plate, a bat in my hand. Coach Kendall was pitching, and Maggie, Sophie, and another girl were on the bases. My hands were shaking, and I felt like I was going to toss my Grainy Flakes all over the field.

"You can do it, Katie!" Alexis called out, and my mind flashed back to our practice session.

Think, I said. *You know what to do. Bend your knees. Don't hold the bat too high. Don't swing too early.*

But when Coach Kendall's first pitch came speeding toward me, I was so scared that I swung before it was even halfway to the plate.

"Just relax, Katie," Coach Adani said behind me. I took a deep breath and tried to focus. When the next pitch came, I forced myself to hold off swinging. Then I swung wildly.

"Foul ball!" Coach Adani called out as the ball veered off sharply to the right. At least I hadn't struck out.

I did strike out on the next turn, though. And then I hit two more fouls before I managed to get one near first base. I ran like crazy, and the only reason I was safe was because poor Maggie dropped the ball three times as she tried to pick it up.

It's over, I thought, my heart pounding. *For better or worse, it's over.*

After all the girls had a turn, Coach Kendall

had us all gather in a circle. "We'll put the team list in the front hall on Monday morning," she told us. "Those of you who don't make the team will be put on our alternate list. But no matter what happens, you should all be proud of how you performed today."

"Thank goodness that's over," I said out loud as the coaches walked away.

"I know, I was so nervous," said a voice behind me. It was Maggie.

"Me too," I agreed. "I almost threw up my breakfast."

Maggie laughed, and we started walking off the field together.

"So, I guess none of your friends are trying out?" I asked, hoping desperately that I would not end up on a team with Sydney.

Maggie shook her head. "Sydney's trying out for cheerleading," she answered. "So is Callie. And Bella is on the swim team."

"How come you're not trying out for cheerleading?" I asked. I thought Maggie did everything that Sydney did.

Maggie looked embarrassed for a second. "I could never do a cartwheel, no matter how hard I tried," she admitted. "Plus, I kind of want to do my own thing, you know? I really like softball. It's fun."

I suddenly realized that talking with Maggie wasn't so bad once she wasn't with the PGC—or making fun of me in gym. But then I heard Sydney's voice.

"Mags! Over here!"

Sydney walked up with Callie and Bella. "Maggie, oh my gosh, you are soooo sweaty!" she said, wrinkling her nose. (Of course, Sydney looked like she just stepped out of a makeup chair on a movie set.) "And, ew, gross, is that grass on your pants?"

Maggie looked flustered. Instead of answering Sydney, she started trying to rub off the grass stain.

"Yeah, you should have seen her," I said. "She dove to make this amazing catch."

Sydney looked at me like she had just noticed I existed.

"And what did you do?" she asked. "Accidentally throw the bat instead of the ball? Or maybe you knocked out the catcher with your silly arms."

Now it was my turn to clam up. I don't know why, but somehow it was easier to stick up for

Maggie than to stand up for myself. Besides, what could I say that would make any difference?

Maggie didn't tell Sydney that I didn't stink at softball, and I couldn't blame her. But I could blame Callie, who just stood there like she did last time and let Sydney be mean to me.

"Come on," Sydney said, nodding to her friends. "We need to get to that sale at Icon. But, Maggie, you definitely need a shower first. And please do not get any gross dirt in my mom's car!"

I really don't get Sydney sometimes. How can someone who looked so pretty and so sweet be so mean? Was she born that way? Did she squirt milk from her baby bottle at the other babies in the hospital? It's a mystery.

"Good luck, Katie," Callie said as she walked away. She said it kind of soft, and it didn't seem like Sydney heard her. She turned back around fast and just then Emma and Alexis ran up to me.

"You did great, Katie!" Emma said.

"I kept a record of how everyone did when they tried out," Alexis said. "I think you're in the top thirty or forty percent."

"So, does that mean I didn't totally stink out there?" I asked.

"Exactly," she answered. "It also means you're

probably good enough to make the team."

"I hope you're right," I said. But now that I was close, I had another reason to get nervous.

If I made the team, I'd actually have to play softball games. In front of people. With rules and winners and losers.

I grabbed my stomach and groaned. "I should never have eaten those Grainy Flakes."

CHAPTER 13

I'm Happy! . . . I Think

So did you have fun at tryouts?" Mom asked as she drove me home.

"Are you kidding? I was so nervous!" I said. "It was fearful, frightening, ferocious, and freaky—but definitely not fun. Why, are they supposed to be?"

"I guess not," Mom said, and she sounded a little worried.

As we drove through town I remembered something that took my mind off of the tryouts.

"Can we make a quick stop at Food City, please?" I asked. "I need to get some blueberries for the cupcakes."

Remember that blueberry frosting? I was going to ask Mom about it, but then I looked online to get some ideas. And I thought I had a way to make the perfect icing.

"Do you think you can help me try out this icing?" I asked Mom when we got home with the blueberries.

"Sure," Mom replied. "But why don't you take a shower first?"

"Good idea," I agreed. "I don't think sweaty cupcakes would taste so good."

A few minutes later I was squeaky clean, and Mom and I were setting up the food processor to begin my icing experiment. First I made a basic buttercream icing with butter, sugar, and vanilla. Normally we add a little bit of milk to make it creamy, but I wanted to hold off on that until I added the blueberries. I didn't want the icing to get too runny.

Then I put the blueberries in the food processor and with Mom's help we pureed them until they were supermushy. Then I put a strainer over the bowl and poured them into the strainer. The blueberry juice went into the bowl and the skins and seeds and stuff stayed in the strainer.

Next I poured the blueberry juice into the icing, a little at a time, and beat it in. It was a pretty, light purpley-blue color. But we were going for robin's-egg blue. So I added a couple of drops of gel color, and the blue became bright and happy—just like a robin's egg.

"What do you think?" I asked Mom.

"I think it's a lovely color," Mom said. "And I also think we need some cupcakes to go with it!"

I thought making cupcakes with my mom would take my mind off of softball, but when I was making the batter, it hit me.

I was making cupcake *batter*—and I was a terrible softball batter. Why could I be good at making batter but not actually be a good batter?

"Batter up!" I said, pouring the cupcakes into the tin, and Mom laughed.

And so I thought about the tryouts for the rest of the weekend. The only thing that cleared my mind was going on a run with Mom.

Monday morning I got on the bus and sat with Mia, like I always do.

"Sorry I missed your tryouts," Mia said. "How did it go?"

"Okay, I think," I said. "Alexis did her magical calculations, and she thinks I'll get in."

"You don't sound happy about that," Mia said, noticing the nervousness in my voice.

"I'm not sure how I feel," I confessed. "If I don't make the team, I'll feel like a loser. Plus, I'll disappoint everybody. But if I make the team, that means I'll have to play in games and that makes me nervous."

Mia nodded. "I get nervous sometimes before a game. But usually it goes away when I start playing."

Then she noticed the cupcake box in my hand. "What's that? It's not Friday."

I opened the lid a little bit. "I tried to get that blueberry icing right. What do you think?"

"It's so pretty!" Mia cried. She reached into her backpack and pulled out a sketchpad. "I did some designs over the weekend."

Mia showed me a sketch in colored pencils of a cupcake cake. On the bottom round layer, the cupcakes had green icing with flowers in pretty spring colors on them. The top two layers of cupcakes had blue icing and little birds on them. It looked absolutely beautiful.

"Oh, Mia, that's perfect!" I cried. "We can leave the blueberries out of the bottom ones and just use green food coloring."

"I found tiny cookie cutters shaped like flowers and birds," Mia said. "We can get different colors of fondant and roll it out and then cut out the shapes."

"Grandma Carole is going to love these cupcakes," I said.

George looked over the back of our seat. "Did somebody say cupcakes?" he said, eyeing the box.

"Sorry, George, these are for my friends," I said.

He made a sad face. "Aw, come on. I'm your friend, aren't I?"

I giggled. "Forget it, George!"

Then the bus pulled up in front of the school, and I started to feel nervous all over again.

"Come on," Mia said. "I'll go with you."

We walked up to the bulletin board in the front hall, and there it was: SOFTBALL TRYOUTS RESULTS. I took a deep breath and stared closer.

The list was alphabetical, so I saw my name right at the top: KATIE BROWN. I couldn't believe that I made it!

"Oh my gosh! I made it!" I said.

"I knew you would, Katie!" Mia said happily, and she gave me a hug.

I scanned the rest of the list and saw that Beth, Lucy, and Sophie had made the team, but Maggie was listed as an alternate. I felt kind of bad for her. I knew how much she wanted to play.

Then the opening bell rang, and I had to run to homeroom. I was dying to text Grandma Carole, but there's no texting allowed in our school.

When I got to the cafeteria later, I saw that Alexis and Emma were at the table already with Mia, instead of in the lunch line. They were all smiling.

"Congratulations!" they cried, and Alexis took her hands out from behind her back and presented me with an open cardboard box with four cupcakes inside. Each one was decorated to look like a softball.

"Thank you!" I cried. "These are so awesome. You didn't have to do that!"

"It's exciting," Alexis said. "Plus, I wanted to test out my cupcake idea."

"But what if I didn't get on the team?" I asked, teasing.

Emma held out another box of cupcakes. These said, "World's Best Friend" on top.

"Alexis had a backup plan," Emma admitted.

"Of course I did," Alexis said.

I held out my cupcake box. "Well, I brought

cupcakes too," I said. "I did a blueberry icing test."

"How are we possibly going to eat all these cupcakes?" Mia wondered aloud.

I had an idea. "I'm going to give one to George."

I picked up one of the blueberry cupcakes and walked across the cafeteria to George's table. On the way I passed the PGC table. Sydney was talking very loudly to Maggie.

"I don't understand why you're upset, Maggie. You're lucky you didn't make the team," Sydney was saying. "Why would you want to wear those ugly uniforms and get all dirty and sweaty just to play that boring game?"

Maggie looked like she might cry. "I—I just like it, that's all," she stammered.

Then Callie spoke up. "Leave her alone, Sydney. Maggie wanted to be on that team really bad."

Well, it's nice that she's standing up for Maggie, I thought as I walked past. *It would be even nicer if she would stick up for me once in a while.*

When I reached George's table, I put down the cupcake in front of him.

"You looked so pitiful before," I teased him.

"Thanks, Katie," George said. "I promise never to call you Silly Arms again."

If I had known that all I had to do was bribe George with cupcakes, I would have done that a long time ago.

"I hope you remember that," I said to George.

Then I walked back to my table, where my friends were waiting to celebrate with me.

CHAPTER 14

Can I Actually Do This?

So practice started on Monday after school and lasted until six thirty. By the time Mom picked me up I was sweaty, starving, and exhausted. And I still had to do my homework!

I have to say that I didn't do too badly in practice. But I still couldn't stop worrying. Every time I was in the field, I kept worrying that I would drop the ball or make a bad throw. And every time I was at bat, all I could think about was striking out. Which I did, a few times, but I got a few hits, too.

I think Coach Kendall knew I was nervous. Whenever I got up to bat, she would say, "Relax, Katie! Just have fun!"

Grandma Carole said the same thing when I called to tell her I made the team.

"You'll do great, Katie! Just have fun!"

Even my Cupcake Club friends had the same idea. One day at lunch, Mia asked me how practice was going.

"It's hard," I said. "And I keep worrying that I'm going to mess up."

"Just have fun," Alexis said. "Like we did when we had batting practice with Matt."

I thought about it. Practicing with Alexis and Matt had been kind of fun. But that's because they're my friends, and it didn't matter if I did good or not.

"I'll try," I said, but I knew I was kidding myself. I mean, how can you "just have fun" if something isn't fun?

Which is exactly what I asked my mom. "Everybody says 'just have fun,'" I said. "But how do I do that? It's not like I can turn on a switch in my brain or anything."

"I think everyone means to just relax and not take it so seriously," Mom said. "It's important to do your best, but in the end, it's just a game."

What Mom said made sense, but it didn't change anything. I still couldn't shut my brain off whenever I was at practice.

I did notice that one person was having a

lot of fun—Maggie. Even though she was an alternate, she came to every practice. Usually she was the first one to arrive. She asked to play different positions, too. One day she was in the outfield, the next day she'd be playing first base or at shortstop.

"You never know when coach will need me to play," Maggie told me. "And I want to be ready."

Maggie messed up a lot on the field, but she didn't let it get her down. She even made friends with the girls on the team really fast. I still didn't know some of their names.

One Tuesday we got our game schedule, and I saw that my first game was just four days away, on Saturday morning. We were playing the team from Fieldstone at their school field.

"Are you sure the game is *this* Saturday?" I asked Coach Kendall. "I mean, we're not actually ready to play another team, are we?"

"Playing another team is the best way to get experience," Coach Kendall said. "And a lot of their players are new, just like you. It'll be fine."

The Friday night before the game I didn't sleep very well. I dreamed that I kept swinging and swinging and striking out, and everyone in the stands was pointing and laughing at me.

The game the next morning was at eleven, but once again I woke up superearly. Thankfully, Mom woke up early too, and we went for a run. The sound of the chirping birds and the gentle breeze blowing through the trees in the park all helped to calm me down a little bit.

When I got home I changed into my softball uniform: gold baseball pants, white socks, black cleats, and a blue shirt that said PARK STREET MIDDLE SCHOOL in gold letters. I put my hair in a low ponytail, so I could fit my hat over it.

I looked at my reflection in the mirror. I looked just like a real softball player.

"This is it, Katie," I whispered to myself.

Even though the game started at eleven, Mom dropped me off at ten, so I could warm up with the team.

"I'll be back later," she promised. "And Katie—"

"Please don't say, 'just have fun,'" I said.

Mom smiled. "I was going to say, just do your best and you won't have anything to worry about."

"Thanks, Mom," I said.

I got out of the car and ran toward my team. On the other side of the field, the Fieldstone girls in their black and gray uniforms were warming up. It might have been my imagination, but I swear they all looked bigger and stronger than all of us.

To warm up, we did some exercises and then practiced throwing and catching. The whole time my head felt like it was full of cotton balls—so full of fear that I pretty much drowned out everything all around me. It was a really weird feeling.

We were walking to our dugout when a loud cheer erupted from the stands, and I looked up. Alexis, Emma, and Mia were holding up a big sign that said, GO, KATIE! Mom was sitting next to Mia, and sitting next to Mom was a lady with white hair, wearing a blue T-shirt and a gold baseball cap.

I couldn't believe it. "Grandma?"

Grandma Carole saw me looking and started waving like crazy. "Surprise, Katie-kins!" she yelled.

I felt like everybody was looking at me, which was embarrassing, but I was still happy to see Grandma. I ran over to the stands, and she climbed down to meet me by the fence.

"I came a week early to surprise you," she said.

"I can't believe it!" I said.

Grandma grinned. "I wouldn't miss this for anything. Go get 'em, Katie-kins!"

I was really happy that Grandma was here, but now I really didn't want to mess up. I gulped hard and ran back to the field.

CHAPTER 15

Are You Sure Those Other Players Aren't Professionals?

It felt good to have my own personal cheering section, but I also felt like it was extra pressure, too. Like everybody would be watching my every move.

They must be wondering, Who is this Katie? I thought. *She must be pretty awesome to have people here holding up such a big sign for her.*

So the game started, and I learned that when you're playing at another field, they have to let you go first. Which meant we were up at bat first.

Luckily, Coach Kendall had me batting sixth.

Maybe I won't have to bat this inning, I thought. *Maybe everybody else will strike out.*

As soon as I had the thought, I felt terrible. Of course I didn't want anyone to strike out. I wanted us to win. Right? Of course I did. Winning was the goal here, wasn't it? Or was it just to have fun, like Mom and everyone kept telling me?

Tanya, the girl who batted first, struck out. I felt really guilty that my first thought was "Good, at least someone else struck out before me." But then Beth got up, and she hit a grounder to left field and made it to first base. Sophie was up next, and she walked, so there was someone on first and second. Then on Lucy's turn she hit a ball way into the outfield. It bounced once, but the fielder got it fast and threw it back to the pitcher, so Beth couldn't make it home and was stuck on third base.

The bases were loaded. My palms were starting to sweat like crazy, and Sam wasn't even around. I held my breath when a girl named Sarah went to bat. She ended up striking out, too.

It was the first inning of my first game, and it was bases loaded with two players out. If you're a superstar hitter, this is your dream situation. But if you're a not so great hitter, like me, it's pretty much your worst nightmare. So you can imagine how I felt.

The fuzziness in my head was worse than ever, and I swear I could have filled a gallon milk jug with all the sweat from my palms. I was so frozen with fear that when the first pitch came at me, I didn't even swing. Unfortunately, it was a perfect pitch.

"Strike!" the umpire called out.

Swing, I willed myself. *Just swing next time!*

So when the next ball came, I swung—way too early, like I do when I'm not focused.

"Strike two!"

When the third ball whizzed at me, I tried to stay focused. But I should have wiped my sweaty palms on my pants, because even though I swung on time, the bat slipped a little in my hands, and I missed the ball.

"Strike three!"

The other team started running off the field, and I was confused for a second until I realized the half was over. We had lost our chance to score, all because of me.

"Good job, girls!" Coach Kendall called out. "Now let's get out there!"

I was still standing at home plate, kind of dazed. "It's okay, Katie!" I heard, and I looked behind me. It was Maggie. "Just shake it off!" Was Maggie pulling a Ms. Chen, telling me to just shake it off? "You're doing great, Katie!" yelled Maggie. Wow, was Maggie actually being nice to me? I was so surprised that I kept standing there.

"C'mon, Katie!" called Coach Kendall.

I put down the bat and helmet, grabbed my glove, and jogged over to my position on second base. I quickly glanced at the stands, where Mom, Grandma, and my friends were still smiling and cheering. Didn't they just see me strike out?

Sarah, the girl who had struck out before me, was pitching. I braced myself as the first Fieldstone batter came up to home plate. She looked about six feet tall and had muscles like a bodybuilder. Okay, maybe that's not exactly true, but that's how she looked in my mind. I was convinced we were playing a team of professionals in disguise.

The Fieldstone batter made contact on the first pitch, whacking the ball way into the outfield. Tanya was out there, and she missed the ball, but Sophie ran and scooped it up. I saw the batter touch first base and figured that was the end of the play.

Then I heard Sophie cry out, "Katie! Katie!"

I turned and saw her throwing the ball to me. To my horror the batter was making her way to second!

My heart was in my throat as I quickly got under the ball and caught it. For a second I stood there, frozen.

"Katie, tag the runner!" Coach Kendall called out.

I had forgotten all about that part. I ran to the Fieldstone player as fast as I could and touched her with my glove about a second before she got to the base.

"Out!" the umpire called, and I almost fainted with relief. Everyone in the stands cheered. Out of the corner of my eye I saw Grandma jump up. Oh boy, I really hope she wasn't yelling "Yay, Katie-kins!" That would be harder to live down than Silly Arms.

I tried to concentrate. Almost messing up the play really bothered me. I kept thinking about it over and over, and so when the next batter hit an easy pop-up, I let it bounce out of my glove. The rest of the inning was brutal. Each Fieldstone batter was stronger than the next, and by the time the inning ended, they had scored two runs.

Lucy tried to psych us up as we ran back to the dugout for the next inning. "It's just the first inning!" she said. "We can come back strong!"

But the game was a total disaster. Every time I was at bat I either fouled out or struck out, and lots of other girls were striking out too. The more runs the other team scored, the worse we played.

We had a chance in the third inning to score some runs. We had a runner on third base. There were two outs. Lucy was up.

"Go get 'em, Lucy!" I cheered. But then the catcher called time out and went to the mound to speak to the pitcher. The pitcher nodded, and the catcher trotted back to her position behind the plate. Then the catcher held her right arm straight out. The pitcher threw the ball to her right hand, far away so the batter couldn't swing. She did this four times; it was an intentional walk. Lucy trotted out to first base.

At first I didn't understand why the pitcher would intentionally want to put another batter on base. And then I understood. They intentionally walked Lucy to get to me because they figured I would be an easy out. Wow, these girls were just as bad as Sydney! Why would they be that mean? I knew it was about winning, but boy that made me even more determined than ever to get a hit. But I was overeager and swung at everything. Three quick strikes, and I was done.

The Fieldstone team didn't even need to go up to bat in the seventh inning, because they had already won the game: 12–2.

We didn't just lose—we lost badly. But I didn't

mind losing as much as I minded how badly I had played. Mom told me to do my best. If that was my best, I was in trouble.

Coach Kendall gave us a pep talk in the dugout. "This was a good first effort, girls," she said. "We're still learning how to play together as a team. You'll see—we'll do better each time we play."

"When's our next game?" someone asked.

"Monday night," Coach Kendall said. "We'll meet an hour early, so we can practice beforehand."

Another game in two days? My stomach hurt just thinking about it. And every time I thought about the pitcher walking Lucy to get to me, my face burned.

But something else was upsetting me even more. Grandma Carole had come out early just to see me play. She had so much confidence in me and was sure I would do well. I felt like I had let her down. She must be so disappointed in me. How could I face her now?

Maggie was trying to cheer everyone up. *Maybe she should have tried out for cheerleading after all,* I thought grumpily.

"Hey, Katie, nice work!" she said. "You really went down swinging!"

I tensed up. Was she making fun of me?

But when I looked at her she looked friendly. "You weren't going down without a fight!" she said.

"Thanks," I mumbled.

Maggie hadn't even played in the game. Maybe that's why she didn't feel so badly. None of the strikeouts were her fault.

"See you on Monday!" she said with a wave.

"See you," I said. Then I turned to face the stands, where my fan club was waiting for me.

CHAPTER 16

I Learn Something New About Grandma

After Coach Kendall finished her speech, I slowly walked to the stands. Mom, Grandma, and my friends were all coming toward me, smiling.

"It's all right, it's okay, you did a great job, anyway!" Mom cheered, and at that moment I wished the ground would open and swallow me up.

"Well, I wouldn't say 'great,' exactly," I told her.

Grandma put her arm around me. "It's just first-game jitters, that's all," she said. "I'm sure you'll do great at your next game."

My next game. The thought made my stomach flip-flop again.

Mom turned to the Cupcake Club. "Can you girls join us for some pizza?"

Vinnie's Pizza was just a few blocks from the

field, so we walked there. We couldn't have all fit in the car, anyway. Mom and Grandma walked ahead of us. Thankfully, we started talking about cupcakes instead of going over that disaster of a game.

"You know, now that your grandma is here early, it will be hard to surprise her with a cupcake cake," Alexis pointed out.

"I didn't think of that," I admitted. "The party's Friday night, so we should bake on Thursday."

"We can probably do it at my house," Mia offered.

"Cool," I said. Then I remembered something. "Mia, aren't you with your dad next weekend?" It made me sad to think she would miss the party.

"Dad said I could come out Saturday morning instead," Mia said with a grin. "So I can bring the cupcake cake with me Friday night."

"Double cool," I said.

We found a big table in the pizza parlor, and Mom ordered one plain pie and one pie loaded with veggies, Grandma's favorite. The pizza was delicious, and of course we ended up talking about softball.

Grandma held up her glass of water. "Cheers to Katie! I'm so proud of you for playing your first game."

Everyone clinked their glasses together.

"I was so nervous," I admitted. "I couldn't focus. And besides, we lost—in a major way."

"You can't win all the time," Alexis said. "Our soccer team lost our last three games. That's just how it is sometimes."

"But don't you get nervous when you play?" I asked.

Alexis shrugged. "Not really. I just play."

I saw Mom and Grandma look at each other. Then Mom got up to pay the bill. Grandma smiled at us.

"I heard you girls are making a cupcake cake for my party," she said. "I can't wait to see it. Maybe you can give me just a little hint about it?"

I shook my head. "Sorry, Grandma. We want it to be a surprise."

"One hint is that it will be delicious!" Mia said.

"Oh, I'm sure it will!" said Grandma.

"Katie told us you used to bake professionally," said Alexis.

"Yes," Grandma said. "But that was a long time ago. And now I'm happy you girls are baking for me. I like eating cupcakes more than I like baking them!"

We left Vinnie's and walked back to the field. Grandma Carole pointed to the grassy lawn, where a gray bird with a black head and a red belly was hopping on the ground.

"There it is! The first robin of spring!" she said. She looked at me. "It always brings me good luck. And I think it's extra lucky that I saw it with you."

Grandma walked ahead, and I looked at the Cupcake Club and smiled. We had definitely designed the perfect cupcake cake for her!

But when we got back home, I wasn't smiling anymore. I kept thinking about Monday's game.

"Katie, come sit down at the kitchen table with us," Mom said.

Uh-oh, I thought. *I must be in trouble for something.* Maybe they were going to tell me all the things I did wrong in the game.

But Mom asked me something I wasn't expecting. "Katie, Grandma Carole and I have noticed that you are not yourself today. Is something bothering you?"

"Well, I guess . . ." I didn't want to disappoint them.

"It's okay, Katie," Grandma Carole said. "We're here to help."

I took a deep breath. "It's like this," I said. "I know I'm okay at softball. And I like playing catch with my friends and even having batting practice with Matt. But being on the team . . . it's so much pressure. I'm not having any fun at all."

"I understand," Grandma Carole said, nodding, and I was kind of surprised.

"You do?" I asked, surprised.

"I do. There's a reason I quit baking professionally," she said. "I love to bake, but once I started doing it as a business, it wasn't fun anymore. I felt all this pressure to make things perfect. One day I was making a cake and I realized that I was hating what I was doing. That's when I knew I had to stop and end the business."

"That's exactly how I feel about softball," I said.

"I figured that because I recognized the look on your face," Grandma said. "I'm sorry if I pushed you into sports at all."

"You didn't, Grandma," I said honestly. "I wanted to try. It wasn't just about making a team. I just don't want to stink at sports anymore. I don't want to be the worst kid at everything in gym class."

"You can be athletic without being on a team," Mom pointed out. "You can still play with your friends for fun. And I'll throw a ball around with you whenever you want."

"And I won't make you play tennis anymore," Grandma said with a grin. "The important thing,

Katie, is that you do things that are good for you and make you happy."

I grinned back. "I just remembered something. There is one sport that I'm good at, and I don't ever need to be on a team. And the two of you are really good at it too."

Mom and Grandma looked at each other, confused.

"Running! Anybody want to go for a run?" I asked.

Mom and Grandma both stood up.

"You bet!" Grandma Carole said. "Let me go get changed."

A few minutes later the three of us were jogging through the park, under the trees.

And I didn't feel nervous at all! In fact, I felt great.

CHAPTER 17

My Moment in Gym Class

When I woke up Monday I knew what I had to do, and it wasn't going to be easy. Instead of taking the bus, I asked Mom to drop me off at school a few minutes early. I had practiced what I was going to say with her. "Take a big breath," she said as I opened the car door. "It will be fine."

"I know," I lied.

"I love you, sweetie!" she called out, and I waved and shut the door fast. I love my mom, but you do not want your mom yelling "I love you" in front of the entire middle school, for goodness's sake.

I took a deep breath. Then I went and found Coach Kendall in the gym office.

I knocked on the door. "Coach Kendall?"

"Oh, hi, Katie," she said, looking up at me. "Come on in."

I sat in the metal chair on the other side of her desk. Then I took another deep breath.

"So, I think I need to quit the team," I blurted out. That is not how I planned to say it, but it just came out.

"Is everything okay?" the coach asked.

"Yeah, I'm fine, except that I just get too nervous when I'm playing," I said. "Everybody says to relax and have fun, but I can't."

"But you've just started, and you've got talent, Katie," Coach Kendall said. "I'm sure you'll feel more confident the more you play."

I shook my head. "I don't think so. It's a lot of pressure. I just don't think I can do it. I like playing in the backyard with my friends, but I really hated playing during the game. I got nervous, and I didn't sleep the night before the game. And, honestly, I just kind of hated every minute of it. And I know we just had one game, but I thought about it all weekend, and I don't think softball is for me. Honestly, I almost threw up thinking about playing a game tonight. I'm sorry. I hope I didn't disappoint you."

Whew, well, at least I finally got out what I practiced with Mom.

Coach Kendall frowned a little and nodded her head. "Competitive sports aren't for everybody. I certainly don't want you to be unhappy. But if you change your mind and feel like trying out next year, I'd be happy to have you on the team."

"Thanks," I said. "And thanks for understanding."

Then I left the gym, and even though I felt kind of bad about quitting, I also felt like a big rock had been taken off my shoulders. Like I could float or fly. What a relief!

Now I just had to tell my friends.

At lunch I waited until Alexis and Emma sat down with me and Mia. Then I just spit it out (not my lunch, my news).

"So I quit the softball team this morning," I blurted out.

"Oh no!" Emma said. "But you tried so hard."

"I know," I said. "But I can't take the pressure. I was miserable. I like playing for fun. But for real in a game, it's not for me."

Mia nodded. "Yeah, you looked pretty miserable on Saturday. Like all of your Katie energy was sucked right out of you."

That's why Mia is my new best friend. She totally gets me.

"Exactly," I said. "Anyway, thanks for helping me

out so much, you guys. And I'll still play ball with you and stuff. I just don't want to be on a team."

"So does this mean you're not going to find another after-school activity?" Alexis asked.

"Well, I have one new activity. I am running now," I said. "I go with my mom or grandmother. I really love it. I just put my sneakers on and go, and there's no pressure or anything. And I feel great afterward."

"Hey, you should try out for the track team!" said Alexis.

"I don't think so," I said. "That's the thing about running. It's just me and my legs taking me along. I'm not worried about teammates or letting anyone down or who is watching me. It feels great to just run."

"We do track as a unit in gym," said Emma. "Just think about how great you'll be!"

"And we have softball, too," said Mia. "So that's a bunch of gym classes you should ace!"

"I hadn't thought about that," I said. But it was true. Some worry-free gym classes wouldn't be too bad.

A lot of surprising things had happened in the last few weeks. I had made the softball team. I learned that Grandma Carole and I were more alike than I thought. And then another surprising thing happened, right there at lunch.

Maggie walked up to me as I went to throw out my garbage—and she wasn't following Sydney or the other PGC girls.

"I heard you quit the team," she said. "Why? You were good."

I nodded. "It's kind of hard to explain, but mostly I just wasn't having fun."

Maggie shook her head. "Are you serious? Because I think it's really fun," she said.

I felt my neck get stiff. "Well it wasn't for me," I said a little defensively.

"My mom says there's enough stuff you have to do that you don't like, and that when you can choose, you should always choose the things you love," said Maggie. "So I get that."

I smiled. "Thanks," I said. Maybe I should be giving Maggie more of a break. What she just said sounded like something my mom would say.

"Anyway, I came to thank you. Coach Kendall gave me your spot on the team. I'm so excited. I'm sorry you didn't like it, but I'm hoping I'll be able to catch as well as you."

I was happy then. Maggie deserved it.

Then she leaned close to me. "And I don't care

what Sydney thinks!" she whispered.

I laughed as Maggie walked away. Alexis raised an eyebrow.

"What was that all about?" she asked.

"Maggie's on the team now," I said. "I'm happy for her."

"But doesn't she torture you in gym?" Emma asked.

I shrugged. "Sometimes. But she's not so bad, especially when she's away from Sydney."

That reminded me of my only lasting problem: Sydney. More exactly, Sydney in gym class. We had been playing flag football for a few weeks, and I hadn't gotten any better. Although ever since I gave George that cupcake, he had kept his promise and stopped calling me Silly Arms.

"If only we were done with flag football," I said with a sigh. "I guess I am doomed to be a flag-football spaz forever."

"I'm sorry," Emma said. "But lately Sydney seems more interested in bumping into the boys than bothering you, anyway."

"Good point," I agreed. "Maybe I can practice turning invisible in gym. I heard if you concentrate long enough, it can happen."

"That can't be true," Alexis said.

"Of course not, but I can try," I said.

When I got to gym class later, Ms. Chen had an announcement to make after we did our warm-up exercises.

"The state physical fitness tests are next month," she said. "We're going to start training today. Let's start with some running. Ten times around the gym. Let's move it!"

I can handle that, I thought with relief. Maybe my worry-free gym class was starting sooner than I thought. But as soon as I started running, Sydney started in on me.

"Be careful, Katie, or you'll trip over your own feet!" she said. Then her voice got louder. "Hey, everybody, watch out for Katie! She might crash into you." She smirked and tossed her long, perfect, shiny hair.

This time Sydney's teasing didn't bother me much—maybe because I knew how wrong she was.

"I think I'll be just fine," I told her, and then I ran right past her. I pretended I was in the park with the birds and started flying around the gym, getting ahead of everybody—even the boys.

"Nice hustle, Katie!" Ms. Chen called out. "Sydney, look alive out there! This isn't a funeral march!"

I looked back and saw that Sydney was one of the last runners, and she actually looked a little bit sweaty. I smiled.

"Go, Silly Legs!" called George. "The girl can run!" *I have to start bringing him more cupcakes,* I thought, and sprinted toward the finish.

In a couple of months we'd be playing basketball or volleyball or whatever, and I'd be back to being a spaz again. But for now, all I had to do was run.

CHAPTER 18

I Don't Mean to Brag, but I Am Pretty Talented After All!

The rest of the week went by very fast. It was nice having Grandma Carole there early, because I didn't have to go to Mom's office after school. She helped me with my homework, and we made dinner together.

Then Thursday was pretty crazy. After school I met Alexis and Emma at Mia's house, and we started on the cupcake cake. Mia's mom was nice and got us Chinese food to eat while the cupcakes cooled down. Then we decorated them with fondant flowers, leaves, and birds in shades of yellow, pink, green, violet, and blue. When we were all done, we boxed them up. Tomorrow, at the party, we would put them on their stands.

Mom picked me up at eight thirty. She had been

decorating the house while we made the cupcakes. Grandma was staying at Uncle Jimmy's tonight. "Everything looks great," she said. "Barbara helped me set it all up. It looks so beautiful."

Barbara is Callie's mom. I knew Callie and her family would be at the party tomorrow, and I wasn't sure how I felt about it. I was still pretty mad at Callie for not sticking up for me.

But I didn't tell my mom that. "I can't wait to see it," I said.

Mom was right about the decorations. The whole house looked like a spring garden, with light green tablecloths and a pretty flower arrangement on each table. The streamers on the ceiling were green and yellow and robin's-egg blue, a perfect match for our cupcake cake.

The next day we got up really early. Mia and her stepdad arrived not long after. Eddie was carrying the cupcake boxes, and Mia had the stands.

"Over there," Mom instructed, pointing to a little round table in a corner of the room. "I can't wait to see them!"

Emma and Alexis arrived next, so all four of us were able to set up the cupcake cake. We started with the green flower cupcakes on the bottom, and the top two tiers were blue with birds on them, just like in Mia's drawing.

"Oh, it's absolutely beautiful!"

Grandma Carole walked in, wearing a blue dress that almost matched the cupcakes. Grandpa Chuck was there too, and he wore a robin's-egg-blue tie with his gray suit.

Grandma walked around the cupcake table, admiring it from every angle.

"This is absolutely perfect!" she cried. "Robin's-egg blue! I love it!"

"And the cupcakes are blueberry, too," I said.

"My favorite!" Grandma said. "You girls are very talented. Your business must be doing very well."

"Our profits are rising every month," Alexis reported proudly.

Then the party guests started streaming in, and Joanne from Mom's office started playing songs from her iPod on a speaker. It really felt like a party.

Then Callie came in with her older sister, Jenna, and her mom and dad. Mr. Wilson gave me a big hug when he saw me.

"Hey there, Katie-did," he said. "My gosh, you must have grown a foot since I last saw you!"

"Not a foot," I said. "But maybe a little."

Then Callie's parents walked off to say hi to my

grandparents, and Callie and I were just standing there, looking at each other. Callie looked kind of embarrassed.

"So, I just wanted to say that I felt kind of bad about the way Sydney's been talking to you," she said. "I wanted to stick up for you, but Sydney . . ."

"It's okay," I said, thinking of gym the other day. "I can take care of myself. Besides, I don't really care what Sydney thinks, anyway."

I didn't believe it until I said it out loud, but it was true. Sydney could say whatever she wanted, but as long as it didn't matter to me, it couldn't hurt me, right?

Callie looked a little surprised. "Um, that's cool, then."

That's when Mia ran up and grabbed me by the arm. "Katie, I looooove this song. Let's dance!"

We all danced and ate a bunch of food, and Mom showed a slideshow of photos of Grandma from when she was a little girl.

"Wow, Katie, you look just like your grandma," Emma remarked.

"I know," I said proudly.

Then Grandpa Chuck walked up to me. "Katie, I hear you're a fine softball player. How about a game outside?"

I hesitated, but then he said, "Just for fun. We won't even keep score."

Then I relaxed. "Sure," I said.

So some of us went outside and played softball for a while, and it *was* fun. And something amazing even happened. I hit a home run!

The ball went way into the outfield, and Alexis ran for it, but couldn't catch it. So I ran around the bases as fast as I could.

"Go, Katie-kins!" Grandma Carole cheered as I crossed home plate. My heart was pounding and I was very sweaty, but not because I was nervous—I was excited.

Finally it was time for cupcakes. After Grandma Carole blew out her candles, everyone dug in.

"Katie, these cupcakes are delicious!" Grandma said. "You could be a professional baker."

"We all made them," I said, blushing.

"Yes, but Katie figured out the frosting," Mia pointed out.

Mom hugged me. "You know what you're great at besides baking cupcakes?" she asked me.

"No, what?"

"You're a good friend," Mom said. "And a wonderful running partner."

"And a pretty good batter," Grandpa added.

"And the best granddaughter ever!" Grandma Carole said, joining me and Mom in a group hug.

I counted in my head—that was one, two, three, four, five talents! Not bad, don't you think? I smiled at everyone around me as they happily ate delicious cupcakes.

Then I remembered to save a cupcake for George. I'd need it—pretty soon in gym we'd be starting basketball!

Mia's baker's dozen

CHAPTER 1

I'll Definitely Finish It Tomorrow . . .

Me llamo Mia, y me gusta hornear pastelitos.

That means "My name is Mia, and I like to bake cupcakes" in Spanish. A few months ago, I could never have read that sentence or even written it. Maybe that doesn't sound like a big deal. But for me, it totally was.

Here's the thing: I'm good at a bunch of things, like playing soccer and drawing and decorating cupcakes. Nobody ever *expected* me to be good at them. I just was.

But everyone expected me to be good at Spanish. My whole family is Latino, and my mom and dad both speak Spanish. I've been hearing it since I was a baby, and I can understand a lot of it and speak it pretty well—enough to get my point across. But reading and writing Spanish? That's a whole other thing. And the fact that I was bad at it got me into a big mess. Well, maybe I got myself into a big mess. But Spanish definitely didn't help.

The whole situation kind of blew up this winter. You see, when I started middle school in the fall, they placed me in Advanced Spanish with Señora Delgado because my parents told the school that I was a Spanish speaker. At first I did okay, but after a few weeks it was pretty clear to me that I was in over my head. I could speak it but not write it. The homework kept getting harder and harder, and my test grades were slipping.

One night in February, I was trying really hard to do my Spanish homework. Señora asked us to write an essay about something we planned to do this month. I decided to write about going to see my dad, who lives in Manhattan. I visit him every other weekend, and we always go out to eat sushi.

It sounds simple, but I was having a hard time writing it. I always get mixed up with the verbs, and that was the whole point of the essay—to use future indicative verbs. (Yeah, I'm not sure what those are either.) Anyway, I was trying to write "We will eat sushi," and I couldn't get the verb right.

"*Comemos*? Or is it *comeramos*?" I wondered aloud with a frown while tapping my pencil on my desk. My head was starting to really hurt, and it wasn't just because of the homework.

"Dan, TURN IT DOWN!" I yelled at the wall in front of me. On the other side of the wall, Dan, my stepbrother, was blasting music like he always does. He listens to metal or something, and it sounds like a werewolf screaming in a thunderstorm. He couldn't hear me, so I started banging on the walls.

The music got a little bit softer, and Dan yelled, "Chill, Mia!"

"Thanks," I muttered, even though I knew he couldn't hear me.

I looked back down at my paper, which was only half finished. Where was I again? Oh, right. Sushi. At least that word is the same in any language.

My brain couldn't take any more. I picked up my smartphone and messaged three of my friends at once.

Anyone NOT want to do homework right now?

I asked.

Alexis replied first. She's the fastest texter in the Cupcake Club.

Mine is already done!

Of course, I should have known. Alexis is one of those people who actually likes doing homework.

It's better than babysitting my little brother! came the next reply.

That's my friend Emma. I actually think her little brother, Jake, is kind of cute, but I also know that he can be annoying.

The last reply came from my friend Katie.

Let's go on a homework strike!

I laughed. Katie is really funny, and she also feels the same way I do about a lot of things (like homework). That's probably why she's my best friend here in Maple Grove.

Where are we meeting tomorrow? I asked.

I think I mentioned the Cupcake Club already. That's a business I started with Alexis, Emma, and

Katie. We bake cupcakes for parties and other events, and we meet at least once a week.

> We can do it at my house, Emma replied.
>
> Works for me! Alexis texted back at light speed.

Alexis always likes going to Emma's house, and it's not just because she and Emma are best friends. She used to have a crush on Emma's brother Matt. He's pretty cute, but Emma's brother Sam is even cuter.

Alexis texted again.

> Everyone come with ideas for the Valentine's cupcakes.
>
> Ugh! I hate that holiday! Emma complained.
>
> But there's candy! Katie wrote.
>
> And everything's pink, I reminded Emma

since pink is her favorite color.

> K, you have a point. But still. We have to watch all the couples in school make a big deal out of it, Emma replied.
>
> And watch all the boys go gaga for Sydney,

Alexis chimed in.

Sydney is the president of the Popular Girls Club, and Alexis is right—lots of boys like her.

Any boys who like Sydney have cupcakes for brains, Katie wrote.

I laughed.

Got to go! Twelve more math problems left! Emma wrote.

I have 2 go study, Alexis added.

I thought you were done? Katie wrote.

This is just for fun ☺, Alexis wrote back.

If u want to have fun u can do my homework, Katie typed.

Or mine, I added.

LOL! CU tom, Alexis typed.

I said good night to my friends and put down my phone. I stared at my paper for a few seconds and then I picked up my sketchbook.

My Spanish class isn't until after lunch, so I figured I could finish the essay then. I couldn't concentrate now anyway. Besides, I was dying to finish a sketch I had started earlier.

My mom's a fashion stylist, and she's always taking the train to New York to meet with designers and boutique owners. I guess I take after her because I am totally obsessed with fashion and I love designing my own clothes.

Once in a while, Mom takes me to meetings with her and I get to see all the latest fashions before other people do.

Lately I've been trying to design a winter coat that keeps you warm but isn't all puffy. I hate puffy coats. I thought maybe the coat could be lined with a fabric that kept you warm *and* looked streamlined. Maybe cashmere? But that would be really expensive. Flannel might work; and it would be so cozy, like being wrapped up in your bed's flannel sheets!

I opened up my sketchbook, a new one that my dad gave me. It's got this soft leather cover and really good paper inside that makes my drawings look even better. I picked up a purple pencil and started to finish my sketch of a knee-length wrap-around style coat.

There was a knock on my door, and then Mom stepped in.

"Hey, sweetie," she said. She nodded to the sketchbook. "Done with your homework?"

"Yes," I lied.

Mom smiled and walked over to look at my sketch. "Very nice, *mija*," she said. "I like the shape of those sleeves. And purple is a very nice color for a winter coat. Most winter coats are black or brown or tan. They're so boring."

"Thanks!" I replied, and she kissed me on the head and left the room. I started to feel a little guilty about lying about my homework, but I pushed the feeling aside. I was definitely going to finish it tomorrow, so no problem, right?

Actually, it *was* a problem . . . a big one.

CHAPTER 2

Señora Is Not Happy

"I know how to say all the colors," Katie said helpfully. "Red is *rojo*. Blue is *azul*. Yellow is *amarillo*. I'm not so good at pronouncing that one because I can't do that thing with the two *l*'s."

It was lunchtime, and I was frantically trying to finish my essay while eating the chicken salad sandwich that Eddie, my stepdad, had made for me.

"Thanks, Katie," I said. "But I don't think the colors will help. I need future indicative verbs."

Katie frowned. "That sounds painful. But maybe you could, you know, pad it. Like say the sushi restaurant has red chairs and a blue rug and yellow walls."

I laughed. "Can you imagine if a restaurant was really decorated like that?"

"Rainbow sushi!" Katie exclaimed. "I think it would catch on."

I sighed. "Anyway, I need verbs."

Alexis and Emma walked up to the table carrying trays of spaghetti and salad. Alexis nodded at my notebook.

"Cupcake ideas?" she asked.

"I wish," I replied. "It's my Spanish homework."

Alexis's green eyes widened in horror. "You mean you didn't finish it?" Most people have nightmares about monsters, but Alexis wakes up screaming if she dreams she hasn't done her homework.

"It's hard!" I complained. "I'm supposed to be writing about when I go see my dad. Now I'm trying to say, 'We will visit my grandmother.'"

Alexis frowned. "We haven't done a lot of future tense in our French class yet. Spanish must be a lot harder than French."

I shook my head. "It's because I'm in Advanced Spanish," I said with a moan. "That's why we're already on this."

"But you speak Spanish, Mia," Alexis said. "I've heard you!"

"Yes," I replied. "But I've never taken a Spanish class. I took French in my old school. And when we moved here, my mom thought I should get some formal training in Spanish. She told the guidance counselor that I spoke Spanish at home, and they put me in the advanced class. Without even asking me!"

"So it's not easier because you already speak it?" Katie asked.

"No way," I said. "It's like, when I hear people talking in Spanish, I can understand most of it. And if someone asks me a question, like my *abuela*, I can answer her. But my main language growing up was English."

I took a sip of my water. "And think about it," I said. "You learned how to speak English before you could learn how to properly write it, right? You can say to a baby, 'Show me your nose,' and the baby will point to her nose. But she isn't able to write, 'My nose is on my face.'"

Katie nodded. "You're right," she said. "I can see why it's more difficult to learn how to write a language than to speak it."

I picked up my sandwich, and Katie eyed it. "Did Eddie make you chicken salad again?"

"Uh-huh," I answered, taking a bite.

"He's a really good cook, isn't he?" she asked.

"His chicken salad's pretty good," I admitted.

"But believe me, you do not want to eat his Mystery Meat Loaf."

Katie looked thoughtful. "Maybe he can be my top chef when I open up Katie's Rainbow Restaurant," she said.

"Ooh, that's a great idea," Emma said. "You could divide the menu into seven colors, and people could pick one food from each color."

"That's way too much food," Alexis objected.

"Well, you wouldn't have to order *all* seven," Katie pointed out. "You could order three dishes of your favorite color, if you want."

Did I tell you that my Maple Grove friends are a little bit crazy? They always make me laugh. Maybe "creative" is a better word than "crazy" to describe them. Everybody always has lots of ideas. A rainbow restaurant! Only one of my friends would dream up something like that.

When I look at our lunch table, I sometimes think we are like a rainbow of hair colors. Emma's hair is pale blond, the color most women in Manhattan pay a fortune to try to get. Alexis has gorgeous, curly red hair. Katie's hair is light brown and wavy, and mine is black and really straight.

"We could all be waitresses," I suggested. "We could each wear a different color uniform."

"I'll be violet!" Katie cried. She loves purple.

Emma frowned. "There's no pink in a rainbow."

"You could be red," Alexis suggested.

"Red is *so* not pink," Emma protested.

"I'll be red," I said. Then I took out my sketchbook and started drawing our uniforms.

Before I knew it, the bell rang. Lunch was over, my assignment wasn't done—and I had to go to Spanish class.

"Wish me luck," I said.

"Everybody forgets their homework at least once," Katie said, trying to cheer me up. "It'll be okay."

The problem was, I hadn't forgotten to do it—I just *couldn't* do it. There's a big difference. If you forget to do your homework, it's a one-time thing. But if you don't know how to do it, it's a huge problem. And I didn't expect things to get easier.

I gathered my books together and headed to Señora Delgado's class. The only good thing about that class is that I sit next to Callie, who's pretty nice. She used to be Katie's best friend, but that's kind of a long story. And she hangs out with Sydney and is in the Popular Girls Club. And Sydney doesn't really like me, but that's another long story.

Anyway, I like Callie, and it's nice sitting next to her in class. Especially when things get confusing. She's really helpful.

Callie gave me a smile when I slid into the seat next to her.

"Nice shirt," she said, admiring my boxy blue knit shirt. I had accessorized it with a necklace one of my mom's designer friends had given me—a silver chain with a chunky silver circle pendant.

"Thanks," I said. "I like your scarf." Callie was wearing one of those loopy big infinity scarves in red and black that looked nice with her black sweater.

"Thanks," she said back.

Callie is into fashion too. That's one of the reasons we get along. But our little mutual admiration session was the highlight of my Spanish class.

"Hola, clase," Señora Delgado said when she walked into the room. That means "Hello, class." In advanced class we're supposed to speak Spanish all the time, which is pretty easy for me. (But since you might not speak Spanish, I'll do all the dialogue in this class in English.)

Señora began by asking us each to say a few sentences about what we did the day before. That's so we could practice our past tense. I was able to do that okay.

"I did my homework, talked to my friends, and drew in my sketchbook," I told her, and Señora smiled.

"Perfect pronunciation and accent as usual, Mia," she said. "Good job."

But Señora wasn't smiling at me after she asked us to hand in our assignments. I handed it in and held my breath. Señora went through the pile of papers and then frowned.

"Mia, this is only half finished," she said.

"I know," I said. "I'm sorry."

Señora shook her head. "You are getting lazy these days, Mia. This is not acceptable. See me after class. I'm giving you an extra worksheet for homework tonight."

"Yes, Señora," I said.

Callie gave me a sympathetic look, and I slunk down in my seat. This was just what I needed. More homework that I didn't understand.

I know what you're probably thinking right now. Why didn't I just tell my parents the truth? That I shouldn't be in Advanced Spanish.

Well, I just felt like I couldn't. What would they think? The truth was that their only child,

Mia Vélaz-Cruz, the daughter of proud Spanish-speaking parents, couldn't read or write the language. I didn't think they could handle the truth. It would have to be my secret. Hopefully they would never find out.

CHAPTER 3

Sweet and Spicy

At least I didn't have to face Mom right after school because we had an official Cupcake Club meeting. Emma lives close to the school, on the same street as Alexis, so the four of us walked to her house. It was cold out, and there was still some snow on the lawns from a storm the week before. My red winter jacket kept me nice and warm, though, and for once I didn't mind its general puffiness.

When we got inside, Mrs. Taylor was sitting at the dining room table with Emma's little brother, Jake. He was taking the books out of his backpack.

"Hi, Mom!" Emma called out. "Did you get off early?"

"I'm working story time tomorrow morning, so I had the afternoon off," her mom replied. She's a librarian, and she's got blond hair just like Emma and all her brothers.

Jake ran up to us. "Are you making cupcakes today?" he asked. "I want a blue one with a dinosaur on it!"

"Sorry, Jake, today we're just talking about cupcakes," Emma told him. "But maybe you can help me make some later, okay?"

Jake got a big smile on his face. "Okay!" Then he ran back to the table.

"There's a pot of hot chocolate on the stove, and some oatmeal bars to go with it," Mrs. Taylor said.

"Thank you!" all four of us said at once. Then we headed to the kitchen for our meeting.

You can tell from Emma's kitchen that everyone in her family loves sports. There are sports schedules tacked to the refrigerator, and her brothers' hockey sticks were leaning up next to the back door. The one thing of Emma's that stands out is her pink mixer. Besides being gorgeous, it's great for baking cupcakes.

"Emma, we should use your pink mixer to make our Valentine's cupcakes," Katie suggested as we grabbed our cocoa and snacks. "Maybe they'll add some extra Valentine's magic or something."

Alexis opened up her backpack and took out her notebook.

"So, the bookstore wants four dozen cupcakes for their event," she said, getting right down to business as usual. "And they want them to be Valentine themed. Any ideas?"

"I was thinking we could do a white cupcake," Emma said. "You know, the kind you make with no egg yolks? They're fluffy and light as air. I think they're called angel's food."

Katie nodded. "My mom showed me how to make those." (Katie's mom is, like, the best cupcake baker in the world.)

"And then we could make some light pink strawberry frosting to go with them," Emma finished.

We all made an *ooh* sound.

"That sounds so pretty!" I said. "I had a different kind of idea. I was thinking about something red—maybe a red velvet cupcake, but with red cinnamon frosting and Red Hots candies on the top."

"Spicy romance!" Katie said, and we all laughed.

And that was exactly when Emma's brother Sam walked in. How embarrassing!

"Spicy romance?" he repeated. "What are you girls talking about? I thought this was a cupcake meeting."

Sam is a junior in high school, and his blond hair is wavy and sometimes falls over his eyes. And he's just as nice as he is cute.

"This *is* a cupcake meeting," Emma said with a huff. "We're trying to invent some Valentine's cupcakes."

Emma's brother Matt walked in just behind Sam. He opened the refrigerator, took out a carton of milk, and drank right from it.

"Valentine's cupcakes?" he asked. "What, for your boyfriends?"

"We're too young to have boyfriends!" Katie blurted out. "At least, that's what my mom says."

Matt shrugged. "Well, then you can make some for me to give to my girlfriend."

Next to me, Alexis suddenly got a weird look on her face.

"You don't *have* a girlfriend," Emma said. "And stop drinking from the milk carton or I'll tell Mom!"

Matt reached over her shoulder and grabbed

two oatmeal bars from the plate on the table. "Well, maybe I'll get one," he said.

Emma shook her head. "Exactly. You don't have one."

Most of the time, Emma is pretty quiet and shy. But when she's with her brothers, she can totally stand up to them. I think that's cool.

Alexis's face was all pink underneath her freckles. I know she used to like Matt (and maybe she still did, a little), so it must be weird to hear him talking about girlfriends.

Sam took the milk from Matt and poured himself a glass.

"There's too much spicy romance in this room," he said. "I'm getting out of here."

Now it was Katie's turn to blush, only she turned as red as the cupcake I was imagining.

"Can we please get back to our meeting?" Alexis asked impatiently.

"We have two cupcake ideas," I reminded her. "Fluffy and pink, and red and hot."

"We should do both," Katie suggested. "One pink, one red. Sweet and spicy."

"Good idea," Alexis said. "Then people will have a choice."

I started sketching a big heart entirely made of

cupcakes. All the pink ones were in the middle, and the border was made with the spicy red cupcakes. "Here's a fun way to display them," I said. I held up my sketch.

"I love it, Mia!" Emma squealed. Nothing like a big pink heart to make a girlie girl happy.

"That's awesome," Alexis said. "Now we have two cupcake ideas and even a cool way to display them. This was a very productive meeting." She nodded approvingly.

"That was easy!" Katie said, leaning back.

Alexis stood up. "I'd love to stay longer, but I think I should go home," she said.

"Already?" Katie asked.

She nodded. "Tons of homework."

"I think teachers get bored in the winter and give us extra homework so they have something to do at night," Katie mused. "It seems like it's double lately."

Suddenly I remembered the extra homework Señora Delgado had given me.

"I should go soon too," I said. "Let me text Eddie."

"My mom can give you a ride," Katie said.

"That's okay," I told her. "He's expecting me to text him to pick me up."

My stepdad, Eddie, is a pretty nice guy. I don't have too many complaints about him, even though it's superweird that my parents are divorced and I have a stepdad in the first place. But one thing that bugs me is that he's way more strict than my dad, and Mom goes along with it.

For example, Mom works at home on her business, but she's out at meetings a lot. And she and Eddie have a rule that I can't be home alone. So if Mom's not home, then Eddie leaves his office, which is here in Maple Grove, and hangs out with me until Mom comes home.

Can you believe that? I mean, I'm in middle school! Emma's mom lets her stay home alone, and she even watches Jake. It's so not fair. When I'm in Manhattan with my dad, sometimes he'll run out to the store or something and *he* lets me stay in the apartment by myself. But not Eddie. And I know Mom's only going along with it because that's what Eddie wants.

I hung out with the Cupcake Club for about fifteen more minutes, and then Eddie called my phone. He doesn't believe in beeping the horn. He says it "disturbs the peace."

I said good-bye to my friends and headed outside. Eddie's car was nice and warm.

"Hi, Mia," he said cheerfully. "How did the cupcake meeting go?"

"Good," I replied. Eddie always wants to have these long, chatty conversations, but sometimes I'm not in the mood.

"Do you have a lot of homework tonight?" he asked as we began the drive home.

"Um, some," I said. There was absolutely no way I was going to tell him what happened in Señora Delgado's class.

"You can start that while I start dinner then," he said. "And don't forget to text your mom as soon as we get home."

"Why do I always have to do that?" I asked. "*You* know I'm home! Why do I have to tell both of you?"

Eddie laughed. "Because your mom likes to hear from you."

I rolled my eyes and stared out the window. Back when Mom and Dad were still together, I had a babysitter who picked me up from school when they were both working late. Her name was Natalie, and she was really nice. She would make me mac and cheese for dinner, and I was usually in bed when Mom came home and kissed me good night. Mom never made me text her then.

But there was no use arguing with Eddie. I texted Mom as soon as I got home, and she said she'd be home by six thirty. Then I decided to text my dad to see if he wanted to Skype. Thinking about those old days in the city was making me miss him really bad.

In a meeting. We'll Skype after dinner, OK? he texted back.

K, I answered, feeling a little sad.

"Guess it's just me and Eddie," I muttered.

There was nothing to do but start my homework. I did my math first and then my vocabulary, and then I started on my Spanish.

Soon a delicious smell filled the air, and I realized that Eddie was making his famous spinach lasagna for dinner. *Yum!*

When I heard the door slam, I knew Dan was home. A little while later, my mom pulled into the driveway.

"I hope I'm not late!" Mom called out.

I ran down the stairs, remembering I should have set the table by now. But when I got into the dining room, Dan was already setting it.

"Hey, thanks," I said.

Dan shrugged. "Dad said you were doing homework."

Eddie walked into the dining room carrying a steaming pan of lasagna. He was wearing my mom's oven mitts with the big red roses on them, and he looked pretty silly.

"Let Family Time begin!" he announced in a goofy voice.

A few minutes later I was eating delicious lasagna and salad and garlic bread, and Mom was telling me about her new client, and then Dan told this story about this guy in his chemistry class who made something explode, and we were all laughing. It was definitely better than eating mac and cheese with Natalie. In fact, it was pretty nice.

But you know what would be even better than that? Having "Family Time" with me and Mom and Dad all together. It doesn't really feel like "Family Time" to me completely without my dad here eating dinner with us. But that's never going to happen again.

And sometimes knowing that really hurts.

CHAPTER 4

Thank Goodness for Cupcakes

I felt a little better after I Skyped with my dad; I always do. And I definitely didn't want to disappoint Señora Delgado again, so I made sure to finish all my homework. They were both worksheets, so I ended up guessing a lot. But at least I finished!

Anyway, tomorrow is Friday, which is my favorite day of the week. For one thing, it's the last day before the weekend, and the best things always happen on weekends. But for the Cupcake Club, it's also Cupcake Friday.

We started Cupcake Friday when school started and we all met. I definitely wouldn't mind eating cupcakes every day, but that's not exactly healthy, you know? So every Friday one of us brings in cupcakes to share. Since we started our business, a lot of times the cupcakes are test runs of the cupcakes we're going to make for an order.

The next day in the cafeteria, we all waited eagerly for Emma to arrive. Last night Emma texted everyone and told us she was going to bake the white cupcakes with strawberry frosting. She came to the table with a pink cardboard box and lifted the lid.

"They're a little messy, because I let Jake help me," she said apologetically. "So I added some coconut flakes to cover up the dents in the icing."

"That looks like snow!" I said. I took my sketchbook out of my bag and started sketching with a pink pencil. "I like how it looks on top, but maybe we could test out some other decorations too. Like some white heart-shaped sprinkles, maybe?" I held up my sketch.

Emma's eyes lit up. "Ooh, I like that idea!"

Katie picked up a cupcake. "They look sooo good, Emma," she said, peeling off the wrapper.

We hadn't even eaten our lunch yet, but none of us could resist trying one. I unwrapped one and took a bite. The white cake was superlight and fluffy, and the strawberry icing was perfect—not too sweet.

"It's almost like eating a cloud," Katie remarked, finishing her cupcake in one big bite.

"It is delicious," I agreed.

"It's perfect," Alexis added. "Now we just need to test the spicy ones. Mia, can we do that at the meeting on Sunday?"

"Oh, I almost forgot!" I said. "My friend Ava is coming out to visit this weekend. Is it okay if she's at the meeting?"

"She's nice," Katie said. "Besides, since we're making cupcakes for her birthday party, she can tell us what she wants."

"She's the one we met at your mom's fashion show and wedding, right?" Alexis asked, and I nodded.

"Of course she can be there," Alexis said. She looked down at her notebook. "Oh yeah, I forgot something. I meant to mention this yesterday."

I smiled. "Yeah, it looked like you were a little distracted."

Alexis blushed. "I told you, I don't like Matt anymore! Besides, you and Katie turn bright red whenever Sam walks into the room."

"Ew! You guys are talking about my brothers, remember?" Emma pointed out.

"Sorry," I said. "So what's up, Alexis?"

"The question should really be, 'What's down?'" Alexis said. "And the answer to that would be 'our sales.' They've dropped twelve percent since the fall. We had a little bump during the holidays, but still, we need to pick up business."

"Maybe we can start promoting the business again," Emma suggested. "Remember when we handed out those flyers? They really worked."

Alexis nodded thoughtfully. "True. We haven't done those in a while. But maybe we could put a coupon on them or something. You know, like a special deal."

"We could do a baker's dozen!" Katie said.

"What's that?" Alexis asked.

"It's when you buy a dozen of something and you get an extra for free," Katie explained. "Like they do at the bagel shop. They give you thirteen bagels for the price of twelve, and they call it a baker's dozen."

"I like it!" Alexis said. "Except for one thing. Our cupcake boxes fit twelve cupcakes exactly. Where would we put the extra one?"

Everyone was quiet for a minute. "Maybe we could wrap the extra one in a clear bag with a ribbon," I said. "Then they'd definitely see that they're getting an extra one."

"So cute!" Emma agreed.

"They also make special boxes that fit exactly one cupcake," Katie said. "I've seen them at the store. But they might be too expensive. I can check."

"Either one of those ideas could work," Alexis said. "And you know, maybe we don't have to do flyers. I was doing some research on advertising, and it costs only ten dollars to put an ad on the school's website for parents. Since we need some new customers, we could offer a baker's dozen to everyone who orders for the first time."

"Sounds like a plan!" Katie said.

"I can write something up and show it to you guys on Sunday," Alexis said.

"And I'll get the ingredients together for the cinnamon cupcakes," I added.

And then I realized that I had spent the whole lunch period without even thinking about Spanish class. That's another reason I love being in the Cupcake Club!

CHAPTER 5

Some Advice from Ava

"Why exactly do I have to sweep the basement?" I complained. "Nobody ever goes down there!"

"Would you take a bath and not wash your feet?" Eddie replied. "A truly clean house is clean all over. And we want things to be nice for your friend."

"But she's not even going to see the basement!" I pointed out.

That was when Mom stepped into the kitchen. "Mia, please don't argue with Eddie. It will only take a few minutes to sweep the basement."

I glared at my mom, but I knew I wasn't going to win this argument. So I grabbed the broom from Eddie and went down the stairs.

"No stomping!" Mom called after me.

"I am *not* stomping!" I called back. (Although to be honest, I was stepping pretty hard.)

I couldn't help it. I was feeling pretty cranky. Ava was due any minute, and I was thinking of changing out of my skinny jeans and black sweater into something different. But no—I had to clean the basement.

When we lived in an apartment, we didn't have a basement. In fact, I don't remember cleaning our apartment. I had to keep my room clean, but the kitchen and living room were always neat. I never thought much about how that happened.

But now I lived in a house, and Eddie believes that "a clean house is a happy house." So every Saturday we wake up at the crack of dawn (which to me is any time before ten o'clock) and clean the house, unless I have a soccer game or a cupcake job. It's just one more way that my new life is worse than my old life.

Even though I hate to admit it, Mom was right about the basement. There's not much down there except Dan's and my sports equipment and a metal shelf with some pots and pans and cans of food. The floor is concrete, and it didn't take long to sweep at all.

But by the time I got back upstairs, the doorbell

was ringing. My heart started to beat extra fast. Ava was here!

Ava and I have known each other since preschool. She was my only best friend in the world until I met Katie. I miss Ava so much! I usually visit her when I spend the weekend with my dad, but she's never been to Eddie's house before—I mean, *my* house. Our house.

I ran to the door and opened it. Ava was there with her mom, Mrs. Monroe. A blast of cold air swept into the room.

"Come in, fast!" I said. "It's cold out there."

Then Mom and Eddie came up, and everybody hugged one another. Ava took off her coat, and I saw she was wearing skinny jeans and a black sweater—just like me.

We pointed at each other and laughed.

"Nice outfit," I said.

"You too," Ava replied.

I've always thought that Ava and I look kind of alike, even though I'm Latina and she's part Korean and part Scottish. We're both the same height, and we both have brown eyes and straight black hair. Oh, and we both have first names that are three letters long. How cool is that?

Eddie took Ava's purple duffel bag from

Mrs. Monroe and brought it over to the stairs.

"Ellie, can you stay for coffee?" my mom asked Ava's mom.

"I wish I could, but I've got to get back for Christopher's hockey game," Mrs. Monroe replied. She hugged Ava and kissed her on the forehead.

"Call me if you need anything, okay? Otherwise I'll see you at the train station tomorrow."

"Okay, Mom," Ava replied.

When Mrs. Monroe left, Eddie said, "Mia, why don't you give your friend a tour of the house?"

"Um, sure," I said. I felt a little awkward. I'd never had to give Ava a "tour" of anything. But everything was different now.

"I'll take you on the grand tour!" I said dramatically, and we both started giggling. "Follow me, madam."

So I showed Ava the kitchen and the dining room, and she kept saying, "Wow! You have so much space!" It's true, I guess. In Manhattan, almost everyone I know has a pretty small apartment.

When we got to the living room, Dan was setting up his video game system.

"Oh, hey, guys," he said, nodding to Ava. "You were at the wedding, right?"

"Right," Ava said, and I saw her cheeks turn pink.

"Ava, you remember my stepbrother, Dan," I said.

Dan nodded and settled down in front of the TV. Then I led Ava upstairs.

"Your brother is so cute!" she whispered when we got to the top.

"He's not cute! He's just . . . regular," I said. Suddenly I knew how Emma must feel with everyone crushing on Matt and Sam. "Besides, he's not my brother. He's my stepbrother."

"Oh yeah, I forgot," Ava said as I opened the door to my room. Then she gasped. "Wow, look at all this space!"

I had been nervous about showing Ava my bedroom. My room in Manhattan has this cool Parisian theme, and it's light pink and black and white. But I haven't decorated my room in this house yet. Right now it has ugly flowered wallpaper on it, but Eddie promised to scrape all that off for me. I still haven't figured out what color to paint it, and none of the furniture matches.

But Ava didn't seem to notice. She went straight for my closet and threw open the door. "Oh wow! This is HUGE!" she exclaimed. "You could fit a whole store in here, Mia!"

My closet isn't really *that* big, but compared to my old one in the city, it definitely is huge. Then Ava frowned.

"Wait! I can't find anything!" she cried. "Where's my favorite top? The one with the butterfly? It used to be next to the red dress!"

"I reorganized it," I told her. "Mom showed me how to do it by color. Look in the blue section."

Ava searched and then pulled out the shirt. She held it in front of her. "You have to let me borrow this again! When it gets warmer, I mean."

"Or you could layer it," I said. I rummaged through the clothes and pulled out a slim-fitting, long-sleeved knit top with purple-and-blue stripes. "See?"

"Cool!" Ava said, grabbing it from me. "Can I borrow them both? I'll give them back next time I see you."

"Of course!" I told her. "You don't even have to ask."

Ava flopped backward on my bed. "Sorry if it was weird that I said Dan was cute. He seems really nice," she said. "It must be fun having an older brother instead of a younger one. Christopher is always getting into my stuff and bugging me!"

"Well, Dan is pretty nice," I admitted. "But wait until you hear the loud music he plays. That's really annoying."

Ava sat up. "So you must like living here, right?"

I shrugged. "It's okay. But I miss not seeing my dad every day. And you and everyone else."

"But you still get to see us," Ava said. "It's kind of like you have the best of both worlds."

"Maybe," I said, a little unsure. "Sometimes I think about what it would be like if things had never changed with my parents. Most of the time I think I would like that. But I'd miss some of this new stuff, like some of my new friends."

"I guess I would be sad if I couldn't see my dad every day," Ava said thoughtfully.

That's what I love about Ava. She gets me, you know?

"So listen to this," I said. "I am failing Spanish class!"

Ava looked surprised, and then she said the same thing everyone else always said: "But don't you speak Spanish?"

"Sí," I replied, and then I explained the situation like I had to Katie and my cupcake friends. Ava nodded.

"It's the same with me," she said. "My dad's a

doctor, and I almost failed science! He was mad at first, but then when he was helping me with my homework, he saw how hard it was, so I had a tutor. It really helped."

I imagined Eddie and Mom sitting in Señora Delgado's class and smiled. "I wonder if Mom and Eddie could even do my homework. It's hard!"

"Just ask for help," Ava said. "They'll understand. I'm sure they'd rather help you than have you fail the class."

"I will," I told her, but I wasn't sure if I meant it. After all, things had been pretty crazy the last few months, with the move and the wedding and everything. Maybe I just needed to catch up, I told myself.

Suddenly a loud screeching came through the bedroom wall, followed by the *thump, thump, thump* of a bass line.

Ava covered her ears. "Oh my gosh! What *is* that?" she yelled over the music.

I grinned. "I told you!" I shouted back.

"DAN! Turn it DOWN!" I yelled, and banged on the wall. "Not so cute now, is he?" I said, and then we both started laughing.

CHAPTER 6

A Different Kind of Cupcake Meeting

Spending Saturday with Ava was awesome. We went to the mall, and after that Mom made spicy chili for dinner. Then we all watched a movie together (well, except for Dan, who was out with his friends). And Ava and I stayed up *way* late talking and talking. I love my cupcake friends, but it's also great to have a friend who knows your history. Someone you don't see all the time, but every time you reconnect, you can pick up right where you left off. Every time I see Ava it's like we just hung out the day before.

In the morning we helped Mom make chocolate chip pancakes, and then we got the kitchen ready for the Cupcake Club meeting. Eddie was making a turkey-and-swiss sandwich on a superlong loaf of bread while I got out the baking stuff.

"I ordered the bread special from the bakery," he told us. "This is a lunch meeting, right? You can't have a lunch meeting without lunch!"

I hadn't even thought about that. Eddie's pretty good that way. I think he likes to take care of people.

To tell the truth, I was a little bit nervous about the meeting. Besides baking the cinnamon-frosted cupcakes, we were also going to talk about the cupcakes we were making for Ava's birthday party in a few weeks. I was invited to the party, but my cupcake friends weren't.

Of course, we bake stuff all the time for events we're not invited to, like that baby shower for our science teacher's sister. So maybe that wasn't such a big deal.

I was also worried that Ava wouldn't get along with my Maple Grove friends. But then I realized that everyone is really nice, so that shouldn't be a problem. At least, I hoped it wouldn't be!

Then the bell rang, and Katie, Alexis, and Emma all arrived at once. It took a few minutes for everyone to take off their coats, hats, gloves, and scarves, but soon we were all around the kitchen table and Eddie was cutting up his giant sandwich for us.

"I like your shirts," Emma said to Ava. She was wearing the striped shirt with the butterfly shirt that she had borrowed from me.

"Thanks! They're Mia's," she replied. "The butterfly one has always been my favorite."

I noticed that Katie suddenly got kind of a weird look on her face. Was she jealous? No, probably not. *Katie's just insecure,* I thought. Her old best friend, Callie, dumped her, so she's always afraid someone else is going to do the same thing.

Then Ava started to talk really fast about stuff, like she does when she's excited or nervous.

"You guys live in such a nice town," she said. "I'm kind of jealous. I sort of wish I had an older brother like Dan too."

Emma rolled her eyes. "You're lucky. They can be *so* annoying."

"More annoying than a little brother?" Ava asked. "'Cause I already have one of those."

Emma nodded. "Worse. At least little brothers do cute things sometimes."

"I tried to tell you, Ava," I said.

"At least none of you have an older sister,"

Alexis chimed in. "She spends hours and hours in the bathroom every day."

"Dan showers longer than any of us," I whispered. "And then he sprays on that cologne for guys that they advertise on TV. Gross!"

I looked at Katie, expecting her to make a joke like she always does, but she was kind of quiet. In fact, she stayed quiet for the rest of the meeting. I decided I'd have to ask her later if everything was okay.

Then Alexis took out her notebook and we got down to business.

"So, Ava, I can show you our most popular cupcake styles," she said.

Ava took her phone from her jeans pocket. "Actually, I have a list of ideas I've been working on," she said. "Mia says you guys can do anything, right?"

Alexis looked flustered—she's used to being the one in charge, and Ava was kind of taking over.

"Well, sure, but sometimes it helps if—"

"Let's hear your idea, Ava!" Emma said, smoothing things over.

"I have a few," Ava replied. "But winter is totally my favorite season, and it almost always snows on my birthday, so I was hoping you could do a snowy cupcake."

Alexis started flipping through her notebook. "Snowy. Hmm, I'm not sure exactly how we'd do that."

All of us were quiet for a minute. A snowy cupcake? That was tough. Then Katie came through, as usual.

"Remember Emma's cupcake from yesterday?" she blurted out. "What if we do coconut flakes on top of vanilla icing? Mia said the coconut looked just like snow."

I nodded. "That could work."

I jumped out of my seat and ran to the kitchen cabinet where I keep all my cupcake supplies. Eddie had cleared out a shelf just for me.

I came back with a big jar of glittery sugar sprinkles.

"How about white icing, coconut flakes, and then some edible glitter, like this?" I suggested. "We could do a silver wrapper."

"That sounds nice," Ava said. "But do I get to see it first?"

"We'll take a photo and send it to you for approval," Alexis said. "But first you need to tell us what flavor of cake you want."

"Would chocolate be okay?" Ava asked. "The brown cake won't show through the vanilla frosting, will it?"

"No way," I said. "Especially if Katie's doing the frosting. She's the best."

"You guys are all just as good," Katie said, smiling a little for the first time.

"We'll do a test run at our next meeting, after we get the ingredients," Alexis said. "Today we've got to do a test batch of Mia's spicy cupcakes."

"I've got the red food coloring and the cinnamon and the Red Hots," I said.

Katie held up the canvas shopping bag she had brought with her. "I was talking to my mom about them, and she thought some other flavors might go nice with the cinnamon frosting instead of the red velvet. Like dark chocolate, maybe, or apple."

"Wow, they both sound good," Ava said.

"I thought we could try a batch of each," Katie suggested. "I brought the dark chocolate, and some applesauce and some extra spices, like ginger and cloves." Everyone agreed to try the two different kinds, and we quickly got to work measuring out the flour and other ingredients for the batter.

"Don't you use a recipe?" Ava asked.

"Sometimes," I said. "But mostly we know how to make a basic batter and then add extra flavors to it."

"Ooh, extra spices! *Muy caliente*, right, Mia?" Emma said, and everybody laughed. But that got me thinking about my Spanish class again. How was I ever going to tell my mom and dad and Eddie that I was failing Spanish? Ava was right. They would make sure I got the extra help I needed. And the longer I avoided telling them, the worse it was going to be. But still, the thought of telling them made my stomach feel queasy. Even though I knew it was crazy, I kept hoping that if I avoided the problem, somehow it would magically disappear.

"Earth to Mia!" said Katie, waving something under my nose. She held up an index card. "Mom gave me her recipe for the dark chocolate ones. The measurements are always a little different when there's chocolate," she explained to Ava.

Chocolate. Now that should have caught my attention. But I couldn't get my mind off my Spanish class. This was awful. Baking cupcakes with the Cupcake Club was one of my favorite things to do in the entire world, and now I couldn't even enjoy that. I kept throwing ingredients into the batter and stirring, stirring, stirring, wishing I could make my problems disappear the way the spices were disappearing into the chocolate batter.

Wait—spices in the chocolate batter? I tasted a little bit. *Whoa.* Intense. And not in a good way.

"Um, sorry, guys," I said. "I think I mixed up the two batters. I added the spices to the dark chocolate batter by accident." Alexis frowned at the waste of ingredients, but everyone else was really nice. We've all ruined or burned batches of cupcakes at one time or another, so everyone was pretty forgiving.

"Maybe you should work on something else right now," Alexis suggested.

I agreed, and so I said, "Ava and I will do the icing." Then we made a double batch of vanilla icing dyed red and spiced with cinnamon.

About forty-five minutes later we were staring at two plates of cupcakes with red frosting and dotted with Red Hots candies. They looked great, and both looked the same—although inside, they were both really different.

"Tasting time!" Alexis announced, and we cut

some of the cupcakes in half so we each ate half of one. Everyone got quiet for a few minutes while we ate. Cupcake tasting *is* fun, but it's also serious business.

"They are both so good," Emma said, wiping her mouth with a napkin. "But I think I like the dark chocolate ones best."

"Me too," I agreed.

Alexis shook her head. "I like the spices in the apple cupcakes."

"I vote for apple too," Katie said.

Alexis frowned. "It's a tie."

"Ava can break the tie," I said. "What do you think, Ava?"

"You know me. I love chocolate!" she replied.

I turned to my friends. "What do you think? Should we do the dark chocolate?"

Katie and Alexis looked at each other and shrugged.

"Fine," Alexis said. "Studies show that chocolate is one of the most popular cupcake flavors, anyway. Maybe we'll get some new customers from it."

"And they're Valentine's Day cupcakes," Emma said. "And you know how everybody goes gaga over chocolate on Valentine's Day."

Katie put her arms around the plate of apple

cupcakes. "Then I guess I'll be taking these home," she joked, and we all laughed.

It felt really good to have all my friends together in one place. But I knew it wouldn't last. In a little while, Ava would have to go back to the city. My cupcake friends would be in Maple Grove. And I would still be stuck with Spanish wherever I went.

CHAPTER 7

Tiny Plates and Tiny Lies

After our meeting was over and the kitchen was clean, Ava and I had to hurry and pack up her things. We had a half hour to get to the train station.

Even though Ava was leaving, there was one good thing about that day. You see, I was supposed to see my dad this weekend, but he had to go on a business trip. He was coming back Sunday afternoon, and Mom had to go to the city to style a client for a party, so she and I were going to take the train in with Ava. Mom would go to work, Ava would go home, and I'd get to have a special dinner with my dad.

It sounds complicated, right? Welcome to my life!

Eddie drove us to the train station and dropped us off. He gave Mom a big hug and a kiss. I looked at Ava and winced.

"He's acting like she's going away for a year or something," I said. "We'll be back in a few hours."

Ava laughed. "I don't know. I think it's kind of sweet."

I rolled my eyes. "Seriously?"

Then the train pulled up, and Mom and Ava and I climbed on. It wasn't as crowded as it usually is when I leave on Friday, so we all found a seat near one another. I don't really love the train, though. The seats are an ugly color, and it always smells like stale bread in there. But it's fast and it gets me to my dad, so I don't mind so much.

Mom shopped for accessories on her tablet on the way to Manhattan, and Ava and I talked about her upcoming birthday party. The snowy cupcakes had inspired her.

"I could get silver and white decorations," she was saying. "And sprinkle silver glitter on the cake table, maybe."

I whipped out my sketchbook. "We could put the cupcakes at different heights, like this," I said, quickly drawing my vision for her.

"I love it!" Ava exclaimed.

"And of course you'll need the perfect dress," I said.

I flipped the page and started sketching Ava in a snowy dress—a sleeveless top attached to a flowing, white knee-length skirt.

"The top could be silver," I said, pointing. "But I'm not sure. It kind of looks like an ice skater's outfit."

"No, it's awesome," Ava said sincerely. "You are such a good designer, Mia! You're going to be famous someday."

I blushed a little bit, and Mom leaned over to see my sketch. She smiled. Being a famous fashion designer would be so cool. But I know that takes a lot of hard work, and a lot of luck, too.

Finally the train pulled into Penn Station. It's always crazy when everyone gets off the train, with people running in every direction, but Dad always waits in the same spot for me, by this big pillar by the ticket counter.

When the doors opened up and we walked to the concourse level, I saw him standing there. Dad always looks like a movie star to me. He had on a warm black coat that wasn't puffy at all, and shiny black shoes and an olive green scarf around his neck. Dad wears glasses with black rims, but on him they don't look old-fashioned, they look smart.

I ran up and hugged him.

"Hello, *mija*!" he said. "It's good to see you."

Ava and my mom walked up behind me.

"Hello, Alex," my mom said. Her voice sounded friendly, but a little cold at the same time.

"Hi, Sara," dad replied, and he just sounded uncomfortable.

Ava looked around. "Where's my mom?" she asked.

"She texted me and said she's a little bit late," Mom answered. "But we'll all wait with you until she gets here."

And so we waited, and it was totally awkward. Mom and Dad were talking to me instead of each other.

"Mia, how are you doing in school?"

"Mia, is it colder in New Jersey?"

"Mia, tell your father about your Valentine's Day cupcakes."

I realized that this was probably the longest time my parents had spent in the same place since their divorce. No wonder it was awkward.

Finally, Mrs. Monroe came rushing up. "I'm so sorry! The subways are so slow on Sunday."

"That's all right," Mom told her. "Thank you for letting Ava stay with us. She's a pleasure to have around."

"And so is Mia," Mrs. Monroe said. She smiled at me. "We'll see you at the party soon. I can't wait to try your cupcakes!"

Ava gave me a quick hug good-bye. "I'll text you later," I said.

Then Mom kissed me. "I'll meet you back here at seven fifteen, okay?"

"I'll make sure she's on time," my dad promised.

"Thanks," Mom said, and managed a smile. She then rushed off, and it was just me and my dad.

"Sushi?" I asked. That's usually our tradition.

"Well, since this is a special visit, I thought we should mix it up a little bit," Dad said. "Try someplace new."

"Where are we going?" I asked him.

Dad smiled. "I want to surprise you."

So we quickly found a cab outside and traveled downtown for a while. Then the cab stopped in front of a restaurant with a red awning. Painted on the window were the words SABOR TAPAS BAR.

"We're going to a bar?" I asked. "Isn't that kind of inappropriate?"

"It's not that kind of bar," Dad said, paying the cabdriver. "You'll see."

We walked inside, and the place looked warm and cozy. Dark wood panels covered the walls, and the booths were made of wood too, with red cushions. The server showed us to one of the booths, and then Dad handed me a menu.

"In a tapas bar, they serve small plates of food," Dad explained. "And then you share. That way you get to try a little bit of a lot of different things."

The server, a woman with dark hair almost exactly like mine, took our drink orders, and then we looked at the menu. Everything on it looked delicious. I was starting to like this idea.

"This is awesome," I said. "But there's so much to choose from! I can't decide."

"I'll order for us, then," he said.

The server brought our drinks, and then Dad ordered a bunch of tapas from the menu: shrimp with garlic and chilies, a potato omelet, sautéed spinach, and a bowl of Spanish olives.

"Anything else, *mija*?" he asked.

I looked at the menu, and one thing caught my eye.

"Croquetas con pollo y plátanos, por favor," I

ordered. (That means "Croquettes with chicken and plantains, please." I wasn't sure what a croquette was, but I love plantains. They're kind of like bananas, but not sweet.)

"Bien. Creo que les gustará," the server replied in Spanish. That means, "Good. I think you'll like them."

"Creo que lo haré," I replied, which means, "I think that I will."

The server left the table, and when I looked at Dad, he was beaming with pride.

"Such good Spanish, *mija*," he said. "Your Spanish teacher must love you."

I smiled, but I didn't say a word. I know what you're thinking. This was the perfect time for me to talk to my dad about my problems in Advanced Spanish. I know Ava told me I should ask for help, but I just couldn't bear to disappoint Dad. Not now, anyway. I just wanted to have a nice dinner with him.

And it *was* nice. It turned out that a croquette is a little fried ball-shaped thing, and it was superdelicious. All the stuff Dad ordered tasted good too.

But it went way too fast, and soon it was time to get back to the train. Dad walked me to the platform, and Mom was already waiting there.

"Get home safe," Dad said, giving me a hug.

"I'll text you when I get home," I promised.

Mom got a funny look on her face. After Dad left, I found out why.

"You always complain when I ask you to text *me*," Mom said.

Yikes. She had a point. I had to think about that for a little bit.

"You have me most of the time, plus Eddie and Dan, but Dad is all alone," I explained. "I feel bad for Dad sometimes."

Mom sighed. "It's hard," she admitted, "but please don't worry about your dad, Mia. I know he misses you a lot, but he's still your dad, no matter where we live. And we're all a lot happier this way."

Happier? I had to think about that one.

As the train sped toward Maple Grove, I stared out the window into the dark sky. Mom and Dad fought a *lot* before they got divorced. They tried to do it at night in their room, when they thought I was asleep, but I always heard them. So I guess they weren't too happy then.

But when they got divorced, things still weren't good. Mom moved out and I stayed with

Dad, but it felt weird and I missed her. And Mom and Dad still argued every time they saw each other. Then I moved into Mom's new apartment, but that was extra weird because it was a whole new place.

So was it still weird? I had to think about that. Living in Maple Grove was starting to feel like home. I had good friends. And Eddie and Dan were nice, and Eddie sure tried to make us feel like a "normal" family as much as possible. But happi-*er*? As in, more happy than before, when we were all together?

Like I said, I'd have to think about that.

CHAPTER 8

Can I Start the Week Over Again?

While I was still on the train, I called Katie. I wanted to reach her before it got too late.

"Hey," I said.

"Hey," Katie replied. "Are you home?"

"I'm on the train," I told her. "Is everything okay? You seemed a little quiet at the meeting today."

"Everything's fine," Katie said, but I could tell by the sound of her voice that she was lying.

"Good," I said. I wasn't going to press her about it. "So anyway, we're still going to see *The Emerald Forest* next weekend, right?"

"Of course!" Katie answered, and her voice sounded like the old Katie again. The Emerald Forest is a fantasy book series that we both love, and they finally made a movie out of it!

"Awesome," I said. "I can't wait to see what kind of costumes they're going to do for the emerald fairies. In the books, the description is totally beautiful."

"I can't wait either," Katie agreed. "We're going on Saturday, right?"

"Mom said she'll take us," I promised.

We said good night, and I hung up the phone. When I got home, I was totally exhausted. I fell asleep dreaming of the Emerald Forest. . . .

If only the rest of the week was as peaceful as that forest. But it was anything but. The next day was Monday, my least favorite day of the week.

I was so tired in the morning that I left my gym uniform home by mistake, and I had to sit out of gym. And Señora Delgado gave us pages and pages of notes for our Spanish test the next day—on verbs.

You have to believe me when I tell you that I studied like crazy. I went straight home after school and studied. I ate dinner and then went right back upstairs and studied. I didn't even sketch! (Okay, I did doodle a pair of boots in the margin of my notes, but I didn't open up my sketchbook, I swear.) When I went to sleep that night, I dreamed of verbs instead of emerald fairies.

I even studied at lunch on Tuesday before the test. I was feeling pretty good—until Señora handed me my test paper. The questions looked like Egyptian hieroglyphics to me.

So I took the test, and I did my best. But as I handed it in, I knew I hadn't done well.

That night Mom asked me about it as we were cleaning up from dinner.

"So how did you do on your Spanish test?" she asked. "You really studied hard for that one."

"I think I did okay," I lied. I thought about spilling everything out, right then and there. *Mom, I think I'm failing Spanish. I know I should have told you sooner. The advanced class is so difficult. I'm still having trouble no matter how hard I try.* I opened my mouth to tell her, but I just couldn't bring myself to say the words. I don't know why it was so hard. Usually I could always talk to Mom about anything.

It was then that I realized that Mom really was a lot happier. She smiled a lot, and she seemed more relaxed than ever, even though she was busy. And she really did seem to love Eddie. Then I wondered if my dad was as happy as Mom. Was I?

Mom smiled at me and kissed the top of my head. "I'm so proud of you, Mia," she said.

Ugh. I felt bad about lying, and then something happened that made me feel ten times worse.

"I have a surprise for you," she said. "Come upstairs with me."

I followed Mom to her room. "So you know that Annie Chang has a line out for teens, right?"

I nodded. Annie Chang is a popular fashion designer, and I absolutely love her clothes. I was psyched when I read that she was putting out a teen line. But I know they are kind of expensive, too, so I wasn't holding out much hope that I'd convince Mom to buy me anything.

Mom unzipped a garment bag hanging from her closet. "I met Annie at an event the other day, and I told her all about you," she said. "So today she sent this just for you."

I gasped. Inside the bag was a totally cool mod-looking sweater dress with gray and black stripes.

"That's from her latest winter line!" I shrieked. "Oh, Mom, it's perfect!"

"Wear it with some black tights—or even a jewel-toned color, for that matter—and black boots, and you've got a killer outfit," Mom said.

I slipped the dress off the hanger and ran to my room. "I'm going to try it on!"

I tried the dress with some solid red tights, and it looked awesome. I ran into my mom's room and gave her a big hug.

"Thank you, thank you!" I said.

"You deserve it, with all the hard work you've been doing," Mom said, and I felt a huge pang of guilt.

You should tell her now, a little voice inside me said. But just like Dad and dinner, I didn't want to ruin the moment.

I loved the dress so much that I wanted to sleep in it, but I didn't want to ruin it. So I wore it to school the very next day. At lunchtime, I was walking past the PGC table when Callie called out to me.

"Mia? Is that an Annie Chang?" she asked.

I walked over to her. "Yes, she gave it to my mom to give to me," I said.

"It's really cool," said Maggie, another one of the popular girls. Maggie's actually pretty nice, but she does everything Sydney tells her to do.

Sydney examined my entire outfit from head to toe. I could tell she was trying to find something wrong with it, but she couldn't. So she just made one of her mean comments instead. "It's nice of your mom's friends to give you their castoffs," Sydney said, tossing her perfect blond hair. I knew she was insulting me, but I didn't care.

I smiled sweetly at Sydney. "Yeah, well, Mom says that Annie *is* really nice," I said. "And it's actually not a castoff. It's a sample. Like the kind they give models to wear. See you."

Then I walked away.

My Cupcake Club friends liked my dress too, even though they didn't know who Annie Chang was. Then it was time for Spanish class. Oh boy.

Señora Delgado handed out our tests as soon as we sat down. I already knew how I did, but I was still shocked when I saw the big red F on my paper. I've never gotten an F in anything before.

"Class, please turn to page fifty-seven in your workbooks and start that page," she said in Spanish, as usual. "Ms. Vélaz-Cruz, please come to my desk."

Uh-oh. This wasn't going to be fun. I walked up to her desk as slowly as I could. What was she going to do? Was she going to yell at me in front of everybody?

Señora Delgado is petite, with short black hair, and she wears big eyeglasses. She looks like a very wise owl. And I know from science class that owls are predators. They eat cute little chipmunks and mice.

"Mia, I think you might need some extra help in this class," she said softly, in English. She wasn't mean or angry at all. It seemed like she really wanted to help me. She started to write on a piece of paper. "I know some excellent tutors. Please give this to your parents and tell them to call me if they have any questions."

"Thank you, Señora," I said quietly, and then I walked back to my seat. I couldn't keep my secret any longer now. I'd have to give my parents the note. But I didn't have to give it to them right away.

I'll give it to them, I told myself, *when the time is right! Because they're all too happy now for me to spoil it.*

CHAPTER 9

Sydney Needs My Help. Really?

Okay, so I technically couldn't give my parents the note that night because my dad was in Manhattan and my mom was working late. It was just me and Eddie and Dan, and Eddie is technically my *step*parent, not my parent. So I left the note in my Spanish book.

We had a Cupcake Club meeting at Katie's house the next day after school. Katie's mom was there. Mrs. Brown has curly brown hair and Katie's smile, and she's really nice. She's the one who taught Katie how to make cupcakes.

"Come on in, girls, I've got it all set up for you," Mrs. Brown said as we went into the kitchen. Katie's kitchen is small, but it's got everything you need to make cupcakes in it. Her mom has every kitchen gadget you've ever heard of—and some you haven't heard of.

We quickly got to work making a test batch of Ava's snowy cupcakes. Katie and I made the chocolate batter, and Emma and Alexis worked on the extra frosting.

"I want to get it extra fluffy," Emma said as they put the ingredients in the mixer bowl. "So it looks like snow."

"Great idea," I said. I opened up my bag. "Good news! My mom found the silver cupcake liners for us."

"She's so nice," Katie said, smiling at me, and I figured that whatever was bothering her wasn't anymore. Maybe she was just uncomfortable around people she didn't know, and that's why she was quiet when Ava was visiting.

As we baked the cupcakes we talked about school and stuff, and then Katie asked me, "So how did you do on that Spanish test?"

I frowned. "I can't bear to say it." Instead, I used the wooden spoon in my hand to draw an *F* in the bowl of batter.

"You failed? No way!" Katie cried. "But you studied so hard."

"I know," I said. "Señora says I need a tutor."

"Will your parents get you one?" Emma asked.

I bit my lower lip. "Well, they kind of don't know yet. I'm waiting for the right moment to tell them."

"That must be so hard," Katie said sympathetically.

"You should tell them soon," said Alexis, always the practical one. "They're going to find out eventually. And the sooner you get some help in Spanish, the better. You've put this off long enough. I thought maybe if you studied a little harder, you'd be okay, but things are obviously getting worse instead of better."

"Just talk to your mom, Mia," Katie said. "I'm sure once you tell her everything, it will be all right."

"I know, I know!" I said crossly. "Can we please talk about cupcakes instead of school?"

Nobody said anything for a while after that, and I felt kind of bad for losing it. But soon we were back in our groove again, and I was decorating our first test cupcake.

"It's perfect!" Alexis said, and I had to admit it looked pretty good. The silver liner was really pretty, the icing was nice and fluffy, and the sparkles looked good on top of the coconut.

"Let me take a picture and I'll send it to Ava," I said.

A minute later Ava texted me back.

It's pretty, but the coconut looks too big or something. Not like snowflakes.

Alexis rolled her eyes. "Great. Another picky client."

"Hey, she's my friend," I reminded her. "Besides, she kind of has a point."

The coconut flakes from the package did look a little big. Luckily for us, Mrs. Brown walked in just then.

"That's beautiful!" she said.

"Except Ava doesn't like it," Katie said, and then explained about the coconut.

Katie's mom looked thoughtful. "I think I have just the thing," she said finally.

She opened up the small pantry closet by the back door and came back with a weird-looking device.

"It's a veggie chopper," she said. "Normally you could use it to chop onions into small pieces. But I bet it will work on the coconut."

She put a pile of coconut on a cutting board,

put the chopper on top of it, and then pressed down a few times. When she picked up the chopper, the coconut underneath was very finely shredded.

"That looks a lot more like snow," Katie remarked. "Let's try another one."

So Katie iced another cupcake, and I sprinkled the coconut flakes and glittery sugar on top.

"Much better," agreed Mrs. Brown. "I'm sure your friend will like it."

"Let's see," I said. I sent another photo to Ava.

This time she was happy. Here was her reply:

♥♥♥♥♥♥♥

"She loves it!" I reported, and we all cheered.

"I think I've got all the details down so we can re-create this for the party," Alexis said. "Otherwise, we're meeting at my house on Saturday morning to do the Valentine's cupcakes, right?"

"Right," Emma said.

"My mom said she'd help us drop them off at the bookstore," I told them.

Alexis shut her notebook. "Just one more thing," she said. She gave each of us a sheet of paper. "Let me know what you think, and then I'll get the ad up on the PTA website next week."

We all read Alexis's ad:

Need a sweet treat for your next party or event? Let us do the baking for you! Click here to contact the Cupcake Club. We can do any flavor or amount you want. And we're having a baker's dozen special for all new customers! Buy a dozen cupcakes and get one free!

"I like the 'sweet treat' part," Katie said.

"It's really good, Alexis," Emma said.

I nodded. "The baker's dozen was a great idea, Katie," I said. "I'll bet we'll get lots of new business from this."

When the meeting was over, Eddie picked me up and brought me home. Mom was home, but she was working in her office. And at dinner she seemed really distracted. So I decided it wouldn't be fair to give her the note while she was so busy.

The next day was Friday, and I was glad it was the last day of the week. No tests, and we had our leftover snowy cupcakes for Cupcake Friday.

But then something really unexpected happened at lunch. Here's how it went down. While I was eating lunch, Sydney Whitman actually came up to our lunch table.

"Mia, can I talk to you a minute?" she asked. "I need a favor."

"Sure," I said. I turned to my friends and raised my eyebrows, giving that *I don't know what she wants* look. Then I followed her over to the wall.

"Thanks," she said. "I got this text from Jackson Montano, and it's in Spanish. Usually I'd ask Callie, but she's home because she's sick today."

What could I say? Should I launch into my entire "I can speak Spanish really well, but I have problems reading and writing it" explanation? Meanwhile, Queen Sydney stood in front of me with her arms crossed, waiting for me to say something.

"Uh, sure," I said, a little nervously. I hoped it wasn't too complicated.

Sydney handed me her phone, and I checked the message.

Te quiero.

Now, if you read Spanish you probably know that this means, "I love you," which is what my parents say to me, and my *abuela* says all the time. But when I saw "*quiero*" I got it mixed up with the word "*queso*," which means "cheese."

Yes, that's right. That's what I thought. And here's what I told Sydney.

"He says you're cheesy," I said.

Honestly, I didn't think that was strange. Jackson is on the football team, and he says mean things to kids all the time. Sydney and Jackson actually would make a perfect couple. Jackson thinks he's supercool just because he's a football player, and Sydney thinks she's supercool because . . . well, because she's Sydney.

Sydney's face turned bright red. "Cheesy? Really? I'll show him!"

Then she stomped away. She went back to her table, and I could see her talking with Maggie. While Sydney talked, she looked shocked and kept glancing down at her phone and looked like she was getting angrier by the minute.

I went back to the table.

"What did she want?" Alexis asked.

I shrugged. "She wanted me to translate some text message for her from Jackson Montano. He told her he thinks she's cheesy."

"Cheesy? That's a weird thing to say," Emma said.

"Hmm. Well, at least that's one less boy drooling over Sydney," Katie said. "So yay for that."

"It figures he's texting her," Alexis said. "Those two think alike."

And then I forgot all about it—for a little while, anyway. In a split second, I had made a terrible mistake—one that would haunt me forever. (I know that sounds totally dramatic, but it's true!)

CHAPTER 10

Katie Is Still Acting Weird

That night at dinner Mom made an announcement.

"I just got the e-mails about the parent-teacher conferences next week," she said. "I can't wait to meet all your teachers!"

I almost choked on my pork chop, and started coughing.

"Mia, are you okay?" Mom asked.

I nodded and took a sip of water.

"Do not believe anything Mrs. Caldwell tells you," Dan said. "She's always accusing me of messing around in class, but it's Joseph, not me."

Eddie raised an eyebrow. "Hmm, we'll see about that," he said. "Any other teachers we should look out for?"

Dan shrugged. "They're all pretty cool, I guess.

Mr. Bender gives us tons of homework, but I always do it all."

"What about you, Mia?" Eddie asked.

I shrugged too. "They're all cool." Normally, I would have told them about how much fun Ms. Biddle's science class is and how strict Mrs. Moore is in math class, but I didn't feel like talking. I couldn't keep my secret about Spanish class much longer. I decided I'd have to tell Mom after dinner.

But then Eddie said something that really made me mad.

"Mia, I'm looking forward to meeting your teachers too," he said.

I almost choked again. Why was Eddie going to my parent-teacher conference? Dad is the one who should be going!

I was too angry to say anything. I kept quiet until the end of dinner. Then after, when Mom and I were cleaning up, I confronted her.

"Why is Eddie going instead of Dad?" I asked her. "Dad's still my parent, right? Shouldn't he be going?"

Mom looked really startled. "Well . . . ," she said, like she was trying to figure out an answer. "I didn't think of it. It might be hard for Dad to get here from the city during the week. I'll ask him. But is there a reason you don't want Eddie to go?"

"Because he's not my dad!" I blurted out.

Mom sat down on the nearest chair. She thought for a minute.

"You're right about that," she said finally. "But he's still your parent. He cares about you very much. And he takes an active role with you. He helps you with your homework and projects. So it's important for him to meet your teachers and know what's going on in your school."

I nodded grudgingly, feeling a little guilty. After all, Eddie did drive me all over the place, and he made me lunch and dinner and snacks. But I was still mad. "Fine. But Dad does those things too. He should be there."

"I promise I'll talk to him," Mom said. "And if he can't go, I'll make sure he gets all the information, okay?"

"Okay," I mumbled. Then I went up to my room. I decided to do some sketching. Sketching always relaxes me and makes me feel better when I'm in a bad mood.

I started to sketch some Valentine's Day outfits. First I drew a really girlie pink dress with a short, full skirt that I knew Emma would love. Then I drew a denim skirt paired with a loose sweater, with a big bold red heart embroidered on the front. It looked very "casual cool." Out of the blue I wondered how I would write "casual cool" in Spanish. I drew a complete blank. I couldn't stop thinking about it, and I found myself getting more and more upset. *Great,* I thought. *Now even my sketch time is ruined by Spanish.* Meanwhile, I had forgotten all about giving Mom the note from Señora Delgado.

The next morning I woke up early, and Mom drove me to Alexis's house. She has the neatest, cleanest kitchen of all of us. We had to get the cupcakes to the bookstore by one o'clock, so we got to work right away.

Katie and I worked on the cinnamon-frosted cupcakes, and Emma and Alexis worked on the pretty pink cupcakes. Emma blasted some music, and we didn't talk much while we worked. Katie calls it "being in the baking zone."

When we were done, we had four dozen perfect, beautiful cupcakes packed neatly into boxes. I had designed labels for us on the computer that said THE CUPCAKE CLUB, and there was a picture of a cupcake on each one. I carefully stuck a label on each box, and we stepped back to admire our hard work.

"Perfect!" Alexis said with satisfaction.

I looked at the clock, and it was ten minutes to noon. "Mom will be here soon. She's going to take Katie and me to lunch, and then we're going to drop off the cupcakes and then see the movie. Are you sure you guys don't want to go?"

"I've got three dog walking clients today," Emma said. "Otherwise I would."

"And we're all going to my grandmother's house today," Alexis said. "But text me when the movie's done! I'm dying to see it."

"Even though I already know how it ends, I still can't wait," Katie said. She looked really excited.

Then Alexis handed me an envelope. "I printed out some business cards on my computer using your label design," she said. "See if you can leave them out on the cupcake table. That way if anyone likes the cupcakes and wants to order some, they know how to reach us."

My mom then came in, and she helped us carry the boxes to the car. We have an organizer in our trunk now, so the boxes don't slide around. The bookstore, Harriet's Hollow, is in downtown Maple Grove. There are a bunch of other stores on Main Street besides Harriet's. There's also a little café where they have the most awesome tuna melts. That's where we went for lunch.

"Mmm, melty!" Katie said when her sandwich came, and we all laughed.

Then it was time to deliver the cupcakes to Harriet's. The owner of the store is named Harriet. She's tall and has long brown hair that she always piles on her head, and she has a very global sense of fashion. Today she was wearing a really flowy purple-and-orange dress that looked like it was made from Indian saris, and she had lots of silver bracelets jangling on her wrists.

"It's the cupcake girls!" she said when she saw us. "And right on time, too. Come here, let me show you the display."

We walked through the store to the place in the back that Harriet called the reading nook. It's filled with comfy couches and beanbag chairs, and Harriet doesn't mind if you sit there and read all day. Today she had decorated it with pink and red flowers on the end tables, and in the middle was a round table with a pink tablecloth on it.

"We'll set them up for you," Katie said, and we started by putting out four round, clear plastic trays that we got from a party store. They don't cost much, and the cupcakes look good on them. Then we carefully placed the cupcakes on them: two trays of my spicy dark chocolate with cinnamon frosting, and two trays of Emma's fluffy pink cupcakes.

"They look too good to eat!" Harriet exclaimed, but then she picked up a spicy one. "But of course I can't resist."

Katie and I held our breath while Harriet took a bite. We always get a little nervous when someone tries our cupcakes for the first time.

Harriet smiled. "Fantastic!" she said. "What's in this?"

Katie and I explained the flavors of the two cupcakes, and Harriet nodded in approval. She walked to the register and came back with an envelope for us.

"Thank you so much, girls," she said. "I'll be sure to recommend you to my friends."

Then I remembered Alexis's cards. "We have some business cards," I said. "Would it be okay if we put some out on the table?"

"Of course!" Harriet said. "My, you girls certainly are professional."

I made a mental note to tell Alexis that later. She would love that compliment!

Next Mom dropped us off at the movie theater, which is in the mall. Now that we're in middle school, our moms have decided that we can go to the movies by ourselves, as long as we don't leave the theater. (Eddie didn't like that idea much, but Mom convinced him.)

Soon Katie and I were sitting in our seats with sodas and a bucket of popcorn between us. They were showing some commercials or something on the screen, so I started to tell Katie about my problems with Mom and Eddie and Spanish.

"It's bad enough that everyone's going to find out that I'm failing, but I don't really get why Eddie needs to go," I said. "My dad should go, right?"

"I guess," Katie answered. She really didn't seem interested, but I kept talking.

"Plus, I have to check in with everyone all the time," I said. "It's like I have three police officers watching my every move or something. I feel like a prisoner sometimes. We're lucky Eddie's not sitting here right now."

"Shh," Katie said. "The previews are coming on."

I have to admit I was a little bit hurt about that. It's like Katie didn't care at all, which isn't like her. Usually she's a great person to talk to.

As the previews played, I tried to figure out what might be bugging her. I know Katie's parents are divorced too, so I figured she'd understand.

Then it hit me—Katie never talks about her dad, ever, and she doesn't visit him the way I do. I don't know why, but she just doesn't. Maybe her dad lives far away or something. I've never really asked her.

So maybe Katie can't understand my problems. Maybe she has some of her own—different ones.

I almost asked her about it but then the lights went dark, and we both got transported to the Emerald Forest.

CHAPTER 11

Sydney's Revenge

Katie was like her old self again after the movie, so I didn't bring up anything about her dad. I figured she'd talk to me when she was ready.

Nothing much interesting happened until Monday morning, during my first period math class. Mrs. Moore was explaining a problem on the board when suddenly a note fell onto my desk.

I looked up, alarmed. Mrs. Moore is superstrict, and it takes guts to throw a note in her class. I looked around and saw Bella looking at me.

Bella is in the PGC (Popular Girls Club) with Sydney and Maggie and Callie. She's pretty quiet, but everyone knows she loves vampires—after all, she changed her named from Brenda to Bella because of that series with the sparkly vampires.

She dresses in black a lot and wears pale makeup.

Bella nodded for me to open the note, and I opened it.

Jackson Montano is going bald!
Seriously, it's true!

I gave Bella a strange look. What was that about? But then I saw Mrs. Moore turn away from the board, and I quickly stashed the note in my book.

As Mrs. Moore kept explaining fractions, I suddenly realized what the note was about. Sydney had said that Jackson would be sorry about calling her cheesy, and she meant it.

I showed the note to my friends at lunch, but nobody was surprised.

"There are these texts going around saying that Jackson has foot fungus," Alexis reported.

"I heard it in the hallway," Katie said. "Sydney, Bella, and Maggie were telling everyone who would listen."

"Poor Jackson," Emma said sympathetically.

"I don't feel sorry for him," Alexis said. "He always calls me 'copper top' and asks if my brains are rusting."

"And George says he's mean to the younger kids on the football team," Katie added. George is her friend from elementary school, and Jackson is one grade above us, so I guess he must pick on George.

"Still, nobody deserves the Sydney treatment," I said.

"Well, nobody actually believes this stuff, do they?" Katie asked. "Maggie told me that he has false teeth. I mean, come on."

"It doesn't matter if they believe it or not," Alexis pointed out. "It still looks bad for Jackson. Just imagine if Sydney were spreading those rumors about us."

I shuddered. "That would be awful. But I guess Jackson brought this on himself. He shouldn't have called her cheesy."

I still didn't know that I was the one who was causing Jackson so much trouble. But in the meantime, I still had plenty of other things to worry about—namely, my Spanish.

I had to tell the truth before the parent-teacher conference. It was the only thing to do. And that wasn't going to make anybody happy.

CHAPTER 12

A Really, Really Bad Day

As you can probably guess by now, I like to avoid bad situations. There didn't seem to be a time all week that I could talk to my mom. But that weekend I went to my dad's, and that's when it all came out.

It was after dinner on Friday, and I knew I had to bring up the note from Señora Delgado. But as you know, I love to put things off. So I decided to bake a batch of cupcakes first. My dad loves chocolate, so I made a quick, easy batch of chocolate cupcakes. Soon a delicious, chocolaty aroma was wafting through the entire apartment.

"Something sure smells good, *mija*," Dad said with a smile as he walked past the kitchen.

"They'll be ready soon," I promised.

When Dad walked out of the kitchen, I took the note out of my notebook. For the millionth time, I replayed in my head what I would say and how I would say it. I remembered how proud Dad had been of my Spanish at the tapas bar. He was going to be so disappointed in me. I dreaded giving him this note, and I dreaded telling my mom, too.

As I sat staring forlornly at the note, my dad came running back into the kitchen.

"Mia! Don't you smell that?" he shouted. I looked up, confused, and was shocked to see black smoke coming out of the oven. The cupcakes were burning! My life really was in shambles. Now I couldn't even bake cupcakes anymore. Dad quickly turned off the oven and turned to look at me.

"*Mija*, is something wrong? You've never burned a batch of cupcakes before—especially when you were sitting two feet away from the oven. Is there anything you want to tell me or talk about?" I couldn't put it off any longer. Taking a deep breath, I took the note from Señora Delgado and handed it to him without saying anything.

Dad read it and raised his eyebrows. "Mia, what is this? You're failing Spanish? How is that possible?"

Tears filled my eyes. I couldn't help it.

"You guys put me in Advanced Spanish," I said. "It's really hard. I know I can speak it, but reading and writing it is different. My essays and homework are just too hard for me."

"They can't be that bad," Dad said. "Can you show me?"

I nodded and brought my backpack to the kitchen table, and Dad and I sat down.

"This is the worksheet she gave us for the weekend," I said, handing him the paper. It was another sheet of verbs.

Dad looked it over for a few minutes, and then he frowned. "You're right," he said. "I speak Spanish too, but this looks hard. Have you told Mom about this yet?"

I shook my head. "No," I admitted.

Dad sighed. "Well, I'll have to talk to her about this. We should talk to your teacher and get you one of these tutors she's suggesting."

"You can talk to her at the parent-teacher conference on Wednesday," I said, and Dad looked surprised.

"Wednesday? I don't think Mom mentioned that," he said.

I started to cry again. "Mom's going to be so mad when she finds out."

"*Mija*, we only get upset when you keep things from us. Having trouble in school is nothing to be ashamed of," Dad said, hugging me. "No matter what, *te quiero*."

Te quiero. Dad had said those words to me a million times, and I knew what they meant: I love you. *Te quiero.*

Suddenly it hit me. "Dad, how do you spell *quiero*?" I yelled, breaking away from him.

"Q-u-i-e-r-o," Dad answered. "That's one I know. Why?"

My stomach dropped down into my black velvet flats. I had made a terrible mistake.

"And how do you spell 'cheese' in Spanish?" I asked him.

"*Queso. Q-u-e-s-o*," he replied.

"Oh no!" I wailed. "Oh no, no, no!"

I should have *known* that *quiero* meant "love," not "cheesy." Now Sydney thought Jackson had dissed her when actually he liked her. I felt awful! And now she was spreading all those awful rumors about him. So even if Jackson had liked Sydney to begin with, maybe I ruined it for her. I don't like Sydney, but I'd never purposely mess up anybody's budding romance.

"What's wrong, *mija*?" Dad asked.

"I made a terrible mistake." I groaned, and then I told him about Sydney and the note. Dad started to laugh and then stopped himself.

"Sorry. I know it's not funny to you," he said. "And I feel sorry for that boy. Sydney sounds like somebody you don't want to mess with."

"You don't even know," I said, shaking my head.

Dad put his hand over his mouth as he started to laugh again. "Oh, Mia. 'Cheese' instead of 'love'?" Then he saw I wasn't laughing. He put his arm around me again. "Come on, let's watch that movie."

Soon we were settled in the living room with some microwave popcorn, and for a little while I forgot about all my problems while we watched a comedy about talking animals in a zoo. Then I got ready for bed.

Before I fell asleep, I heard Dad call Mom. He was talking in Spanish, but I heard most of it. His voice drifted in and out as he paced across the floor.

"You need to tell me these things, Sara! Just because I'm in Manhattan doesn't mean I don't want to be involved! You're the one who moved away, not me!"

For a second, it reminded me of a few years ago all over again, when Dad and Mom were fighting all the time. I put the pillow over my head, so I wouldn't hear.

See what happens when I tell the truth? It always ends up badly. I told you nobody would be happy.

CHAPTER 13

Just Like Old Times . . . Or Is It?

Saturday was a much better day. Mrs. Monroe took me and Ava to see the Costume Collection at the Metropolitan Museum of Art. Ava and I took lots of pictures, and I spent about an hour sketching shoes from the 1920s. I liked the really cool buttons on them. Saturday night Dad and I went out for sushi, and everything felt like normal.

Then Sunday morning at eleven thirty, Dad said, "Mia, please pack your bag."

"But it's too early for the train," I told him.

"We're not going right to the train," he said. "Mom's meeting us for lunch at Johnny's Pizza."

At first I wasn't sure I'd heard right. Meeting Mom for lunch? Dad and Mom and I hadn't had lunch together since they got divorced.

I must be in big trouble, I thought. So I packed my bag and put on my coat, and then Dad and I headed out to Johnny's.

Johnny's has the best pizza in our neighborhood, and maybe even in the whole city. They cook it in a brick oven with real wood, and the crust gets nice and crispy. Mom and Dad and I ate there a lot when we all lived together.

I shivered the whole walk there, but once we got inside it was warm and toasty. Mom was already sitting at a table, waiting for us. She had her hair pulled back, and she looked kind of tired.

Mom stood up when she saw us. "Hi, Mia," she said, giving me a hug. But she didn't hug Dad.

Dad draped his coat around the chair. "I'll go place our order," he said, and then he got in line.

Mom looked at me and shook her head. "Mia, your father told me about that note from your Spanish teacher. Why didn't you tell me?"

"I don't know," I said, looking down at the table. It was too hard to explain.

"You know can talk to me about these things, Mia," Mom said. "I just don't understand."

Dad sat down. "It should be ready in a few minutes," he said. "So, Mia, I guess you know why we're all here."

I nodded.

"It's like I said the other night," he said. "You can't keep secrets from us. Especially when it's about school and especially when you need help."

"That's right," Mom said, and she sounded angry. "Mia, your only job right now in life is to do well in school. Baking cupcakes, going to fashion shows, that's all good, but school is the most important."

"I know!" I said. "I really do. I'm doing well in my other classes. But you guys put me in Advanced Spanish without asking me. It's not my fault."

Dad and Mom looked at each other.

"I'm sorry about that," Dad said. "We didn't realize we were pushing you into something too hard for you. Sara, can they put her in a different class?"

"I'm not sure," Mom replied. "But I'll ask. I don't know if they can switch her schedule until the spring."

"In the meantime, we can get you a tutor," Dad said. He handed Mom the note. "Her teacher suggested a few."

"We might not need one," Mom said. "Eddie majored in Spanish in college. He's a translator at the company he works for."

I was surprised. "He is?" I asked.

"I thought you knew," Mom said. "What did you think he did?"

I shrugged. I knew Eddie was a lawyer, but I didn't know he also translated. "I don't know. I thought he just went to an office and . . . did stuff." Now I felt kind of silly not asking for help when I had an honest-to-goodness translator living right under the same roof as me.

"Then let's see if Eddie can help," Dad said. "But if not, we'll get you that tutor, okay?"

"Okay," I said.

"And no more secrets," Mom said sternly. "In fact, you can live without screens this week while you think about that. No phone, TV, music, or computer. And if you keep any notes from teachers from us in the future, it will be *two* weeks."

I saw her look at Dad, and Dad gave a little nod.

I didn't even protest. With a sigh, I handed over my music player and earbuds, and my phone.

Luckily, Dad saw our order appear at the counter right then. "Food's ready! I'll be right back."

The rest of the lunch was a lot easier. We ate salads with vinegary dressing and these light green peppers that were sweet and hot at the same time. Then we had our usual—pizza with mushrooms and olives. (I know it sounds weird, but it's really good, trust me.)

For a minute, it almost seemed like old times, like nothing had changed. Except really, everything had. Before, Mom and Dad would have been talking and laughing the whole time. Now they couldn't even look at each other. Just like that other day, they both talked to me instead of each other.

And then, instead of all of us going back home, Mom and I got into a cab and headed to the train station. Back to Maple Grove. Back to our new life.

Things were never going to be the way they'd been before. I knew that. But knowing that didn't make it any easier. Was everyone really happier?

CHAPTER 14

A Cheesy Problem

When we got home, Mom and I met Eddie in the kitchen, and she told him the whole story.

"I think I can help you," Eddie said. "Let's take a look at your homework together after dinner, okay?"

I nodded, grateful that Eddie didn't give me a hard time about it all. After dinner that night, he and I sat at the kitchen table, and I showed him my worksheet.

"It's verbs I have trouble with," I told him. "There's, like, a million different ways to say and spell each one, and I can't keep them straight in my head."

"Let me see," Eddie said, taking the sheet. He looked it over and then smiled. "I used to have trouble with this too. But let me show you a trick I figured out."

So, I won't bore you with a whole Spanish lesson, but you need to know that by the time Eddie was done helping me, I actually understood what was on the sheet. I answered every question, and Eddie didn't even have to help me with the last two. It was the first time I'd ever felt good about handing in my Spanish homework.

"Thanks, Eddie," I said when we were done.

Even though the tutoring went well, I was still feeling pretty down that night. That's because I knew that tomorrow I'd have to tell Sydney about the *quiero/queso* mistake.

I could keep the Spanish secret for so long because I was only hurting myself. But the *queso* secret was hurting Jackson, and it would be wrong if I didn't say anything.

But I was dreading it. I saw what Sydney did to Jackson when she was mad at him. She was going to destroy me, I just knew it.

So the next day, Monday, I knew what I had to do. As soon as I got off the bus, I walked up to Sydney. She and Maggie were hanging out by the tree in the front school yard, texting.

"Sydney, can I talk to you?" I asked.

"Busy," she said, not even looking up from her phone. "Later, okay?"

I tried again in the hallway, when I ran up to Sydney at her locker. She was talking to Eddie Rossi, but I interrupted her.

"Can I please talk to you?" I asked.

Sydney rolled her eyes. "Excuse me? Talking!"

My face turned red, and I walked away. For a second, I thought I might give up and let her keep torturing Jackson. But I just couldn't do that.

So at lunchtime, I marched up to the PGC table.

"Sydney, I need to tell you something really important," I said.

Sydney turned to Maggie and rolled her eyes. Then she looked at me.

"What's the emergency?" she asked.

"It's about that text message Jackson sent you," I said. "I made a mistake. He didn't say you're cheesy. He said he loves you."

Sydney looked absolutely shocked. "He *what*?" she shrieked.

"*Te quiero* means 'I love you,'" I explained. "I got it mixed up with the word *queso*, which means 'cheese.' I'm sorry."

Sydney stood up. "Are you kidding me?" she

asked, her voice rising. "Are you trying to ruin my life or something? Are you jealous? I bet you did that on purpose."

I shook my head. "No. I wouldn't do that. I'm just bad at Spanish."

Sydney sat down and looked at her friends. She looked kind of embarrassed.

"Can you believe I ever asked Mia to join this club?" she asked in a loud voice. "I must have been crazy!"

"I'm really sorry, and I wanted you to know," I said. Then I turned and walked away. I had one more person to tell.

Jackson Montano sat at a table in a corner with a bunch of other football players. I usually never went near that table, because you always get pelted with spitballs when you walk past. But today I had to go there.

Sydney ran up behind me. "Mia, no!" she hissed. But I ignored her and walked up to him.

"Jackson, a few days ago Sydney asked me to translate that text you sent her," I said, talking fast so I wouldn't chicken out. "I thought *quiero* was *queso*, so I told her that you said she was cheesy. That's why Sydney's been spreading those rumors about you."

Jackson put down his sandwich. "Is she making you say this?"

I shook my head. "No, it's true," I said. "I should have known that *queso* was cheese."

"Yeah, you really stink at Spanish," Jackson said.

"I know," I admitted.

Jackson stared at me for a minute and glanced over at Sydney. He didn't look mad. In fact, he had a little smile on his face, as if he thought the whole thing was sort of funny. At least that's what I hoped. "I'm really, truly sorry," I said again.

Then I quickly walked away, leaving Sydney and Jackson to work things out—or not. I'm not sure what I would do if I were in Jackson's place.

When I finally made it to my regular lunch table, all my friends were staring at me.

"What was *that* all about?" Alexis asked.

I sank into my chair. "You are not going to believe this," I said, and then I told them the story.

For a moment, everybody was quiet. Then we all started laughing at the same time. Katie put her arm around Emma.

"I cheese you, Emma!" she said.

"I cheese you, too, Katie!" Emma said back.

Then Katie picked up her sandwich. "Look! My mom packed me a love sandwich for lunch."

Alexis held up the wrap on her lunch tray. "Mine's turkey and love with a little mayo."

"Really? Yum, I really cheese turkey," Katie said.

"Okay, okay!" I cried. I was laughing so hard, it was starting to hurt. "It was a colossal mistake, I know."

"So I hope you finally got a Spanish tutor," Alexis said. "You can't afford to make this kind of mistake again."

"Eddie's tutoring me, and he's actually pretty good," I said.

"Yeah, I hear he really *cheeses* tutoring Spanish," Katie said, and we collapsed into giggles.

I was embarrassed. I had no idea what kind of revenge Sydney was going to take on me. But for the first time in a long time, I felt . . . free. And pretty happy.

I grinned at my friends. "I cheese you guys so much!"

CHAPTER 15

I Figure Out Some Things

The next night Eddie helped me with my homework again, and it went really well. Eddie seemed happy.

"I knew you could do it, Mia," he said. "Keep this up and maybe you can stay in that advanced class."

"You're really good at explaining things, that's why," I said. "You should have been a teacher."

Eddie looked really pleased. "I always thought about being a teacher. Who knows? Maybe I'll give it a try someday."

As I was closing my book I heard a little ringing sound from my cell phone, letting me know a text came in. I flipped open the phone and saw a message from Katie.

We're having macaroni and love for dinner tonight. I really cheese that stuff!

I laughed out loud.

"What's so funny?" Eddie asked.

"You're not going to believe this," I said, and then I told him the whole story.

When I was done, Eddie started to laugh, and he didn't hold it in. Soon tears were running down his cheeks from laughing so hard.

"Oh, that poor, poor boy," he said. "I hope you told him what happened."

I nodded. "I did. He seems okay with it. But I'm still worried about what Sydney will do to me."

Eddie nodded. "No wonder, after what she did to Jackson."

Then I found myself talking to Eddie about Sydney—stuff I hadn't even told Mom about. Like how Sydney wanted me to be in the PGC, but I didn't like how she bossed everyone around. And how she's nice to me sometimes and says insulting things at other times.

"I agree that you shouldn't have joined her club, but you might have hurt her feelings when you did that," Eddie said. "Sometimes when people are hurt, they act sad, but other people get angry and lash out."

I might have hurt Sydney's feelings? Now there was a new thought. I realized that Eddie was probably right. I had never really thought about Sydney's feelings before. I guess I figured she didn't have any.

"By the way, don't forget to ask Señora if she wants you to double-space that report that's due Friday," Eddie said as I packed up my homework.

"I don't have Spanish tomorrow because it's a half day," I said. "But you can ask her tomorrow night when you meet her."

Eddie paused. "We can ask your mom to do that," he said. "Your dad's going to go with her."

"Um, okay," I said, and I was remembering what Mom had said before about Eddie and how he should meet my teachers because he helped me with my homework. I realized now that she was right.

"And Mia?" Eddie said.

"Yeah?"

"Turn off your cell phone before your mom sees you. Remember, no screens for a week."

"Oh!" I said. I had forgotten. I turned off my phone. Then I smiled at Eddie. "Thanks," I whispered, and ran up to my room. Eddie has a lot of rules, but he can also be pretty cool, I guess.

After I went up to my room, Mom came in carrying a garment bag.

"I've got another sample for you, Mia," she said. "This one's leftover from Nathan Kermit's fall line, but I think it's pretty timeless. And cute, too."

She opened the bag to reveal a really awesome blue boyfriend-style jacket with rolled-up sleeves, a plaid lining, and what looked like vintage silver buttons.

"I love it!" I exclaimed, trying it on. "I have just the shirt to go with it."

"I knew you would," Mom said, and she turned to leave.

"Hey, Mom," I said, and she stopped. "I wanted to ask you something. I think Eddie should to go the parent-teacher conference tomorrow."

Mom looked surprised. "Instead of Dad?"

I shook my head. "No, *with* Dad," I replied. "Especially since he's tutoring me in Spanish now and everything."

Mom smiled. "Let me make sure it's okay with Dad. But I'm sure he won't mind."

I hadn't even thought that Dad might be

uncomfortable being around Eddie. I guess divorce is weird for everybody involved. And it's definitely complicated! But I had a feeling that Dad would be cool with it.

The next morning I woke up feeling pretty happy about things. I was nervous about what Señora might say to my parents—all three of them—but at least everyone knew the truth now. And I got to wear my awesome new outfit.

When I got to my locker, Sydney and the PGC walked right by me.

Callie stopped. "Mia, I love your jacket," Callie said.

"Thanks," I said.

Sydney kept walking like I didn't exist, and Maggie and Bella followed her. That was just fine with me. Sydney had been totally ignoring me, but at least she wasn't telling everyone that I was going bald.

Then, on my way to homeroom, I passed Jackson Montano. He smiled at me, and I knew that everything was cool between us.

"Hey, Queso!" he said, teasing. But I totally didn't mind.

Since it was a half day, we all went to Alexis's house for lunch and a Cupcake Club meeting.

Alexis's dad took the day off, so he was there when we walked in the door.

"Hope you're hungry!" he called out when he heard us. "I'm making my famous grilled cheese sandwiches and tomato soup."

"Dad, that soup comes from a can," Alexis said, rolling her eyes.

"Hey, you're going to ruin my reputation," Mr. Becker said. "Well, the sandwiches are all mine."

Mr. Becker reminds me of Eddie sometimes. He's really friendly, and he's always joking around. We took off our coats and sat down in Alexis's neat-as-a-pin kitchen. Alexis's dad already had a bowl of soup and a sandwich at each place on the table.

"Nice service, Mr. B.," Katie said. "When I open up a restaurant someday, you can be a waiter."

"I'll do it if I can be *head* waiter," he said.

Katie nodded. "Deal."

We sat down to eat. The grilled cheese was crunchy on the outside and gooey on the inside, just the way I like it. Of course, Alexis opened up her notebook while we were eating.

"I have good news," she reported. "We already have three new orders based on our baker's dozen offer!"

"Woo-hoo!" Katie cheered, and we all started clapping.

Alexis told us about the orders, and we came up with some ideas. Then we just started talking about regular stuff.

"You'll never believe what Jackson Montano called me today," I said. "Queso!"

Everybody laughed.

"I guess there are worse nicknames," Emma said sympathetically.

"Anyway, I'll never forget what that word means," I said. "Plus, Eddie's tutoring is really good. He's even going to the parent-teacher conference tonight. My dad is too. That's kind of weird, isn't it?"

"It sounds kind of nice to have an extra dad," Emma said.

Katie didn't say anything. Remember how she was joking around and cheering just a minute before? Well, she was quiet for the rest of lunch. Just like before. I had a feeling I knew why, but I didn't want to bring it up in front of everybody.

Then my cell phone rang, and it was Dad. (Eddie actually told Mom that I should have my phone on when I was out of the house for emergencies, and Mom totally agreed.)

"I'll be right back," I said, and walked into Alexis's living room.

"Hey, Dad," I said. "What's up?"

"I'm leaving the city now," he said. "I'll be there in plenty of time for the conference."

"Yay!" I said. Then I thought of something. "Did Mom tell you that Eddie was coming too?"

"She did," Dad replied. "It's fine with me if that's what you want, *mija*."

I had to think of a way to explain it without hurting Dad's feelings.

"Well," I began, "you're my dad, and you'll always be my dad. But when you're not here, Eddie's like a spare dad. Kind of like a baker's dozen. Most kids only get two parents. But I have three right now."

Dad laughed. "Baker's dozen, huh?"

I could hear in his voice that he was okay with that. And that was better than anything—even an extra cupcake.

CHAPTER 16

Katie Tells Me What's Wrong

Now that all three of my parents were going to the conference, and Dan had basketball practice, they didn't want to leave me home alone. At our school, they do the conferences over three nights. Since Katie's mom was going on Thursday, I got to hang with Katie that night.

After we ate chicken tacos and rice with Katie's mom, we went up to Katie's room. There's never a lot of homework when there's a half day, so I was showing Katie sketches I'd made of the *Emerald Forest* costumes.

"These are so cool!" Katie said, looking at a drawing of a fairy in a green sparkly dress. "You have to teach me how to sew sometime. Then we could make awesome costumes for Halloween."

"My mom's a better sewer than I am," I admitted. "Maybe she could teach both of us."

It was nice and quiet in Katie's room, with no distractions—no cupcakes, classrooms, or popular girls to bother us. I figured I might as well talk to Katie about what was bothering her.

I just came right out and said it. "Are you okay?" I asked. "'Cause it seems like something's been bothering you lately. Especially when you're talking to me. And I just hope I'm not doing something to hurt your feelings or anything."

Katie didn't look at me right away. She didn't say anything right away either.

"Don't worry, it's not your fault or anything," she finally said. "It's just . . . hard to talk about, I guess."

"You can talk to me about anything," I told her. "After all, you've been hearing me complain about Mom and Dad and Eddie all the time lately. And I guess . . . I guess I thought maybe something about that was bothering you."

"Kind of," Katie admitted, turning to me. "I never see my dad. He moved away when I was a baby and has this whole other family now."

"Wow," I said. Right away I imagined what it would be like if I never saw Dad anymore. If he spent all his time with other kids, brothers and sisters I didn't even know. "That sounds awful."

"It is," Katie said. She started talking faster, like she couldn't hold in the words. "And every year I used to get a card from him at Christmas, but this year there was no card. Nothing. And it really hurts."

I felt so bad for Katie. "That's horrible."

She took a deep breath. "So when you were complaining about having *two* dads getting into your business, it kind of made me upset. I would give anything just to have one dad in my life. You're really lucky that you have two, you know?"

"I know," I said, nodding, and for the first time I really understood that I was. Having a bunch of parents can be a real pain sometimes, but it's way better than not having any. In a way, I guess I'm very lucky.

"And I know it's hard for you too," Katie told me. "It's just a different kind of situation. So I'm not mad at you at all. I'm mostly just sad for me."

"Hey, if you want, you could borrow one of my dads sometime," I said.

Katie smiled. "It all depends on how I do on my next Spanish test!"

We both laughed, and then everything felt

pretty much normal for us again. It amazes me how Katie can be such a positive person when I know how sad she must be sometimes.

I opened my sketchbook. "Let's design matching costumes for this year. You can be the Emerald Fairy, because you look fantastic in green. And I'll be the Ruby Fairy, because I look great in red."

"Wait, won't we be too old for trick-or-treating next year?" Katie asked.

"Maybe," I said. "So we'll throw a costume party! Then we'll *have* to make costumes."

Before I started sketching, my phone beeped. I jumped, thinking maybe the parent-teacher conferences were over. I was still worried about what would happen with Señora Delgado.

But it was Ava.

Avaroni: Can't wait for the party Saturday!
FabMia: Me 2! Nervous tho. Will everyone remember me?
Avaroni: RU kidding? We all miss u and can't wait to c u.
FabMia: Good!
Avaroni: How r cupcakes coming?
FabMia: We're baking them fresh for Saturday.
Avaroni: Yum!

FabMia: Katie says hi.
Avaroni: Hi Katie!
FabMia: Got to go! Dad's texting.

My text conversation with Dad was much shorter.

Your math teacher really is strict! I love all the others. Let's talk tomorrow.

"Looks like it's all over," I told Katie, after I replied to Dad. "Dad didn't say much, but it sounds like everything's all right."

"Excellent!" Katie said.

A few minutes later Mom and Eddie came to pick me up.

"How did it go?" I asked as soon as I got into the backseat.

Mom turned to talk to me. "We had a long talk with Señora Delgado. She says with the tutoring, you've been doing a lot better lately. So she's going to give you some extra assignments to help you bring up your grade."

I wasn't crazy about getting extra work, but it could have been a lot worse.

"She actually seems very nice," Eddie said. "And

I love your math teacher, Mrs. Moore. She seems like she runs a tight ship."

I shook my head and laughed. "You wouldn't like her so much if you were a student!"

It was pretty much bedtime by the time we got home. After I showered and got into my pj's, I climbed into bed and got out my sketchbook. I just wanted to finish that ruby costume before I fell asleep.

Then there was a knock on the door, and I said, "Come in!" But it wasn't Mom, as usual. It was Eddie.

"Your mom will be up in a minute," he said. "I just wanted to say that I'm glad you wanted me there tonight. I liked getting to know your teachers."

"No problem," I replied.

"Okay, then," Eddie said. "Good night, Queso!"

I groaned and pulled the covers up over my head.

See? I told you that mistake was going to haunt me forever! But like Emma said, I guess there are worse nicknames.

CHAPTER 17

Extra Good

Avaroni: Did you make my cupcakes yet?
FabMia: It's 2 early!
Avaroni: Sooooo excited!
FabMia: Me 2!
Avaroni: Wait till u see my outfit. You'll love it!
FabMia: I bet it's gorgeous. Can't wait to see u!

I yawned and rolled back over in bed. It was only eight a.m.! Ava must be really excited if she was up so early on a Saturday.

I had to get up soon anyway. We were going to make the cupcakes this morning at Emma's house, and then Eddie was going to drive me into the city so the cupcakes wouldn't get bumped around on the train.

That meant I had to pick out two different outfits—one for baking cupcakes and one for the party. What an excellent problem to have! I threw open my closet and stared at it.

Cupcake baking was easy. I pulled out my favorite pair of jeans and a long-sleeved henley top with tiny flowers on it. If I got batter on it, it would be easy to clean.

Then there was Ava's party. That was harder. First, I had to make sure I wore something that went with the party decorations. But also, I wanted to look extra nice. I hadn't seen some of my Manhattan friends in a long time, and I was a little nervous about it.

I changed into my cupcake clothes while I thought about the party outfit. I finally decided to wear my fuzzy white V-neck sweater with a denim skirt, boots, and lots of silver jewelry. My boots are black, but the sweater and jewelry would be very snowy. I put the outfit on my bed to change into later.

After breakfast Mom took me to Emma's house, and pretty soon the Cupcake Club was busy baking. Katie and I made the batter, Emma made the frosting nice and fluffy, and Alexis used the chopper to make the coconut like snow.

We baked two dozen, even though Ava ordered only one dozen. Most recipes make twenty-four cupcakes anyway, and this way we'd have extra if we messed up. (And Emma's brothers will always eat any leftovers we have.)

Matt came into the kitchen while we were all carefully dusting the tops of the cupcakes with coconut and edible glitter.

"More cupcakes for your boyfriends?" he asked, looking over Emma's shoulder.

"No," Emma replied firmly. "These are for a birthday party."

Matt reached to grab one, and Emma pushed his hand away.

"Not yet," she said. "We have to make them all first and pick out the best twelve for the party."

"Thirteen," Alexis corrected her. "This is Ava's first order, so she gets a baker's dozen."

Soon we had a dozen cupcakes carefully stored in a box, and one extra cupcake in a clear bag with a silver ribbon tied around it.

"Now?" Matt asked impatiently.

Emma sighed. "Now."

Matt grabbed one, unwrapped it, and then put the whole thing in his mouth.

"Good!" he said, with his mouth full.

Then Mom picked me up and brought me and the cupcakes back home. I got changed for the party, and then it was time to go into the city.

"Your chauffeur is waiting!" Eddie called up the stairs.

I ran downstairs and put on my coat. We carefully put the cupcakes in the trunk, but I knew the extra one wouldn't be safe there. So I held it in my lap the whole way to the city.

There was a lot of traffic, but Eddie let me pick the music on the radio. Then, before I knew it, we were in my dad's neighborhood.

"Call your dad and let him know we're near," he said. "I don't think I'll be able to park, so I'll drop you off in front of the building."

So I called Dad, and he was waiting outside when Eddie pulled up. He popped up the trunk, and Dad moved to get my bag and the cupcakes. I was about to open the door when I thought of something.

"Thanks for all your help with Spanish," I told Eddie. I handed him the cupcake. "This is the extra baker's dozen cupcake. 'Cause you're kind of like an extra dad for me."

Eddie smiled so wide I could see every one of his teeth.

"Thanks, Mia," he said.

I quickly scooted out of the car and waved good-bye to Eddie, my extra dad. Then I ran to hug my Dad Who Will Always Be My Dad, No Matter What. It wasn't easy because he was holding the cupcakes, but I managed anyway.

I knew Ava wouldn't mind about the extra cupcake, and I was right. I got to her apartment early to help set up, and she practically screamed with happiness when she saw them.

"Mia, they're beautiful!" she cried.

"Thanks. The apartment looks great!" I said.

There were little white lights, those icicle lights, strung all around the living room. Silver snowflakes hung from the ceiling. There was a long, thin table under the window for the food and stuff, and it had a white tablecloth on it with silver glitter dusted over it.

Ava looked just like a decoration herself. She wore a silver tank top with a sequin design and a fluffy white skirt, almost like the one I had drawn for her.

"Ava, you look like a snow princess!" I exclaimed.

Ava smiled and twirled around. "Mom and I looked all over for a dress, but this worked out perfectly. It really reminds me of the dress you drew for me."

By the time I had carefully set up the cupcakes on the table, the buzzer rang and the rest of the party guests started to arrive. Some of my friends from my old soccer team were there, like Jenny and Tamisha. Then there were friends of Ava's that I had never met before—new friends she met after I'd left. Just like my Cupcake Club friends.

I was a little nervous at first, but I fit right in. Tamisha and I were talking and laughing like we had just seen each other yesterday, and Ava's new friends were nice too.

It wasn't exactly like before, when Ava and I were best friends and I lived in Manhattan. But I was starting to think that's maybe just how life is—things keep changing, and there's nothing you can do about it. Sometimes the changes are bad, but mostly they're good, or good things can come out of them. And if something bad happens, sometimes you can learn from your mistakes and start fresh. The way my friends and I do when we make a bad batch of cupcakes.

Take right now, for example. I was having a good time at a party. I had lots of friends. I had three parents who loved me. And I wasn't failing Spanish anymore. In fact, you might say things were very good—*muy bueno*. Just don't ask me to spell that!

CC
bff

KB
ET
AB
MV
cute!

Want another sweet cupcake?

Here's a sneak peek

of the next book in the

CUPCAKE DIARIES

series:

Emma all stirred up!

Little Brother, Big Problem

My name is Emma Taylor, but a few weeks ago I was wishing it was anything but! I was pretending that the little boy who was outside the school bus, wailing that he did not want to go to day camp, was *not* my little brother, Jake Taylor, and that those desperate parents who were bribing and pleading with him were *not* my parents, but rather some poor, misguided souls whom I would never see again.

In fact, I was wishing that I was already an adult and that my three best friends and I—the entire Cupcake Club—had opened our own bakery on a cute little side street in New York City, where none of my three brothers lived. The bakery would be all pink, and it would sell piles of cupcakes in a rainbow of lovely colors and flavors, and would cater mainly to movie stars and little girls' princess birthday parties. That is my fantasy. Sounds great, right?

But oh, no, this was reality.

"Emmy!" Jake was shrieking as my father gently but firmly manhandled him down the bus aisle to where I was scrunched down on my seat, pretending not to see them. I could literally feel the warmth of all the other eyes on the bus watching us, and I just wanted to melt away. Instead I stared out the window, like there was something really fascinating out there.

"Emma, please look after your brother," said my father. How many times have I heard that one? My older brothers, Matt and Sam, and I take turns babysitting Jake, but somehow the bad stuff always happens on my shift. My dad gave Jake one last kiss, reached to pat me on the head, and then dashed off the bus. I wished I could've dashed with him.

A counselor sat on the end of the seat, scrunching Jake in between us, so he couldn't run away. Jake was wailing, and the counselor—a nice girl named Paige, who is about twenty-one years old and probably wishing she were somewhere else too—was speaking in a soothing voice to him. She looked over his head at me, smiled, and then said, "Don't worry. This happens all the time. We always get one of these guys. He'll settle down within the week."

The week?! I wanted to die, but instead I nodded and looked out the window again. I also wanted to kill Jake that moment, but it was only seconds later that his wails turned to quiet hiccups. Then he slid his clammy, chubby little hand into mine and squeezed, and I felt a little guilty. "It's going to be okay, Jake," I whispered, and squeezed his little hand back. He snuggled into me and looked up at me with these really big eyes that get me every time. It's not the worst thing in the world to have a little someone in your life who looks up to you.

I sighed. "Feeling better, officer?" Jake is big into law enforcement, so it usually cheers him up if we play Precinct. At least he wasn't crying anymore. Paige gave him a pat on the head and then went to help some other kids get on the bus. But Jake wasn't feeling better. I could tell just by looking at him.

"I feel sick," he said.

Oh no. Jake isn't one of those kids who fakes being sick. My mom always says on car trips that if Jake says he feels sick, we pull over, because he *will* throw up, 100 percent of the time.

I jerked the bus window open and quickly flung

Jake over me, so that he was sitting in the window seat. "Put your head out the window, buddy. Take deep breaths—in through your nose, out through your mouth. We're going to start moving soon, so the wind will be in your face. . . . Deep breaths."

I rubbed his back a little and looked up to see if anyone I knew was getting on at this stop. My best friend and co–Cupcake Clubber Alexis Becker was going to the same camp, but her parents were dropping her off on their way to work. I fantasized about them driving me, too, and leaving Jake to his own devices. Ha! As if my parents would let me get away with that! At the very least, I did have our Cupcake Club meeting to look forward to later today. Just quality girl time, planning out the club's summer schedule and reviewing the cupcake jobs we had coming up. Chilling with my best friends—Alexis, Katie, and Mia—and brainstorming. It was definitely going to be fun.

A bunch of little kids streamed on and sat mostly in the front of the bus. Suddenly I spied a familiar shade of very bright blond hair, and my stomach sank. Noooo!!! It couldn't be.

But it was.

Sydney Whitman, mean-girl extraordinaire and head of the imaginatively named Popular Girls

Club at school, came strolling down the aisle, heading straight for the back row, where only the most popular kids dared to sit. I quickly looked out the window and pretended I hadn't seen her. But no luck.

"Oh, that's so cute! You and your little brother sitting together! I guess that's easier than trying to find someone your own age to sit with?" She smiled sweetly, but her remark stung just as it was meant to.

Jake hates Sydney as much as I do, if not more, so when he turned his head to look at her, he began to gag. Sydney's eyes opened wide, and her hand flew up to cover her mouth. "Oh no! He's going to—"

Luckily, Jake turned to the window just in time and hurled the contents of his stomach out onto the road.

"Disgusting!" shrieked Sydney, and she fled to the back of the bus.

I didn't know whether to laugh or cry. It's just one more nail in the coffin of my possible popularity, not that I ever really stood a chance. And not that I really wanted to. But it was also kind of hilarious to have Jake take one look at Sydney and then throw up. Definitely not her desired effect on men. I made a mental note to tell the Cupcake Club later. They'd love this.

Jake barfed a couple more times and then sat back down, looking as white as a sheet. The good news about Jake's car sickness is that after he's done throwing up, he's always fine. I pulled a napkin from my lunch bag and gave it to him to wipe his face. Then I cracked open his thermos and gave him a tiny sip of apple juice. I felt sorry for the poor guy. I hate throwing up.

Jake smiled wanly. "Thanks, Emmy. Sorry."

I laughed. "I feel the same way when I see Sydney Whitman." I wasn't sure I would have been so psyched about going to this camp if I'd known Sydney was going—or at the very least that she'd be on my bus. It definitely put a cramp in my happiness.

Jake rested his head back against the seat and promptly fell asleep. In a minute his head was resting, sweaty and heavy, against my shoulder. First days can be hard for anyone, especially little kids. At least tomorrow we wouldn't have the same problem. I said a silent prayer that Sydney wasn't in my group.

At camp, we got off the bus and a crowd of cheering counselors with painted faces was there to greet us. My mom must've called ahead to tip off someone, because one really pretty counselor was holding up a sign, like people do at the airport. It read OFFICER JAKE TAYLOR. That at least allowed me to peel him off and hand him over to the counselor, so I could go with my group, Team Four, to our rally zone (whatever that was) at the arts-and-crafts center.

The boys and girls have separate areas at camp, so I wouldn't see Jake again all day, thank goodness. And thank goodness again, because Sydney headed off with Team Five in the opposite direction. I didn't have a minute to review who was on whose team. Anyway, I didn't know a lot of the kids, but I did know that wherever Alexis was, she and I would be together. (We requested it, and my mom promised me she had spoken with the camp director.) That's all that matters.

As I headed across the green lawn to the arts-and-crafts center, I heard someone calling my name. I turned, and, of course, it was Alexis! I had never been so happy to see her in all my life.

"Thank goodness!" I cried, and threw my arms around her, like a shipwreck victim who has finally been saved.

Alexis isn't much for big displays of affection, so she patted my back awkwardly, but I didn't mind. In any case, she just saw me a few days ago.

"What's going on?" she asked as we separated and followed our counselor.

"Jake drama. Screaming, puking—the whole deal." I lowered my voice. "And Sydney Whitman saw the whole thing."

Alexis waved her hand in the air, as if to say *whatever!* That is just one of the many things I love about Alexis. She doesn't care at all what other people think. "Too bad he didn't puke *on* her," she said with a laugh. "Or did he?" Her eyes twinkled mischievously.

"No such luck. But the good news is, we aren't on the same team as her."

We'd reached the log cabin that was the headquarters for our team. On its porch stood two teenage counselors—a guy and a girl. As the crowd amassed in front of them, I counted twelve campers: all girls, of course. Yay! Finally! A break from all the boys in my life!

"Hello, people! Listen up!" The guy counselor was clapping his hands and kind of dancing around in a funny way to get our attention. Everyone started laughing and listening.

He bowed and said, "Thank you, ladies! My name is Raoul Sanchez, and this is my awesome partner, Maryanne Murphy."

Maryanne did a little curtsy, and we all clapped. She was pretty—short and cute with red hair and freckles. Raoul was tall and thin with rubbery arms and legs, and his face had a big goofy smile topped off by black, crew-cut hair. It was obvious neither of them was shy.

"We are going to have the most fun of any team this summer! Raoul and I personally guarantee it!" Maryanne said enthusiastically.

Raoul nodded. "If this isn't the most fun summer of your life, when camp is over I will take you to an all-you-can-eat pizza party, on me."

There were cheers and claps.

"Okay, we have a lot to tell you, so why don't you all grab a seat on the grass and get ready to be pumped!" said Maryanne.

Raoul and Maryanne then proceeded to tell us how we'd get to pick our own team name. ("Team Four" was just a placeholder, they said.) They told us about all the fun activities we'd do: swimming, kayaking, art projects, team sports, field trips, tennis, and more. Then they told us about the special occasions that were scheduled: Tie-Dye Day, Pajama Day, Costume Day, Crazy Hat Day, and finally, the best day of all . . . Camp Olympics, followed by the grand finale: the camp talent show!

Ugh. The camp talent show? Getting onstage in front of more than a hundred people? *So* not up my alley. I made a face at Alexis, but she was listening thoughtfully, her head tilted to the side and her long reddish hair already escaping its headband. She was probably wondering if there was any money to be made here; business was mostly all she thought about. In fact, her parents said if she did an outdoor camp for part of the summer, she could go to business camp for two weeks at the end of the summer. Sometimes I wonder how we are friends at all; our interests are so different!

"Thinking of signing up?" I whispered.

"Myself? No. But you should," she whispered back.

I laughed. "Yeah, right. What's my talent? Babysitting?"

Alexis raised her eyebrows at me. "Maybe. But I'm sure you can come up with something more marketable than that."

Right. I can't even keep the kid I babysit for from throwing up.

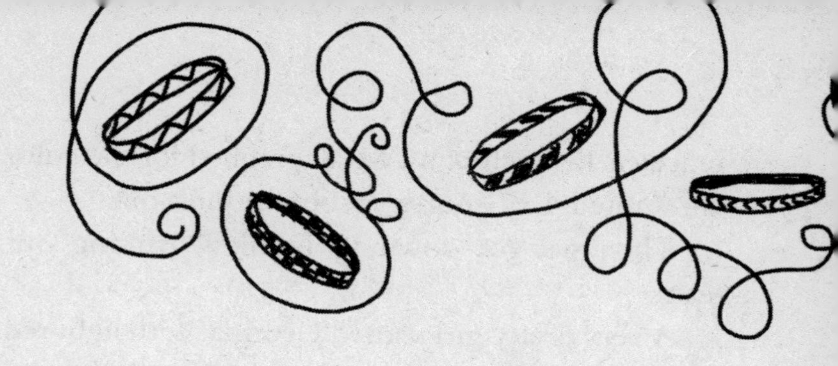

The Hotcakes

First we played a getting-to-know-you game called Pass the Packet. We had a mystery brown bag filled with something, and we each took turns holding it and telling the group about ourselves and then said what we wished was in the bag. (I told the group I had three brothers and I wished the bag had tickets to a taping of *Top Chef*.) When it was Alexis's turn, she told the group how she, Mia, Katie, and I had a Cupcake Club and about all the business we do, baking cupcakes for special events. The other girls in the group thought it was so cool. I felt great, and Alexis and I promised to bring in cupcakes for the group.

At the end, Maryanne opened the "packet," and it was filled with these awesome friendship bracelets for each of us. We all grabbed for the color we wanted. I, of course, grabbed a pink one.

Then we got down to business, naming our team.

A very pretty girl named Georgia, with light red hair and dark eyes, suggested we be "Rock Stars." I thought it was a great idea, but because it was the first idea, everyone still wanted a chance to make their own suggestions.

A girl named Caroline, who turned out to be Georgia's cousin, said, "How about the 'A-Team,'" which everyone thought was funny. Alexis suggested "Winners," because the power of positive branding would intimidate our competitors. I had to laugh. Then a girl named Charlotte—with bright blue eyes and dark, dark hair—suggested that since we would be having cupcakes a lot (she laughed and looked at me and Alexis when she said it), we should be the "Cupcakes." Right after she said it, a funny girl named Elle said, "No, the 'Hotcakes'!" and that was it.

"The Hotcakes! I love it!" cried Raoul. He and Elle high-fived. "Let's take a vote, girls! All in favor of the 'Hotcakes,' put your hands in the air!"

Everyone screamed and waved their hands high,

and that was that. Maryanne announced it was time for the Hotcakes to change for swimming, then lunchtime.

Alexis and I grabbed our backpacks and headed to the changing rooms.

"This is superfun, don't you think?" I asked as we walked across the central green.

"Yes, *and* I think we have the best group," said Alexis in a sure voice.

I laughed. "How do you know?"

She shrugged. "I counted how many girls we have versus the other two teams in our age group, then I evaluated how many of our girls are nice and smart. As a percentage, we have the nicest team by far. I would also venture that one hundred percent of our team is smart, and with Sydney on Team Five and stupid Bella on Team Three, their intelligence rate is at least ten percent below ours."

"Alexis! You are too much!" I shook my head. "The only bad part is, I wish the others were here."

She knew who I meant. Katie and Mia from our Cupcake Club were doing different things from us this month. Alexis frowned thoughtfully. "Yeah. But we'll see them plenty. And maybe it's good for us to branch out a little. It will generate some new business strategies and connections!"

I swatted her. "Is that all you think about?"

She pushed open the door to the locker room with a grin. "Pretty much!"

"I just hope they don't replace us with new friends."

Alexis shrugged. "Maybe they're thinking the same thing."

I thought back to last fall, when Katie had been dumped by Callie, her old best friend, so that Callie could hang with Sydney and the Popular Girls Club. New friends and old: a tough thing to balance. I sighed after just thinking about it.

When I came to the open house they had in March, one of the things I liked about this camp was that they have private changing rooms in the locker room, so you don't have to strip naked in front of strangers. I could never change in front of other people. Forget about being naked and getting into a bathing suit—I can't even change into pj's at a slumber party or try on clothes at the mall if someone else is in the room. Except for Mom. It's just a personal thing. I am very private about my body. Maybe it comes from being the only girl in a family of boys or from having my own room, but I just like privacy.

Alexis and I changed in rooms next to each other, and were chatting through the opening at the top of the dividers.

"Wait till you see my new suit!" she said. "It's so cute!"

"Me too! My mom brought it home as a surprise!"

We came out and took one look at each other and then started laughing our heads off. We had on the exact same bathing suit! They were tankinis, navy blue with white piping and a cool, yellow lightning bolt down either side. Alexis is kind of muscular from soccer, and I'm kind of thin (I play the flute, but that doesn't exactly build muscles!), so the suit fit us way differently. We couldn't stop giggling, though. We looked like total dork twins.

Georgia and Elle, and Charlotte and Caroline all gathered around, and we admired what everyone was wearing. We all had on new suits. Then one girl named Kira, who was shy and superpretty, came out. She had her towel draped around her shoulders, and she wasn't smiling.

"Let's see!" said Elle, clapping.

Kira shook her head. "Uh-uh." She bit her lip, and we instantly realized we shouldn't push her.

She looked like she might cry at any second.

"Okay!" Alexis said quickly. I could tell she was desperate to make Kira feel better, but couldn't think of how. Suddenly she hoisted her towel across her shoulders, to cover herself like Kira. "Capes it is!" I was so proud of her right then for her idea.

Everyone followed suit. Georgia yelled, "The Hot*capes*!" and we all hooted. I glanced at Kira and saw relief on her face, and we all marched out to meet Maryanne and Raoul, who were waiting outside to walk us to the huge pool. I had to wonder how bad Kira's suit was, though.

We sat for a water safety lecture by the lifeguard and swim director, Mr. Collins, a really nice gym teacher from the elementary school whom I recognized. The safety talk was a little boring (yeah, yeah, don't run, no chicken fights, no diving in the shallow end, swim with a buddy), but then we were in the water for free swim, and it was heavenly! The water wasn't too cold and the pool was huge, with a supershallow end and a superdeep end with a diving board!

In my excitement to get in the water, I had forgotten to check out Kira's suit, but I stole a glance the first chance I could. She was kind of cringing in the shallow end, and her suit was a one piece with Hello Kitty on it, and it was way too small for her. I felt terrible. It was babyish and it looked bad. I wondered why she didn't just swim to the deep end to cover it up.

"Okay, people! Now it's time for some fun!" Mr. Collins blew a whistle and beckoned us all over to the wall in the shallow end. I love to swim and I'm pretty good at it, so I did a loopy backstroke, kind of hamming it up, and Alexis did her old lady breaststroke, where she keeps her head out of the water the whole time. We cracked each other up.

Once everyone had reached the side of the pool, Mr. Collins whistled again to get our attention, then he spoke. He had a very kind voice, and was very quiet and patient.

"Okay, kids, today we're going to just get a feel for skill level and what we need to work on with each of you. One of the great things about Spring Lake Day Camp is that you will all leave here swimming really well by the end of the summer, and you'll have fun learning! So let's break you into four groups of three, and we'll have each of you swim a length of the pool in three heats. Count off by threes, then come down to the shallow end and we'll get started."

Alexis and I swam stood next to each other in the lineup, so we would be on the same team. I was first, and Charlotte was the third in our group. The other girls arranged themselves, and Maryanne and Raoul followed, walking along the edge of the pool. The counselors were in bathing suits, but I guess they didn't have to get in the water since Mr. Collins taught this part of camp.

"Okay, girls. Everyone settled? Any stroke you like, no rush. We're not racing. On your marks, get set . . . *bweeet!*" He blew his whistle hard, and I took off, swimming freestyle, all the way to the deep end. I knew we weren't racing, but it felt good to try hard and swim fast. I hated knowing people were watching me, but at least three other girls were swimming at the same time as me, so the bystanders weren't watching *only* me the whole time, which made it okay.

I got to the deep end and slapped my hand against the wall. First! (Not that we were racing!) I hung on to the wall and watched Georgia, Jesse, and Caroline come in right after me. I was breathing hard, but it felt good. Next up was Alexis, along with a girl named Tricia, a girl named Louise, and Kira in the fourth group. Mr. Collins blew the whistle, and they were off.

Alexis is a great swimmer too. Just what you would expect: efficient; not show-offy; fast, clean strokes. Tricia and Louise were doing fine too. But . . . uh-oh. Kira wasn't.

She had pushed away from the wall fine and was gliding, but then when the water got deeper and her glide wore off, she started to flounder. She put down her feet and tried to push off again, but that only got her into the deeper end, to where she couldn't stand. She started to sink.

Mr. Collins was in the water in a flash, as was Raoul. They both dove from opposite sides of the water and reached her at the exact same moment. I was frozen to the spot, watching as they grabbed her and hauled her toward the side of the pool. *Oh my goodness,* was all I could think. Kira can't swim!

When they reached the wall, Kira was sputtering and coughing. They each had an arm around her, and had towed her to the side in a flash. Mr. Collins lifted her onto the deck and pushed himself up and out of the water. Maryanne came running over with her own towel, and put it over Kira's shoulders. Kira started to cry. Tricia, Alexis, and Louise had reached the deep end's wall (they'd been oblivious to what had happened), and now everyone was just silent, watching.

At first, we were all scared for Kira, and then as it became clear that she was okay, we were all really embarrassed for her.

Mr. Collins quickly established that Kira was not hurt or in danger, then stood and called out to the group, "She's fine! Just a little rusty, like the best of us after a long winter! Everything's okay. Just swim for a minute while we change our plan." He and Maryanne and Raoul chatted in whispers, then Raoul jumped back into the pool and swam to the shallow end.

Mr. Collins called out again, "Now is there anyone else who'd like a little extra practice with Raoul? It's fine! Just raise your hand." He looked around. No one was raising their hand. But then Elle, who was still in the shallow end, raised her hand.

"Great! Go with Raoul to the corner and you'll work on it a little. Kira"—Mr. Collins reached down and patted Kira's head—"just come on over and join Raoul and . . . what's your name, young lady?"

"Elle," called Elle.

"And Elle while they practice at this end, okay? The next group, get ready to swim."

In a few moments Kira was back in the water

with Elle and Raoul. Now, if there is one thing I noticed when we were having free swim, it's that Elle is an amazing swimmer. After what she did for Kira, I knew she'd make an amazing friend, too.

How about a

BONUS

CUPCAKE DIARIES?

Alexis

cool as a cupcake

Partners? What Partners?

Business first. That's one of my mottoes.

When my best friends and I get together to discuss our cupcake company, the Cupcake Club, I am all about business. My name is Alexis Becker, and I am the business planner of the group. This means I kind of take care of everything—pricing, scheduling, and ingredient inventory—the nuts and bolts of it all. So when we actually go to make the cupcakes and sell them, we're all set.

Mia Vélaz-Cruz is our fashion-forward, stylish person, who is great at presentation and coming up with really good ideas, and Katie Brown and Emma Taylor are real bakers, so they have lots of ideas on ingredients and how things should taste. Together we make a great team.

But today, when we were having our weekly meeting at Mia's house, they would not let me do my job. It was so frustrating!

I had out the leather-bound accounts ledger that Mia's mom gave me, and I was going through all our costs and all the money that's owed to us, when Mia interrupted.

"Ooh! I forgot to tell you I had an idea for your costume for the pep rally parade, Katie!" said Mia enthusiastically, as if I wasn't in the middle of reading out columns of numbers for the past two jobs we've had. The high school in our town holds a huge parade and pep rally right before school starts. It's a pretty big deal. One year some kids decided to dress up in costumes for the parade, and now everybody dresses up. The local newspaper sends reporters, and there are usually pictures of it on the first page of the paper the very next day.

"Oh good, what is it?" asked Katie, as if she was thrilled for the interruption.

"Ahem," I said. "Are we conducting business here or having a coffee klatch?" That's what our favorite science teacher, Ms. Biddle, said when we whispered in class. Apparently, a coffee klatch is something gossipy old ladies do: drink coffee and chatter mindlessly.

"Yeah, c'mon, guys. Let's get through this," said Emma. I know she was trying to be supportive of me, but "get through this"? As if they just had to listen to me before they got to the fun stuff? That was kind of insulting!

"I'm not reading this stuff for my own health, you know," I said. I knew I sounded really huffy, but I didn't care. I do way more behind-the-scenes work than anyone else in this club, and I don't think they have any idea how much time and effort it takes. Now, I *do* love it, but everyone has a limit, and I have almost reached mine.

"Sorry, Alexis! I just was spacing out and it crossed my mind," admitted Mia. It was kind of a lame apology, since she was admitting she was spacing out during my presentation.

"Whatever," I said. "Do you want to listen or should I just forget about it?"

"No, no, we're listening!" protested Katie. "Go on!" But I caught her winking and nodding at Mia as Mia nodded and gestured to her.

I shut the ledger. "Anyway, that's all," I said.

Mia and Katie were so engrossed in their sign language that they didn't even realize I'd cut it short. Emma seemed relieved and didn't protest.

So that's how it's going to be, I thought. *Then*

fine! I'd just do the books and buy the supplies and do all the scheduling and keep it to myself. No need to involve the whole club, anyway. I folded my arms across my chest and waited for someone to speak. But of course, it wasn't about business.

"Well?" asked Katie.

"Okay, I was thinking, what about a genie? And you can get George Martinez to be an astronaut. Then you can wear something really dreamy and floaty and magical, like on that old TV show *I Dream of Jeannie* that's on Boomerang?" Mia was smiling with pride at her idea.

"Ooooh! I love that idea!" squealed Katie. "But how do I get George to be an astronaut?" She propped her chin on her hand and frowned.

"Wait!" interrupted Emma. "Why would George Martinez need to be an astronaut?"

Mia looked at her like she was crazy. "Because a *boy* has to be your partner for the parade. You know that!"

Emma flushed a deep red. "No, I did not know that. Who told you that?"

I felt a pit growing in my stomach. Even though I was mad and trying to stay out of this annoying conversation, the news stunned me too, and I couldn't remain silent. "Yeah, who told you that?" I repeated.

Mia and Katie shrugged and looked at each other, then back at us.

"Um, I don't know," said Katie. "It's just common knowledge?"

I found this annoying since it was our first real pep rally and this was major news. "No, it is *not* common knowledge." I glared at Mia.

"Sorry," said Mia sheepishly.

I pressed my lips together. Then I said, "Well? Who are *you* going with?"

Mia looked away. "I haven't really made up my mind," she said.

"Do you have lots of choices?" I asked. I was half annoyed and half jealous. Mia is really pretty and stylish and not that nervous around boys.

She laughed a little. "Not exactly. But Katie does!"

Emma and I looked at each other, like, *How could we have been so clueless?*

"Stop!" Katie laughed, turning beet red again.

"Well, 'fess up! Who are they?" I asked.

Katie rolled her eyes. "Oh, I don't know."

Mia began ticking off names on her fingers. "George Martinez always teases her when he sees her, which we all know means he likes her. He even mentioned something about the parade and asked Katie what her costume was going to be, right?"

Katie nodded.

Mia continued, "And then there's Joe Fraser. Another possibility."

"Stop!" protested Katie. "That's all. This is too mortifying! Let's change the subject to something boring, like Cupcake revenue!"

"Thanks a lot!" I said. I was hurt that she said it because I don't find Cupcake revenue boring. I find it fascinating. I love to think of new ways to make money.

How do my best friends and I have such different interests? I wondered.

"Sorry, but you know what I mean," said Katie. "It stresses me out to talk about who likes whom."

Still.

"Well, no one likes me!" said Emma.

"That's not true. I'm sure people like you," said Mia. But I noticed she didn't try to list anyone.

"What do we do if we don't have a boy to go with?" I asked.

"Well, girls could go with their girl friends, but no one really does that. I think it's just kind of dorky. . . ."

I felt a flash of annoyance. Since when was Mia such a know-it-all about the pep rally and what was done and what wasn't and what was dorky and what wasn't?

"I guess I could go with Matt . . . ," said Emma, kind of thinking out loud.

"What?!" I couldn't contain my surprise. Emma knows I have a crush on her older brother, and in the back of my mind, throughout this whole conversation, I'd been trying to think if I'd have the nerve to ask him. Not that I'd ever ask if he'd do matchy-matchy costumes with me, but just to walk in the parade together. After all, he *had* asked me to dance at my sister's sweet sixteen party.

Emma looked at me. "What?"

I didn't want to admit I'd been thinking that *I'd* ask him, so I said the next thing I could think of. "You'd go with your brother? Isn't *that* kind of dorky?" I felt mean saying it, but I was annoyed.

Emma winced, and I felt a little bad.

But Mia shook her head. "No, not if your brother is older and is cool, like Matt; it's not dorky."

Oh great. Now she'd just given Emma free rein to ask Matt and I had no one! "You know what? I'm going to check with Dylan on all this," I said.

My older sister would certainly know all the details of how this should be done. And she was definitely not dorky.

There was an uncomfortable silence. Finally, I said, "Look, we don't have to worry about all this right now, so let's just get back to business, okay?" And at last they were eager to discuss my favorite subject, if only because the other topics had turned out to be so stressful for us.

I cleared my throat and read from my notebook. "We have Jake's best friend Max's party, and Max's mom wants something like what we did for Jake. . . ." We'd made Jake Cakes—dirt with worms cupcakes made out of crushed Oreos and gummy worms for Emma's little brother's party, and they were a huge hit.

"Right," said Emma, nodding. "I was thinking maybe we could do Mud Pies?"

"Excellent. Let's think about what we need for the ingredients. There's—"

"Sorry to interrupt, but . . ."

We all looked at Katie.

"Just one more tiny question? Do you think Joe Fraser is a little bit cooler than George Martinez?"

I stared at her coldly. "What does that have to do with Mud Pies?"

"Sorry," said Katie, shrugging. "I was just wondering."

"Anyway, Mud Pie ingredients are . . ."

We brainstormed, uninterrupted, for another five minutes and got a list of things kind of organized for a Mud Pie proposal and sample baking session. Then we turned to our next big job, baking cupcakes for a regional swim meet fund-raiser.

Mia had been absentmindedly sketching in her notebook, and now she looked up. "I have a great idea for what we could do for the cupcakes for the swim meet!"

"Oh, let's see!" I said, assuming she'd sketched it out. I peeked over her shoulder, expecting to see a cupcake drawing, and instead there was a drawing of a glamorous witch costume, like something out of *Wicked*.

"Oh," I said. Here I'd been thinking we were all engaged in the cupcake topic, and it turned out Mia had been still thinking about the pep rally parade all along.

"Sorry," she said. "But I was *thinking* about cupcakes."

"Whatever," I said. I tossed my pen down on the table and closed my notebook. "This meeting is adjourned."

"Come on, Alexis," said Mia. "It's not that big a deal."

"Yeah, all work and no play makes for a bad day, boss lady!" added Katie.

"I am *not* the boss lady!" I said. I was mad and hurt. "I don't want to be the boss lady. In fact, I am not any kind of boss. Not anymore! You guys can figure this all out on your own."

I stood up and quickly gathered my things into my bag.

"Hey, Alexis, please! We aren't trying to be mean, we're just distracted!" said Mia.

"You guys think this is all a joke! If I didn't hustle everything along and keep track, nothing would get done!" I said, swinging my bag up over my shoulder. "I feel like I do all the work, and then you guys don't even care!"

"Look, it's true you do all the work," agreed Emma. "But we thought you enjoyed it. If you're tired of it, we can divvy it up, right, girls?" she said, looking at Mia and Katie.

"Sure! Why not?" said Mia, flinging her hair behind her shoulders in the way she does when she's getting down to work.

"Fine," I said.

"I'll do the swim team project, okay?" said Mia.

"And I'll do the Mud Pies," said Emma.

"And I'll do whatever the next big project is," said Katie.

I looked at them all. "What about invoicing, purchasing, and inventory?"

The girls each claimed one of the areas, and even though I was torn about giving up my responsibilities, I was glad to see them shouldering some of the work for a change. We agreed that they would e-mail or call me with questions when they needed my help.

"Great," I said. "Now I'm leaving." And I walked home from Mia's quickly, so fast I was almost jogging. My pace was fueled by anger about the Cupcake Club *and* the desire to get home to my sister, Dylan, as quickly as possible, so I could start asking questions about the pep rally parade and all that it would entail.

A Little Sweet Talk!

There are 18 words in this puzzle, and they all have something to do with your four favorite Cupcake girls! Can you find them all?

(If you don't want to write in your book, make a copy of this page.)

WORD LIST: ALEXIS, BACON, BAKE, BATTER, CARAMEL, CHOCOLATE, CINNAMON, COCONUT, CREAM, CUPCAKE, EGGS, EMMA, FLOUR, ICING, KATIE, MIA, MILK, SUGAR

N	O	C	A	B	I	C	I	N	G
B	C	A	R	A	M	E	L	J	M
A	S	E	V	E	M	M	A	P	I
T	B	A	K	E	A	R	I	S	A
T	R	U	O	L	F	M	I	L	K
E	C	H	O	C	O	L	A	T	E
R	A	G	U	S	K	A	T	I	E
A	L	E	X	I	S	S	G	G	E
G	C	O	C	O	N	U	T	W	D
E	K	A	C	P	U	C	G	H	I
M	C	I	N	N	A	M	O	N	T

Mia is always sketching! She has dreams of being a world-famous fashion designer someday. In this story, she sketches a sleek winter coat, a birthday party dress for her friend Ava, and a Valentine's Day outfit.

Designed by . . . YOU!

Do you think you could be a fashion designer? Draw your sketches here. (If fashion isn't your thing, use the space to draw a picture of you with your BFFs!) (If you don't want to write in your book, make a copy of this page.)

B
F
F

Two for the Price of One!

The Cupcake Club is having a sale: two cupcakes for the price of one! The only catch is that you have to find the two cupcakes in this dozen that are decorated exactly alike. Can you find and circle them?

(If you don't want to write in your book, make a copy of this page.)

Are you an Emma, a Mia, a Katie, or an Alexis? Take our quiz and find out!

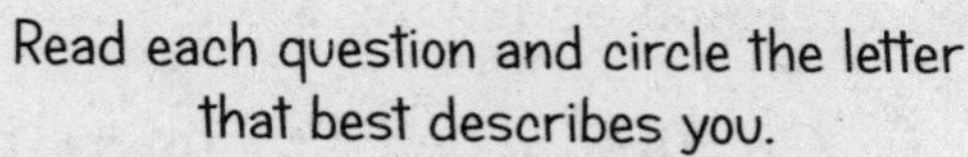

Read each question and circle the letter that best describes you.

(If you don't want to write in your book, use a separate piece of paper.)

1. You've been invited to a party. What do you wear?

A. Jeans and a cute T-shirt. You want to look nice, but you also want to be comfortable.

B. You beg your parents to lend you money for the cool boots you saw online. If you're going to a party, you have to wear the latest fashion!

C. Something pretty, but practical. If you're going to spend money on a new outfit, it better be one you'll be able to wear a lot.

D. Something feminine—lacy and floral. And definitely pink if not floral—a girl can never go wrong wearing *pink*!

2. Your idea of a perfect Saturday afternoon is:

A. Seeing a movie with your BFFs and then going out for pizza afterward.

B. THE MALL! Hopefully one of the stores will be having a big sale!

C. Creating a perfect budget to buy clothes, go out with friends, and save money for college—all at the same time—and then meeting your friends for lunch.

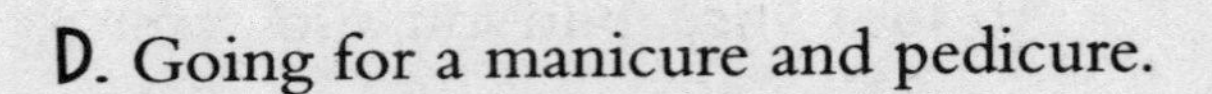

D. Going for a manicure and pedicure.

3. You have to study for a big test. What's your study style?

A. In your bedroom, with your favorite music playing.

B. At home, with help from your parents if necessary.

C. At the library, where you can take out some new books after you've finished studying, or anyplace else that's absolutely quiet.

D. Anyplace away from home—away from your messy, loud siblings!

4. There's a new girl at school. What's your first reaction?

A. You're a little cautious. You've been hurt before, so it takes you a while to warm up to new friends.

B. You think it's great. You welcome her with open arms. (Maybe you can share each other's clothes!)

C. If she's nice and smart, maybe you'll consider being friends with her.

D. You'll gladly welcome another friend—as long as she really wants to be friends with you—and not just meet your cute older brothers!

5. When it comes to boys . . .

A. They make you a little nervous. You want to be friends first—for a long time—until you'd consider someone a boyfriend.

B. He has to be tall, trustworthy, sweet—and of course, superstylish!

C. He has to be cute, funny, and smart—and he gets extra points if he likes to dance!

D. He has to be loyal and true as well as good-looking. You look sweet, but you're tough when you have to be.

6. When it comes to your family . . .

A. You come from a single-parent home. It's hard for you to imagine your parent dating, but you will try to get used to it.

B. You come from a mixed family with stepsiblings and a stepparent. At first it was overwhelming, but you're starting to get used to having everyone in the mix!

C. You get along okay with your parents, but your older sister thinks she's queen of the world. Still sometimes you ask her for advice anyway.

D. You live in a house with many brothers—dirty, sticky, smelly boys! You love them all, but sometimes would give anything for a sister!

7. Your dream vacation would be:

A. Anyplace beachy. You love to swim and also just relax on a beach blanket.

B. Paris—to see the latest fashions.

C. Egypt—you'd love to see the pyramids and try to figure out how they were constructed without any modern machinery.

D. Holland—you'd love to see the tulips in bloom!

Which Cupcake girl are you?
What your answers mean:

Mostly *A*s:

You're a Katie! Your style is easy and comfortable. You always look good, and you always feel good too. You have a few very close friends (both girls and boys), and you like it that way. You don't want to confide in just anybody.

Mostly *B*s:

You're a Mia! You're the girl everyone envies at school because you can wear an old ratty sweatshirt and jeans and somehow still look like a runway model. Your sense of style is what everyone notices first, but you're also a great friend.

Mostly *C*s:

You're an Alexis! You are supersmart and not afraid to show it! You get As in every subject, and like nothing more than creating business plans and budgets. You love your friends but have to remember sometimes that not everyone in the world is as brilliant as you are.

Mostly *D*s:

You're an Emma! You are a girly-girl and love to wear pretty clothes. Pink is your signature color. But people should not be fooled by your sweet exterior. You can be as tough as nails when necessary and would never let anyone push you around.

ANSWER KEY:

A Little Sweet Talk!

N	O	C	A	B	I	C	I	N	G
B	C	A	R	A	M	E	L	J	M
A	S	E	V	E	M	M	A	P	I
T	B	A	K	E	A	R	I	S	A
T	R	U	O	L	F	M	I	L	K
E	C	H	O	C	O	L	A	T	E
R	A	G	U	S	K	A	T	I	E
A	L	E	X	I	S	S	G	G	E
G	C	O	C	O	N	U	T	W	D
E	K	A	C	P	U	C	G	H	I
M	C	I	N	N	A	M	O	N	T

Two for the Price of One!

Still Hungry?

There's always room for another Cupcake!

CUPCAKE DIARIES
7
Emma
all
stirred
up!
by coco simon

CUPCAKE DIARIES
8
Alexis
cool
as a
cupcake
by coco simon

CUPCAKE DIARIES
9
Katie
and the
cupcake war

CUPCAKE DIARIES
10
Mia's
boiling point

CUPCAKE DIARIES
11
Emma,
smile and say
"cupcake!"

CUPCAKE DIARIES
Alexis
gets
frosted
by coco simon

CUPCAKE DIARIES
13
Katie's
new recipe

CUPCAKE DIARIES
14
Mia
a matter of taste

CUPCAKE DIARIES
15
Emma
sugar
spice
and
everything
nice

CUPCAKE DIARIES
16
Alexis
and the
missing
ingredient
by coco simon

CUPCAKE DIARIES
17
Katie
sprinkles & surprises

CUPCAKE DIARIES
18
Mia
fashion
plates
and
cupcakes

cupcake DIARIES
Emma: lights! camera! cupcakes!

cupcake DIARIES
Alexis the icing on the cupcake

cupcake DIARIES
Katie starting from scratch

cupcake DIARIES
Mia's recipe for disaster

cupcake DIARIES
Emma's not-so-sweet dilemma

cupcake DIARIES
Alexis's cupcake cupid

cupcake DIARIES
Katie sprinkled secrets

cupcake DIARIES
Mia the way the cupcake crumbles

cupcake DIARIES
Emma raining cats and dogs . . . and cupcakes!

cupcake DIARIES
Alexis cupcake crush

cupcake DIARIES
Katie just desserts

cupcake DIARIES
Mia measures up

Coco Simon always dreamed of opening a cupcake bakery but was afraid she would eat all of the profits. When she's not daydreaming about cupcakes, Coco edits children's books and has written close to one hundred books for children, tweens, and young adults, which is a lot less than the number of cupcakes she's eaten. Cupcake Diaries is the first time Coco has mixed her love of cupcakes with writing.

If you liked

CUPCAKE DIARIES

be sure to check out these

other series from

Simon Spotlight

sew zoey

Zoey's clothing design blog puts her on the A-list in the fashion world . . . but when it comes to school, will she be teased, or will she be a trendsetter? Find out in the Sew Zoey series: